# THE BETHLEHEM SCROLL

Bill Thompson

**Outskirts Press, Inc.**
**Denver, Colorado**

This is a work of fiction. The events and characters described herein are imaginary and are not intended to refer to specific places or living persons. The opinions expressed in this manuscript are solely the opinions of the author and do not represent the opinions or thoughts of the publisher. The author has represented and warranted full ownership and/or legal right to publish all the materials in this book.

The Bethlehem Scroll

v3.0

Cover design by Ariamedia



Outskirts Press, Inc.
http://www.outskirtspress.com

ISBN: 978-1-4327-3892-1

Library of Congress Control Number: 2009925514



PRINTED IN THE UNITED STATES OF AMERICA

*To Marilyn*
*My Proofreader and Critic Extraordinaire*
*Still the one . . .*
*. . . after all these years.*

# Prelude

THE QUMRAN HILLS NEAR THE DEAD SEA
LATE 2003

It was hot, blisteringly hot, on the canyon floor. The afternoon sun beat mercilessly on the rocky hillside. Only insects and reptiles had the stamina to venture about outdoors in this heat. Mammals stayed under cool rock overhangs or sought shelter in one of the many small caves dotting the landscape.

Deep in the darkness of this particular cave the temperature was below seventy degrees Fahrenheit, far less than the searing heat outside its obscure entrance. Other than the occasional desert fox or snake seeking refuge from the afternoon sun, nothing had ventured into the cave for hundreds of years. This was no place for men.

The cave consisted of two small areas – the space inside the room farthest from the cave's entrance was tight – less than eight feet lay between the tiny entrance and its rear wall. The room's ceiling was no more than three feet above its floor - not even a child could have stood erect. That was part of the reason why the jar had remained untouched for these many years. The larger caves nearby were occasionally used as shelters by the bedouin, but this small indentation went unnoticed.

The jar sat on a small ledge behind some rocks. Its tight seal, put into place long ago, guarded its contents well. Neither searing desert heat nor the cool cave created a problem. There was neither humidity nor dampness to damage anything. So the jar sat, hidden behind two stones at the back of the cave, exactly as the boy had carefully placed it two thousand years ago.

*National Museum of Antiquities*
*Cairo, Egypt*
*May 3, 2004*

The translator had sat for two hours bent over the table, painstakingly examining the ancient manuscript which lay flat on the table in front of him. He had made astonishing progress, although translating from Aramaic into Egyptian was a slow process, made more difficult by the partial deterioration of the document on which he was working. He had to work very carefully, unrolling with painstaking care the two thousand year old scroll.

Achmed thought to himself how much easier this scroll was to handle than the others which had been found back in the forties. Many of them were mere fragments, eroded by the passing of time. This scroll obviously had been cared for much differently, he thought. Although its condition was rough, it still was intact. He wanted to know more about its provenance, but knew the man sitting behind him wouldn't tell him anything.

Earlier today, Achmed had been sitting at his desk, working on the translation of an old Greek parchment which had been brought in by one of the museum's financial supporters. The benefactor said it had been found at a dig in Alexandria. He purchased it from one of the workmen, who apparently had whisked it away from the site in his pocket. Achmed had barely gotten started on the document – just far enough to know it was some sort of shipping manifest – when the museum director had burst into his workroom, accompanied by a pockmark-faced man who now sat behind him.

The man had produced an identity card and badge, identifying him as a Detective Inspector with the Ministry of Interior, the agency which controlled all police activity in Egypt. Achmed found that strange. He had had no interaction with the police in his entire career here. The museum director instructed Achmed to stop what he was doing and to do a quick translation of the document now before him. "He wants to know what it says," the director said. "Not word for word, but an overview of what the scroll is all about."

So began the ordeal which had gone on for hours. The swarthy inspector sat in a chair behind Achmed, occasionally taking or making a call on his cell phone, talking quietly while Achmed worked. His face had startled Achmed when they met. The scars might have been from smallpox, he thought. Once, when Achmed arose to go to the lavatory, the Inspector questioned him, then said, "We will both go, but do not enter this room again until I am with you." It was obvious the man would not allow Achmed to be alone with the document.

What Achmed had translated had astounded him. Now he understood why the man was so protective of the scroll he had brought to the museum. There were groups – governments even – who would do almost anything to get their hands on this parchment.

"I have important work to do," the inspector said to Achmed. "Finish up now, and give me the parchment." Achmed had only a few lines left. He had hurried through the lengthy manuscript, and knew he had missed some of the words, but the meaning was as clear as day to him. His body shuddered involuntarily as he thought of the importance of what he had in his hands.

Achmed made notes on a legal pad next to him as he carefully read the ancient language. Although he wanted to make sure he got the meaning, he wasn't concerned about every word. The document was long . . . a story with no ending. He struggled to contain the excitement that grew within him as he read sentence after sentence.

"What's taking you so long?" the inspector asked Achmed. "I only want to know what it means, not to have you translate the whole thing." *I know exactly what you want,* Achmed thought to himself. *And I may never see this scroll again, so I'm going to take my time and see everything it says.*

"Aramaic is a difficult language, sir," Achmed replied to the man. "And the parchment is lengthy." The man responded gruffly, impatiently. "Tell me, then, if the name Yahweh appears in the text."

*I knew it, Achmed thought. He wants to know if God's name is in the document.* To the inspector, he replied, "I have seen no such name so far, sir." But Achmed also knew from what he had seen that it was only a matter of time until the name appeared.

"I will be finished momentarily," Achmed said to the policeman. He watched out of the corner of his eye as the man turned to retrieve the topcoat he had laid on a counter by the door. There was something unusual going on, Achmed felt.

Finally Achmed put down his pen, turned to the man and said, "I am finished. The document is a scroll which appears to be ancient. It is written in Aramaic, a language common two thousand . . ." "I don't want a history lesson!" the inspector interrupted. As he stood, his voice became louder and more menacing. "What does it say?"

*It's after 6 pm, Achmed thought. I am likely the only person still in the building.* He nervously stammered, "The . . . the scroll resembles those from the Dead Sea discoveries. It speaks of a birth in

Bethlehem. The last sentence calls him a King – Yahweh." Since Achmed knew that was the name this Inspector was seeking, he decided not to tell him the other name which appeared in the scroll, the name Yeshua, or Jesus. This was an important scroll, without a doubt. This scroll mentioned God and Jesus, Yahweh and Yeshua, together in a single document.

The Inspector smiled. "You have done well, translator," he said quietly as he pulled a pistol from his coat pocket. Achmed had no time to think even of his wife and child at home, and he barely felt the bullet enter his chest. He died before he hit the floor.

The pockmarked man who had called himself an Inspector stepped over the body, rolled up the parchment carefully, and took Achmed's notepad. Opening the door, he looked up and down the quiet hallway. He could hear no sounds. He moved to the museum's entrance and left the building, making sure the door locked behind him.

The director of the National Museum prided himself on his early arrival each day. He unlocked the front doors as he did every morning. There were no guards here overnight. The last massive round of budget cuts had eliminated that luxury. All the security cameras were still in place, but no one sat at the guard station watching the activity on monitors.

He wondered how Achmed's translation had gone. That whole situation was strange - an inquiry about an ancient scroll from a policeman? It was very unusual indeed. And he had stayed in the same room with the translator all afternoon, taking a break only when Achmed did. He must have thought the scroll to be very valuable.

As he turned a corner to go to his office, he glanced down the hallway toward Achmed's small workroom. The door was open, and light spilled out from the office into the hallway. That was strange. He knew Achmed to be a fastidious person, one who never left his office with the door open. He must be there, the director thought, but it was certainly early for him. "Achmed," he called. "Did you get finished last night?" He turned to enter Achmed's office and saw the body lying on the floor in a pool of blood. A few flies buzzed around the room. It was obvious this must have happened several hours ago. He turned and ran to his office to place a call to the National Police.

*The Judean hills near Bethlehem*
*Late March, 3 B.C.*

The shepherds spoke quietly among themselves, as they sat on the ground around a small fire. As the sheep settled in for the night, the men smoked and talked. It was a warm spring night, and a light breeze fanned the flames. Overhead, the cloudless sky was as black and brilliant as Joab had ever seen it. "What a night," he thought to himself as millions of stars twinkled above him. "What a beautiful, incredible night."

Benjamin, son of Joab, was only twelve, but he had been with these men many times before as they tended the flock of sheep, which was their livelihood. Although he was often unable to join them because he attended school, this was one night he was glad he had been asked to come. He lay on his back on a small mat as he gazed upward, his pack beside him. A shooting star burned a path rapidly across the sky. Benjamin closed his eyes and made a wish. "I wish for many more nights here, on this hill with my father," he thought.

Joab had been a shepherd since his youth, trained by his father as

Benjamin had in turn been trained by Joab. As he watched his son staring up into the skies, Joab's mind wandered from the discussion in which the other shepherds were engaged. Joab hoped Benjamin could do more with his life. It had been a struggle to send the child to synagogue school, because Benjamin could have lent a much-needed hand to the growing flock of sheep Joab owned. Instead, however, Joab and his wife had decided the boy's education was the key to his future. Perhaps he could become a rabbi, Joab mused. Or maybe a shopkeeper in Bethlehem. Whatever the future held, Joab wanted Benjamin to have the chance to do something meaningful. Little did he know how important Benjamin's education would prove to be.

The embers of the small fire died down. One of the shepherds took a stick and stirred the fire, tossing the twig on it. The talk had turned to politics, a subject on which it seemed everyone in the small group had an opinion. "The Sanhedrin are becoming far too powerful," Joab commented. "Yes," another replied, "but what can we do? They have the education . . . the power. Simple shepherds such as we must be content with our lot in life. But also we have the best of all worlds – we can sit here, far from the crowds below in Bethlehem, enjoying life to its fullest."

They discussed the census that was underway. Since the Romans had occupied Judea, taxes had progressively increased for the Jewish population now under their control. "I think Caesar Augustus is going to use the census as a means to raise taxes once again," Joab said to the group. "I've never seen taxes go down, and the legions of soldiers they're sending to our country require a lot of money to maintain."

The others agreed. One of them spat on the ground and cursed. "I've no money for taxes," he said. "What do we receive from this Roman government? Nothing. They take, but they never give in return." "True," another responded, "but we can't fight them, and it appears the Sanhedrin have aligned themselves with the Romans." "The Sanhedrin are crafty," a third man said. "They watch the wind, and they shift with it."

The census had created havoc in small towns such as Bethlehem, because every person of a certain bloodline was required to register in his own place of birth. This often meant travel for great distances on foot or by donkey. Since travel outside one's own town was rare, the trip to Bethlehem and other cities where the census was taken was a diversion for many people, a time for revelry and a change of pace. The usually quiet towns swelled with people virtually overnight as they thronged in, filling the streets.

The shepherds' city was no exception. People from miles around were crowding into the small hamlet, swelling its population to three or four times its normal size. The streets filled with masses of people. Inns, eating and drinking places teemed with tourists, and many of these visitors became loud and unruly as the long nights wore on.

From their vantage point on the hill above Bethlehem, which lay less than a mile below them to the east, the shepherds could easily hear the noise from the city. It wasn't normal, and the shepherds hoped it wouldn't be long before the visitors would leave and things got back into a routine. At this time, it was difficult to navigate the narrow streets of the town, because crowds moved about, drinking and talking loudly, unconcerned about the disruption they created among the residents. It was as though a holiday were underway, with all the reveling, Benjamin thought. Having never ventured more than a couple of miles from Bethlehem, he had never seen such activity, and it frightened him somewhat, although his father had told him to merely avoid the strangers as much as possible, and things would be fine.

Yesterday when Benjamin had gone to the synagogue for school, two burly strangers had stopped him in the street, loudly asking him if he knew a lodging place in the area. Benjamin hesitantly responded that, as far as he had heard, everything was completely full. "We'll just stay at the Four Horsemen," one laughed to the other. The Four Horsemen was a drinking place not far from Benjamin's school, and he wondered how someone could stay there, since there were only a couple of shabby rooms that the owner occasionally rented to those who had imbibed enough that they could not make it to their homes afterwards. Maybe they weren't going to sleep, he thought, but just drink and be noisy instead. It was a time of change, the boy mused, and his father always told him change might be good, or bad, but it would always occur nonetheless.

None of the shepherds on that starlit hill could have conceived what changes they would see over the next few hours, and how much a part of it they would become.

Benjamin lay on his back on the soft grass. A few of the sheep milled about, bleating softly, unable to settle down for rest. Another shooting star streaked across the crisp, clear night sky and Benjamin waited for its filmy trail to begin to evaporate. Suddenly he became aware that, instead of disappearing at the end of its journey through the heavens, the star had instead become brighter. In fact, it had stopped, and seemed to be directly overhead!

"Look, Father," Benjamin said to Joab. "This was a shooting star, and now it's the brightest one in the sky!" Joab and the other shepherds stopped talking to look up. The star was pulsating and had become so luminous that it lit up the entire field on the top of the hill as if it were midday, but without the searing glare of the sun. It was a soothing glow but equally bright as the sun's rays.

"What do you make of this?" Joab asked the other shepherds, all of whom appeared awestruck at the sight. No one had an answer.

No one had ever seen a phenomenon such as this before. "God is giving us a sign," one whispered.

Benjamin stood. The bright light from the star shone around the men, but outside its circle of light the area was dark, from the hill down to Bethlehem. "Father!" Benjamin shouted. "Look at Bethlehem!" Joab and the shepherds turned their eyes away from the heavens to behold a most unusual sight.

The same star whose rays created a bath of light directly on the Judean hilltop now had developed a second shaft. Piercing the darkness like the first, this second ray of bright, glowing light shone down into the bustling town of Bethlehem below. It seemed to pinpoint one area of town, an area Benjamin knew well. It was the part of town through which he walked to synagogue each morning, his part of town, near the inn known as The Four Horsemen.

As the shepherds stood on the hillside, their sheep, thinking it was daytime, were now fully awake. Both men and animals were perplexed and afraid, not knowing what was happening to them. Joab became aware of movement in the sky above them, and could hear a soft sound of singing through the quiet night. His mouth fell open and he grabbed Benjamin to his side as he knelt with the other shepherds, the sheep now forgotten.

High above the men, seemingly floating in the night sky, were several ethereal figures. Although they were human in appearance, they were the most beautiful creatures the men had ever seen. Their garments were golden and behind them, barely visible in the light, were what appeared to be wings, moving slowly about as they smiled down on the small band of shepherds kneeling on that lonely hilltop. The men felt a warmth from these figures such as they had never experienced before. Their fear had been transformed into a sense of wonder.

"Hosanna, Hosanna," the figures sang, in voices that sounded so beautiful the men could hardly believe their ears. "Tonight is the most special of nights," they announced. "Tonight in Bethlehem the Messiah comes to men, just as it was prophesied." As the shepherds stared, astonished, the beautiful figures began to ascend, directly toward the light, until they were so high it was impossible for the men to see them any longer. When they were gone, the light on the hilltop disappeared suddenly, leaving only the small campfire to light the night.

The shepherds knelt in silence for several minutes. They were awestruck and each man knew something had happened tonight, something that would make things different for time immemorial. But none understood what he had seen.

Benjamin spoke first, hesitantly. "Father," he stammered, "do . . . do you think we should follow the light from the star to Bethlehem? The star still shines there." He pointed toward the hamlet, where the second stellar shaft was still beaming down.

"Yes, my son," Joab answered. "It may be that we are the only people who were given this sign from the heavens, and I think we must go and see for ourselves what is happening in the town." He instructed Benjamin to take his pack, knowing that the boy's parchment, quill and ink rested inside, and knowing that on this special night, a record of the events transpiring would be required.

The dazed shepherds arose and uncharacteristically left their sheep to graze on the Judean hillside as they moved down toward the bustling town. It was well after midnight, a time when on an ordinary night the town would be dark and quiet, its residents slumbering. The shepherds knew that many of the inns and taverns remained open late now, since the tourists were in town. As they approached the low gates that marked the edge of Bethlehem, the group noticed that the streets were as busy as if it were midday, but no one seemed to have noticed anything unusual. "They do not know of the sign," Joab murmured. "They go about as if nothing has happened."

It was harder to discern the destination marked by the star from this vantage point, since the streets of Bethlehem were lit by oil lamps and were crowded with drunken revelers. People pushed and shoved. "Where are we going?" one of the shepherds asked.

"I know," Benjamin answered. "I think I can get us very close to where the star's light was shining." He moved to the front of the group and led them through narrow, winding streets, making one turn after another through the familiar avenues of his birthplace. Several times they pushed through throngs of pilgrims laughing and talking among one another. "I think it's just around the next corner," Benjamin said at last to his father.

They turned the corner and immediately noticed a significant change. For about three blocks in front of them, the street was strangely quiet. Several shuttered businesses stood on the left side of the street, and most of the next block was taken up by The Four Horsemen, the old tavern that had been in existence for many years on that site. The few people in the area were staring, dumbfounded, at the tavern. Most nights this area was dimly lit but tonight the area shone with an unearthly glow. Benjamin looked up. There was the shaft of light coming from the bright star overhead, shining down directly on The Four Horsemen!

Benjamin's father Joab knew Ishmael, the proprietor of the inn. He occasionally went there to catch up on the news and talk politics with other patrons of the tavern. As the group moved to the entrance of The Four Horsemen, they encountered a small throng of people milling around, looking inside. "What goes here?" Joab asked the people.

"We don't know," a tall bearded man said. "We were drinking inside, when suddenly everything got very bright, and I was struck down. I fell to the floor and saw that my friends had done the same. In fact, everyone in the tavern was lying on the floor as though we were unable to stand." He continued, telling the shepherds that after a few moments the group felt able to stand, and had moved outside the tavern, where they were astounded by the brightness of the sky, as though it were morning. Something else happened, the man related, something involving another person who came into the tavern. But he was unable to put his thoughts into words.

"From whence do you come?" one of the tavern patrons asked Joab. "We were tending sheep on a hill west of town," he responded. "We too saw a light, and followed it here." Looking around, the men from the tavern suddenly realized that the light was in fact a shaft, and that by moving only a few feet away, they could step out of the bright glow, and the street became as dark as it had been before. Only directly around the tavern was the beautiful light streaming down from the biggest, most splendid star any of them had ever seen.

"Why is this happening?" they asked. Joab told them he wanted to learn more. He took Benjamin's hand and walked into The Four Horsemen. Ishmael, the inn's owner, was standing behind the empty bar, wiping his brow with a towel. He was perspiring heavily and was obviously in a state of shock.

"Ishmael, it's Joab, the shepherd. What has happened to you?"

"Joab," Ishmael responded. "I don't know. I just don't know. One minute I was serving drinks to a crowd of people, the next minute my place was lit up as though a thousand candles were burning. Look at the place now – it's brighter in here than it usually is on the street at noontime!"

Joab led Ishmael by the arm to a nearby table. He and Benjamin sat with the innkeeper and asked him to recall anything unusual that happened during the evening. "At first there was nothing different," Ishmael said. "This is the best time of all for me. Every room in town is full of out of town guests, here for the census, you know. A man did come to the bar a couple of hours ago, looking for a room. He was very tired and said he had come a long way, from Nazareth, I believe he said. I brushed him away – I was busy at the time – and told him there were no more rooms available here. He was insistent, however, saying that his wife was about to deliver a child after having ridden on a donkey all day. He was concerned for her welfare."

"What did you do?" Joab asked.

"I started to tell him to leave, but I looked up for a moment, into his eyes. Then I saw his wife standing in the doorway. She was about to have her baby, all right. But," Ishmael stopped for a moment, "but Joab, she looked like an angel. Her face glowed. She was a plain village girl, but at that moment, for some reason, she looked like the most beautiful woman on earth to me. I felt sorry for the couple, and something in my heart told me to take care of them."

"But you had no rooms," Joab responded.

"No," Ishmael said, "but you know that little cave off the courtyard, behind the tavern? We used to store food in there, and now I use it as a stable for my cows. I told the man – Joseph, I think he said his name was – that he and his wife could use the stable for the night, at no charge. I gave them some blankets and sent my servant out to fluff up the hay. He came back and told me the man and woman had settled in and seemed content with the accommodation." Ishmael stopped talking and looked up at Joab. "What have I done?" he said despairingly. "The light. The light."

"What do you mean?" Joab asked.

"After the couple went to the stable, about an hour passed. I had completely forgotten about them. This was the busiest night

I've had in years, Joab, and I was serving drinks and food as quickly as I could prepare them. I sensed another patron standing at the bar, and looked up to serve him. I . . . I can't tell you what happened next," Ishmael said, stammering his words.

Joab coaxed the rest of the story from Ishmael. As the innkeeper looked up, he saw a figure standing in front of him, dressed completely in golden robes and bathed in an unearthly light. The figure appeared to be a man, although his skin was whiter than anything Ishmael had ever seen. Ishmael recalled being able to see through the man, as though he were a specter. But Ishmael was not afraid. He felt, instead, an incredible sense of peace and well-being as the figure smiled at him. Ishmael was aware that every other person in the room had fallen to the floor for some reason. He was standing, but he felt as though he should be kneeling before this most unusual apparition.

Ishmael had become aware of the bright, soothing light which filled the room and, through the windows, made the outside look as clear as daytime. The light had begun when the figure had approached Ishmael's bar.

He said that the figure then spoke to him in a melodious voice which sounded incredibly beautiful. "Hosanna," the figure said. "Innkeeper, you have joined the historical thread of the Messiah on this night. You have given the birthplace to the Savior of the World."

"What does it mean, Joab?" Ishmael cried. "I'm afraid to go out in the back courtyard. The light's so bright around the stable that it scares me. But the animals aren't afraid. I can see my cows, and Joseph's donkey, milling about. What does it all mean?"

Joab told Ishmael what he and the shepherds had seen on the hilltop less than an hour before. It seemed that at the exact time the shepherds were being visited by the heavenly angels, the ethereal figure was speaking to Ishmael in his inn. "Do you know what I think, Ishmael?" Joab said. "I think we are part of prophecy fulfilled. I think the Messiah has returned. It must have been Him you saw – that man Joseph – and He must be in the stable now!"

Despite the late hour, Benjamin was wide awake. Ishmael, the proprietor of The Four Horsemen, stood aghast as he listed to Joab's words. "You think . . . you think . . ." Ishmael stammered. "You think that man in my stable is the Messiah?"

"I have no other explanation, my friend," Joab replied. "If we both believe our eyes, if you believe that the man in your tavern was not of this world, if I believe the figures we saw in the sky were from Heaven, then I have no other answer. Look outside even now."

The men stared through the open window into the rear courtyard and the rude stable on the other side. It wasn't a deep room, and the shaft of light shining into the courtyard made things very bright. "The light seems to be centered on the stable itself," Joab noted. "Let's go have a look."

The patrons in the street were slowly making their way back into the tavern. They seemed dazed by the events of the last ten minutes, and were talking among themselves, trying to make sense of something they had never experienced before. Ishmael sent his daughter out into the room to take orders from the patrons, as Joab, Benjamin and the other shepherds walked through the back door into the courtyard. While he was inside the tavern, Benjamin had felt afraid, not knowing what awaited them if they ventured outside. But once they were in the courtyard, they all remarked about the incredible sense of peace and well-being they felt as they stepped into the bright light.

The courtyard was fairly small – no more than twenty meters separated the back door of the inn from the small stable. Benjamin saw two adults – a woman and the man his father had said was the Messiah, kneeling beside a small manger. As the shepherds drew closer, they too knelt – not from a sense of obligation, but because something inside caused them to drop to their knees. Benjamin felt his skin tingle, and he became light-headed. As he drew closer, he saw a tiny baby lying in the makeshift crib on a bed of hay, wrapped in a beautiful white cloth.

The man and woman looked up at the shepherds who now knelt in front of the manger. Joab spoke first. "Messiah," he said to the man. "We have seen your heralds in the skies outside Bethlehem."

The man smiled. He spoke with a soft, gentle voice. "Good shepherd, I am not the Messiah whom you seek." Gesturing before him, he continued, "The King lies before you."

Benjamin's mouth opened in astonishment. It was the baby whom they were claiming as the Messiah! His mind was filled with the things he had been taught in synagogue school about the coming of the Messiah. Never had anyone dreamed it would be a small baby. How could this be? What did it mean?

Joab and the other shepherds had the same thoughts. Although these were not educated men, all Jews awaited the Messiah, and all knew he was to come one day. "Joab," one of the shepherds whispered, "should we believe the man?" "I think we had better," Joab responded. "Look at the back of the stable."

In the rear of the stable stood a figure whom the shepherds had not noticed previously – in fact, Benjamin was certain it had not been there a few seconds ago. It was in the form of a man, but its countenance was so bright that its clothes and skin literally shone with light. Although it stood behind the man and woman, out of the light of the piercing shaft from above, it radiated light itself, so that the immediate area surrounding the figure was bathed in a soft glow.

The figure spread its arms wide, encircling both the woman and the man, and smiling down upon the baby lying before the three of them. "Behold," the figure said in a melodic voice which seemed to Benjamin to be the essence of joy itself. "Behold your Messiah! Bow down and honor Him, sent by the Father to fulfill the promises of the scriptures!"

Without willing it, the shepherds and Benjamin found themselves prostrate on the ground in front of the baby's manger. After a few seconds, they looked up. The figure of light was gone. "Rise up," the man in the stable said. "Worship the King. Yahweh is with us."

# PART ONE

## Chapter One

OVER THE ATLANTIC OCEAN
THE PRESENT

As soon as the huge British Airways 777 lifted off the runway, Brian Sadler had reclined his first class SleeperSeat. His body was tired and his muscles tense. Only hours ago he had completed the most important deal of his life. His limo driver had raced down the corniche to deliver him to the Cairo airport, dropping Brian off just in time to check in and make the flight.

Since he'd taken over Bijan, flying was becoming old hat to Sadler. He knew all the tricks. All the luggage he'd needed for the trip to Cairo was securely stowed in the overhead bin above him. Any more, he never checked bags, reasoning that he'd rather spend a fortune on the hotel laundry than take the time to retrieve his gear, or lose it. He couldn't have checked the briefcase anyway, especially not on this trip. It was uncomfortable having it lightly tethered to his wrist, and the pliable plastic was a constant reminder that he was attached to the case, but it was essential this time.

Since he'd joined the gallery, not a day passed that Brian didn't unconsciously think about the sad turn of events that resulted in his incredible good fortune. As he lay in the seat, almost fully reclined, he mused once again about the future he would have once he finalized The Project. Brian Sadler was a satisfied man. He was thirty-five years old and on top of his game.

As CEO of Bijan Rarities, Brian had participated in the purchase and sale of some of the most priceless items ever to appear in an auction house or a museum's collection. His computer contained profiles on Trumps, Rockefellers, Hunts and Buffetts. He knew them all – knew what they collected, what they wanted, what they couldn't live without. He knew other collectors too – the ones who would pay a fortune for an item that was unique, even if it meant it could never be seen by the public again. Those people didn't ask the questions that might break a deal. Questions like "How did you get this piece?" or "Wasn't this in the Children's Museum of Baghdad before the war?" They wanted the best, at any price, no questions asked.

# Chapter Two

Thirty minutes behind schedule, the plane landed at Kennedy Airport. It was a gorgeous autumn day. The New York skyline had been breathtaking as the plane banked for landing. Brian never stopped loving New York. It had been a couple of years since he had moved here from Dallas, but the Big Apple had become Brian's home.

As the jet bridge was moved to the plane's door, the flight attendants blocked the rear of the forward cabin, so the first class passengers could disembark quickly. Brian stood in line. A family of Middle Eastern descent was just in front of him, the women covered head to toe in the usual bhurka. They talked excitedly, and he wondered how they'd enjoy New York, so different from their part of the world, yet still a melting pot that welcomed everyone.

The passengers moved quickly along the passageway that snaked through the bowels of the airport, heading toward Immigration. Eventually the hallway opened into a wide room with separate aisles for U.S. Citizens and Non-Residents. Brian moved around the Arab family but a Customs officer, noticing his briefcase, stopped him briefly and asked for his declaration form. "You'll have to remove the tether from your case now, sir," he said, "and use Lane 4 at Customs." He made a mark on Brian's form and returned it to him.

As Brian Sadler stood in line, he removed a small key and unlocked the band from the handle of the briefcase. It looked thin and pliable, but had the tensile strength of steel. The handle would have broken before the tether, and he would have had plenty of warning that someone was tampering with it. He bent, set it on the floor and stood, putting his customs declaration form in his jacket pocket so he wouldn't lose it. He saw the Arab family from the plane move by in a line just next to him, separated only by a thin cloth rope that allowed American citizens to use what was normally the faster lane. Today, however, the slight delay in Brian's arrival time meant that three other planes had unloaded hundreds of passengers simultaneously. The arrivals hall was teeming with people and the line for citizens was slower than the one for foreign nationals.

After a few minutes Brian moved to the Immigration desk and presented his form. "Welcome home, Mr. Sadler," the agent said. "What countries have you visited on this trip?" Brian told the agent that he was on a business trip and had been to Egypt and England. "And what business are you in, sir?" "I own an auction house and trading company," Brian replied.

After determining that Brian had only carry-on luggage, the officer again glanced at his form and advised him to go directly downstairs to customs, proceed through the hall and take Lane 4. Brian knew that lane would get him more than the usual wave-through, and that he'd be talking to an inspector. However, there was no alternative this time, since the tether from hand to case was required, and it had obviously raised red flags in customs already.

As he came to the Arrivals Hall exit, just in front of him stood a bank of doors which automatically opened and closed as people approached. Beyond the doors were hundreds of well-wishers, meeting and greeting their passengers who had just come through immigration and were now in New York City. At the final checkpoint, an officer took a look at Brian's paperwork and motioned him to Lane 4, where a number of inspectors stood behind low counters.

He approached a counter and the officer there asked him to put his luggage on the table. Taking Brian's customs form, the officer asked, "Do you have anything to declare?" "Yes, I am a dealer in antiquities and I have three items I am legally importing into the United States." The agent asked to see the items and his paperwork. Brian took the small key he had used to remove the tether from his briefcase handle. It also opened two locks on the case itself. He stuck the key into the first lock. It wouldn't fit. As the agent watched closely, Brian snapped open the lock. His adrenalin began flowing; he knew without a doubt he had locked the case in Cairo after clearing customs there, and now it was unlocked. His heart sinking, he opened the other lock and raised the lid of the case.

His face turned ashen as he stared into the empty briefcase. His mind raced. "Stop the Arab family!" he yelled at the officer. "They've switched my briefcase!" He ran from the inspection area toward the exit doors. Two armed officers grabbed his arms and held him as he yelled, "You don't understand! You have to let me find them!"

As he fought them, one agent removed a set of plastic cuffs, much like the tether Brian still had around his wrist, and shackled his hands behind him. "Let's get your luggage, sir," the officer said. "You're coming with us."

# Chapter Three

BETHLEHEM
MARCH, 3 B.C.

Benjamin held his father's hand. The shepherds stood in a semi-circle in front of the manger, where the child lay on a blanket. His face shone radiantly.

As they stood in silence, a commotion of sorts arose in the courtyard behind the small cave. Benjamin was astounded to see three camels in the courtyard - they must have been allowed in through a gateway to the street – and a trio of tall men dressed in fine clothing. These men were obviously wealthy and deserved respect. The shepherds bowed their heads in the presence of the three, and moved away from the child's crib.

Joseph, the child's father, said, "Enter, strangers. All who have seen the star are welcome here." "How did you know about the star?" the tallest of the men asked. He was of African descent and Benjamin thought he was the most impressive man he had ever seen. "We were traversing the countryside near your town when we saw the shaft of light shining on this place. We felt compelled to come here. What magic is afoot?"

"There is no magic, sir," Joseph answered. Then the woman looked up. She spoke in a voice which sounded almost musical to

Benjamin. "This is the Messiah," she said softly as she smiled at the baby. "Come worship him."

The important men fell to their knees as had the shepherds moments earlier. They believe her, Benjamin thought. But in his heart he knew it wasn't like that. It wasn't that they believed. It was as though it WAS. It was as though they had known it before they arrived. *It is in their minds and hearts too,* Benjamin thought, *just like mine.*

The men rose and went into the courtyard. They rummaged through their saddlebags for a few minutes, each returning with an item in his hand. As they knelt before the small child, they made offerings of the things they had brought into the stable. They laid them before the Messiah.

Benjamin wanted to offer a gift too. They were poor people, and he knew he had nothing which would possibly equal the value of the things those three men had given. In his pocket was a single shekel, a coin he carried for luck, which Joab had given him long ago. He came forward and said to the child's mother, "May I give him my gift?"

"Look at him, child," the mother said. "He accepts your gift." The child looked into Benjamin's eyes and reached his hand toward him. Benjamin placed the coin in the child's hand, and he clutched it to his chest for a moment. Then he reached out again to Benjamin. "The coin is blessed by the Messiah," the lady said. "Take it and keep it safe. The hand of God has held this coin." "I . . . I will," Benjamin stammered. He put the shekel in his pocket and stepped back. Joab smiled at him and patted his head. "That was a wonderful gift, son," he said to Benjamin. "My, we will have much to tell your mother when we get home tonight!"

# Chapter Four

DALLAS, TEXAS
EIGHT YEARS AGO, FEBRUARY 2001

The oil boom was making millionaires overnight and nowhere was it happening as fast as it was in Dallas. A major financial publication listed the metroplex as home to more millionaires under thirty than any other city in the USA. The dot.com boom, which had made literal billionaires of a few twenty-somethings, had begun to fizzle in California, but it was still in full swing here in Texas, where it seemed everyone had more money than sense. They called oil Black Gold. For thousands of Texans in the right place at the right time, the gold was there for the taking. And now was the right time.

Brian Sadler saw all this happening from his vantage point as a stockbroker at Merrill Lynch in Dallas. To look at Brian across a room, six feet tall, brownish blond hair, a physique kept honed by three days a week at the gym . . . he looked like a football player. And he had been, back in Longview, Texas. He played high school ball before heading to the University of Oklahoma. He had been good, but not great. Good was enough some places, but at OU, consistently ranked in the top two or three teams nationally, Brian hadn't even gotten a glance.

He majored in finance and minored in archaeological studies. It was an odd combination, but archaeology was something Brian had always been interested in. Not so much the digs, but the results – he loved to read and watch documentaries showing the incredible finds that archaeologists made. People such as Howard Carter with King Tut, Schliemann with the city of Troy and even Napoleon's team of mummy hunters who dug up Egypt in the nineteenth century – all of this fascinated Brian.

After graduation, Brian knew making a living involved using his finance degree, not his archaeology minor. He interviewed and landed an entry level job as a stockbroker at Merrill Lynch. After being at the firm two years, he now had settled into a routine which paid the bills, but, he thought, was never going to make him rich.

Since he had been at Merrill, Brian noticed a phenomenon which was accompanying the steady rise in oil prices - the Rolls Royce and Bentley automobiles appearing regularly at Capital Grille and Del Frisco's. At these trendy restaurants, the booze flowed freely until the wee hours. And the prices were as high as oil futures, with the customers often equally as high. But it wasn't drugs fueling those people – it was money, deals and more deals. Everybody, it seemed, lived for the next deal. Kids as young as twenty lit Cuban cigars with hundred dollar bills while beautiful girls hung on their every word. Brian vowed to be one of those people.

Amid some fanfare, two Merrill Lynch brokers had defected a month ago, moving to Warren Taylor and Currant. W&T, like Merrill, sold stocks to customers too, but the similarity ended there. Merrill managers talked openly about the firm's rumored problems with regulatory agencies like the Securities and Exchange Commission. "You go there, you sell your soul to the devil," one manager remarked disdainfully about the departure of the two brokers.

Brian listened, but he also had heard the rumors about how

people made incredible incomes at W&T just by selling the deals they were always doing.

Last week Brian had met the two defectors at Martini Park, a hip new bar in Legacy Town Center not far from Brian's apartment. Sipping XO Vodka martinis and sitting on the patio, the guys told Brian about life at Warren Taylor and Currant. "W&T is a crazy place, Brian," Jeff Spivey said. "We're raising money for everything you can think of. I'm working on a deal right now to help a guy who's twenty-five buy an electronics manufacturing company in Austin. He hasn't got a dime, and we're doing a public offering to raise $25 million for the acquisition. And he'll own 70%! Instant millionaires, Brian. We're a factory creating instant millionaires!"

The other broker, Sam Cooper, was thirty, five years older than Jeff. "I'm the old man on the trading floor," he said. "The other guys make fun of me. It's like a party all the time – they brought me a cane last week so I could get around the office." He told Brian that he was on the oil and gas team. Their job was to identify companies that could be acquired, and make the deals happen. "I'm working on a deal now to take Marciano Resources public," Sam said. "It'll happen in the next sixty days, and I'll get a hundred thousand bucks bonus, plus a million options. If the stock jumps on opening day like our one last week did, I'll be a millionaire on day one!"

It all sounded too good to be true. Jeff and Sam talked about the party atmosphere at W&T, the excitement when the company's deals came to market, the champagne that flowed like water after the closing bell, and the chance to make real money.

"Brian, you should come over," Jeff said. "This won't last forever. While it does, you should be on the bandwagon."

Jeff had picked up the two hundred dollar tab at Martini Park. When they ordered their second round, Brian had fervently hoped he would. Brian's credit card was close to the limit, and he had over a week left until payday. "No big deal, a tab like this," Jeff joked to Brian. "You'll find out for yourself if you come over and join the A-Team!"

Driving back in his Jeep, his mind raced with thoughts about everything he had heard. That had been a sleepless night for Brian. He lay in bed, thoughts racing through his head. Sure, it sounded good. But there were no free lunches. At what price did that kind of money come? What was the cost to risk everything?

# Chapter Five

BETHLEHEM
MARCH, 3 B.C.

The sun was rising, its first rays casting a dim light into the courtyard where perhaps twenty people stood as though in a daze. They had been that way all night, occasionally speaking quietly to each other about the event they had witnessed. They had learned that of the three wealthy individuals who had come by camel, only the dark-skinned man spoke their language. Sitting at a table in the inn, he conversed easily with his two friends in a tongue none of them could understand.

Benjamin and Joab looked at one another, suddenly aware that the sun was rising above the buildings in Bethlehem. It was as though they had awakened from a dream, one in which all who were standing around them had participated.

"We must return to our sheep," Joab said, getting his wits about him. He turned to gather his fellow shepherds, and Benjamin went back to the small cave once again.

Standing by the door so he could see in the half-darkness, Benjamin watched the baby sleep in the manger. His father slept on a mat nearby, and his mother sat behind the cradle, smiling as she softly sang to her newborn baby. Looking up, she saw Benjamin. "Yeshua sleeps," she said.

"Is . . . is that his name, Yeshua?" Benjamin asked. He felt so small in front of this woman and child, even though they were obviously not people of high standing, by their dress and situation. No wealthy person would have dreamt of delivering a baby in a stable!

The woman looked at him, and Benjamin averted his face. He found he could not look her in the eyes – they glowed with both a sweetness and an intensity he had never imagined before. "Yes," she responded to him. "The heralds from heaven told me he will be called Yeshua."

Bowing his head, Benjamin approached the child once more, wondering if he would ever see him again. He touched the baby's soft cheek and felt electricity in his fingers. "Thank you for coming to see our child," the mother said to him. "God bless you all." Benjamin turned and went back into the courtyard.

Ishmael, the proprietor of The Four Horsemen, had made pots of steaming coffee for everyone, and delicious pastries cooked by his wife were on the bar. Benjamin found his father and the others drinking and eating. Benjamin joined them at a table and shortly they left The Four Horsemen to return to the hills outside of town.

# Chapter Six

DALLAS, TEXAS

Brian looked at the employment ad he had pulled up on Monster.com. Two of his co-workers at Merrill had gone to this place already, and although you couldn't believe what anybody said in this business, if they were even half right, they were making much more than Brian was. And not just a little more – they could make more in a month than Brian could hope to make after years of service.

So Brian called Warren Taylor and Currant. Since he held a Series 7 securities license, he was given what the firm called a fast-track interview, which, if he accepted a job there, could put him on the floor at W&T in less than two weeks. Unheard of in the traditionally stuffy, get-to-know-you world of investment banking.

Brian struggled with his wardrobe the morning of his interview. He had told his boss he had to take care of some personal business – he didn't think now was the time to tell him what he was really doing – and as he stood in his bathroom in his boxers, Brian wondered what was appropriate dress for an interview at Warren Taylor. In the end, he decided conservatism was best. It wouldn't be good if he were in jeans, and everyone else was dressed in a suit. The other way around was much safer. So he brought out one of the Brooks Brothers pinstripes that was part of his daily regimen.

Brian hit the Dallas North Tollway at 8:15 a.m., an hour later than he usually did. Traffic was light as his Grand Cherokee moved toward downtown. The traffic on the Tollway always invigorated Brian – he thought of the drivers around him as his competition, fighting him for deals and dollars. He had read somewhere that you need to picture yourself in a situation, in order to make it happen. He tried to picture himself as a W&T broker, but he was really unsure what that picture actually looked like. He had no idea what he would see, and how different the operation would be from Merrill Lynch. He figured it would be pretty remarkable. And he would be correct.

W&T's offices occupied the thirty-fifth floor of The Strand, a new office building on McKinney Avenue in the Uptown district, where Dallas' construction boom was in full swing. On almost every block there were high-rise apartment buildings and offices, restaurants, bars and glitzy shops. Walking through the firm's glass entry doors, Brian could hear a faint rumble coming from inside the office suite somewhere. Two receptionists sat behind a massive curved desk made of stainless steel. The firm's name was emblazoned across ten feet of wall behind them. Both were answering calls as Brian approached. Glancing around the lobby, he saw half a dozen people, some dressed in suits, some in jeans, all obviously waiting for one appointment or another.

Closing a call, one of the receptionists took Brian's name and paged Carl Cybola. "What position does Carl hold?" Brian asked her.

"He's the floor manager," she replied. The other receptionist, who had also finished her call, laughed and said, "We call him the ringmaster. He's in charge of the circus!" As they returned to their frenzied answering of incoming calls, Brian took a seat.

Right on time, a gorgeous girl dressed in Seven Jeans and a top probably from Bebe, came to the lobby to retrieve Brian. She opened a door, holding it for him. The noise suddenly increased tenfold as they entered a cavernous room perhaps 200 feet long and 100 wide, crammed with cubicles. Each held a guy or girl, most standing with phones in their hands, shouting. The ones who weren't on calls were yelling at others in the room.

From his work at Merrill, he understood the lingo. They were taking orders from customers – although in a way 180 degrees opposite to Merrill's style. "Don't call me bitching about this deal if you miss it today," one shouted. He heard, "Think it over? Are you a wimp? Make a damned decision and be a man!" And it was working. They were closing deals in record time, quickly moving to the next one. His bosses as Merrill would have been horrified, Brian thought, if they could see these techniques. But, he had to admit, being on the trading floor gave him an incredible rush.

The interview was in a glass conference room, insulated from most of the noise, but situated so a candidate could watch the action while the meeting took place. Carl Cybola, the floor manager who met with him said, "We make dreams come true here. Our clients' dreams come true, but yours can too. We're going to give you a base salary of $25,000 a year." Seeing Brian's face fall, Cybola said, "What's the matter? "

"That's less than half the base I'm making at Merrill," Brian replied. "My friends who work here talk about making six figures already."

"The base is nothing. It won't make the payments on my Maserati," Carl responded, laughing. "The base pay only serves to weed out the stars from the rest of the pack." He went on to explain that Brian would be working on deals he found himself, but also would make money when existing customers did deals. The red-hot oil market in Dallas meant there were lots of people with lots of money, and Warren Taylor and Currant had ways for them to make a great deal more.

They discussed what was expected of a W&T broker. Carl said they were looking for young, motivated self-starters who wanted to get rich quick. "We make no bones about it," he said. "If you aren't primarily motivated by doing deals and making big bucks, you don't belong here." Then he looked Brian in the eye and said, "Do you do drugs?"

The question shouldn't have taken Brian by surprise; it came up frequently in interview situations, he knew. However, he figured it wasn't a big deal here, given the frenzy and pace of the sales floor.

"I've tried stuff," he responded. "But I don't do drugs now. If you're asking me if I can pass a drug test, yes I can."

Carl leaned back in his chair, letting out a booming laugh. "No, that really wasn't the reason I asked," he responded. "A lot of guys and gals here use drugs recreationally. Some of our people are pretty strung out on drugs sometimes. I just wanted to tell you if you use drugs, you might want to tone it down during the workweek. You'll get plenty of high here without 'em, and in my opinion all they can do is make you not think as straight, or as fast, as you should."

Brian assured him it wasn't a problem – and it wasn't. Brian's experiments into drugs in college and afterward left him with an empty feeling every time he came down off a high. And the loss of control while he was doing drugs was something he just wasn't willing to allow, even for the short-term rush.

The interview drew to a close, and Carl said, "I want you here, Brian. Go back and think about it . . . but don't take much time. I have seats to sell in that room out there and if you don't want one, there's a dozen more just like you salivating at the opportunity to be a W&T broker." He tossed what looked like a credit card across his desk to Brian. "Here," Carl said. "When you show up the first day, don't be wearing that Brooks Brothers suit. Go to Stanley Korshak and ask for Doug. Tell him you're a W&T broker now, and he'll fix you up. When you work here, you gotta look like one of us."

Stanley Korshak, the upscale men's clothier in the Crescent Court Hotel, was a place Brian couldn't afford. Although it would help, he figured the Korshak gift card he held in his hand wouldn't pay for all of a suit – and the rest would surely be out of Brian's reach.

He had more to think about than that. A move from Merrill to W&T was a big decision. The W&T firm had a reputation for being cutting edge – not always a good thing. The old-school traditional brokers were conservative. You developed a client base and slowly built a book of business, often becoming a client's broker for life. The big brokers considered Warren Taylor a bucket shop – a place where deals got done by hook or by crook.

# Chapter Seven

THE JUDEAN HILLS NEAR BETHLEHEM
LATE MARCH, 3 B.C.

When the shepherds arrived at the hillside where they had abandoned their flock, they found the sheep milling around, grazing, as though nothing had happened. Not one was missing. Joab remarked that it was as though someone had watched over the flock while they were in Bethlehem all night.

As they walked down the hill, leading the flock to a nearby stream, Joab and Benjamin walked together. "Father," Benjamin said, "what we saw last night was a miracle, was it not?"

"My son," his father responded, "I am still not sure what to make of it. I must have time to think, and perhaps talk to the Elders at the synagogue about what we saw. Whether to mention it, I am not sure. However, one thing I do know. You must take your quill and parchment and write the events of last evening."

Joab instructed Benjamin, the only member of the group who could write, to record everything, beginning with the bright light that had first alerted the shepherds. Leaving a couple of men to continue to tend the flock, Joab and Benjamin walked the dusty road about a mile to their home. When they arrived, Joab said, "Go, son. Record your thoughts now, lest you forget even a single event of last night. I must speak with your mother."

Rachel, Joab's wife, was washing clothes in the yard behind their small house. They had two hectares of land – not much, but enough to raise some sheep and a small garden of vegetables for the family to eat. "Good morning, husband," she said when she saw him. "Did you and Benjamin have a good night's rest?"

Joab took her in his arms and held her tight. "My," she said, smiling. "What is that all about?"

"My darling," he said. "Neither Benjamin nor I slept for one moment last night. I have something to tell you which I hope you will believe. Even though I saw it myself, I hardly can believe it."

It took nearly an hour for Joab to relate his story. Rachel sat, hands folded in her lap, saying nothing until he had finished. By this time, Benjamin had joined them. When Joab was finished, Rachel said, "I think we must pray now. For if you speak the truth, you and Benjamin have witnessed a miracle which will change the world forever."

# Chapter Eight

Brian started at Warren Taylor and Currant four days after his interview. He had thought about the offer all that day, and spent most of the afternoon at Merrill online, researching deals W&T had done in the past year. He was astonished. The firm had done ten times more deals than Merrill had. They were far smaller, Brian noticed, but none was less than $10 million, and most of the companies W&T had taken public were trading higher than the offering price, which meant that investors had to be happy because they were making a profit on their investments with W&T.

The next morning Brian gave his two weeks' notice to his own manager, whose response surprised Brian. "If you're going to W&T," he said, "you're not the guy I thought you were. We don't need you here any more. You're released today."

"Wha… what do you mean?" Brian blurted out. "I'm not the guy you thought I was? I'm who I am." His manager looked at him and said, "Get out, Brian. I'd wish you good luck, but what you need is a bulletproof vest. I've always liked you. I hope you can stay out of trouble."

Stunned, Brian cleaned out his desk and walked out of Merrill

Lynch for the last time, convincing himself as he got in his Jeep that the Merrill guy was just spouting sour grapes, and that every broker had to play by the same rules as the others. Trouble? Brian thought to himself as he pulled out of the parking lot. Bullshit. I can handle anything.

Intrigued by the gift card Carl had given him, Brian dropped by the Stanley Korshak men's store after he left Merrill's downtown office. He asked for Doug, and when the impeccably dressed salesman approached him, Brian decided he must have been a linebacker in college. He was a rugged, handsome guy. He took a look at the gift card Brian offered, and laughed. "So Carl sent you my way? You think you can cut it at W&T? Make a million like the others?"

"Sure," Brian replied confidently. "But if it's the place to make a million, why are you selling suits instead of stocks?"

"The truth?" Doug replied. "W&T's the hottest place in town. You can make a killing there faster than anywhere else – even faster than the oilies can. But I'm looking at tomorrow. I can make my fortune selling clothes to you guys who have to have it all, and I'll still be here when it's all over." He smiled broadly and Brian wondered how much of the revelation had been a joke, or if any of it had.

"So how much will this card buy me?" Brian asked.

Doug laughed. "Pick yourself out a couple of suits," he replied, explaining that the card itself had no value at all. It was a ticket – a passport - carte blanche for the holder to buy up to $5000 in clothes from Stanley Korshak, all charged to Warren Taylor and Currant. Two Hugo Boss suits later, Brian left the store, and left his old life behind.

Driving up the Tollway after his first day at Warren Taylor, Brian thought of the differences. In fact, he couldn't think of a single thing that was remotely similar to this first day and that day at Merrill two years ago.

At Merrill, Brian Sadler's first six weeks had been spent in training sessions, where he learned the basics of the company and its modus operandi. Observed by a supervisor, he had made calls to existing customers who had been reassigned to him, and to potential new customers who had been identified from various advertising methods. Not a stone was left unturned to make a professional from a novice. Brian was self-assured and confident as he was released to become a broker on Merrill's sales floor.

A little of W&T scared Brian. Most of it fascinated him. He knew this place could be his stepping stone to the stars. He also knew he would make that happen.

When he accepted Carl's offer, Brian was told when to report to the office for his first day of work. He rose early that morning, showered, shaved and had a bagel and coffee. He donned his new shirt, tie and Hugo Boss suit, and drove to work.

Brian pulled his Jeep into the garage under W&T's office building and took the elevator to the thirty-fifth floor. Although the receptionists had not yet arrived, the front door was unlocked. He walked to the sales floor, heading for Carl's office. "Fresh meat! Fresh meat!" he heard catcalls from the salespeople as he made his way through the office. Several stood, pointing and laughing. He smiled at them and made his way to Carl's office. Carl was there, along with three guys. As one told a story, the rest were laughing uncontrollably. He stuck his head in, and Carl waved him to an empty chair. "Sit and give me one sec," Carl said. Brian took an empty chair in Carl's office.

"So he took my dare," the storyteller continued. "While we sat in the bar having drinks, he left, then came back a half hour later in jeans and a t-shirt, wearing one of those tool belts like he was a damned plumber or something! He walked over to the painting, took it off the wall, and just walked out with it. He just walked out. Everybody there thought he was a maintenance man or something. Nobody challenged him. Nobody said a word!" The guys were almost bent double, laughing at the story. "Then he came back, ten minutes later, in his suit and tie. He sat down at our table, told me the painting was in the parking garage under my car, and held out his hand."

"Did you pay off on the bet?" one broker asked him.

"Yep," he responded. "A thousand bucks. Laid it right in his hand. I never in a million years thought he could get away with that. And I never thought he would even try it! He stole a damned painting which had to be worth thousands!" The guys guffawed while Brian smiled in astonishment, not only at the deed done, but at the size of the bet made and paid, for such a stupid stunt.

Turning to Brian, Carl introduced him to the group, pulled two sheets of paper from his desk drawer, then said, "Sign this. It's a confidentiality agreement required on the first day of everyone's employment. It's no big deal – just says you won't leave here and steal our stuff." Brian wanted to take a few minutes to read the document, which was in small print and had the usual "whereas" and "therefores" that indicated it had probably been created by a law firm. Carl saw him start reading. "Just sign it, and let me show you where you are going to be sitting," Carl said impatiently. "You can read it later. It's bullshit anyway." Brian signed, gave Carl one copy and kept the other.

Carl led Brian to the sales floor, to a group of cubicles with a huge sign hanging above them that said "Team Bravo." Carl introduced him to Randy Perkins, Team Bravo's group leader. "You guys are going to be stars by the end of the week," Carl said to the team. "So get off your butts and get that Malco Energy deal done!"

"You got it, boss," Randy shouted to him. "Team Bravo – start those calls. It's 9:30 a.m. in New York City. The market is O-PEN! Let's get it done NOW!" A frenzy erupted among the ten or so cubes that made up Team Bravo. Randy turned to Brian. "Here's home, buddy," he said, pointing to a cubicle nearby. It was about six feet square, just like the other hundred or more in the room, with a computer monitor, keyboard and mouse. There was nothing else.

"W&T's intranet will be your homepage," Carl said, gesturing to the monitor. "Look up Malco Energy and read the S-1 there. Get yourself up to speed fast, pardner. You got a million bucks to make."

Guiding the mouse, Carl clicked on his computer screen, bringing up the internal website of Warren Taylor and Currant. "Pending Deals" was one of the selections he saw; clicking it, he chose "Malco Energy" and brought up a folder of documents. He clicked on "S-1 Registration Filing" and brought up a document over a hundred pages long. This was the filing that a law firm had prepared for Malco Energy and filed with the Securities and Exchange Commission. Through W&T, Malco Energy was going to go public very soon.

It was hard to concentrate at first. Having come from the quiet of a small office at Merrill, he was now thrust into the circus of a hundred voices in a cacophony of noise. He could hear the broker next to him shouting, "You can't afford NOT to do this! I guarantee you Malco will be up ten bucks the day we bring it public. It can't lose." Then he heard, "Ten thousand shares. Done, Dr. Samuelson. Drop me a check – do it today. We have to have everything in house by Friday."

Brian looked back at the screen and the registration document open before him. Malco was projected to come to market at twenty dollars a share. The doctor had spent two hundred thousand dollars. Sweet, Brian thought. That broker must have a great relationship with his customer to get a deal that big, that fast.

Sticking his head up over the cube wall, Brian said, "I couldn't help overhearing your quick sale. Nice job. How long have you worked with the doctor?"

The broker stood, introducing himself as Jim Palmer. "About ten minutes," he responded, laughing. "You heard the entire relationship in that one call."

Brian thought about what he had heard. That a broker could get an order from someone he had never talked to before, and could guarantee the stock would go up on offering, was incomprehensible to Brian. "Can I ask a quick question?" Brian said to Jim.

"Shoot," he replied.

"When do I do my initial paperwork, like my withholdings, and sign an employment agreement, and everything?"

Jim responded that W&T wasn't much into things that didn't make the firm money. He said he had been with the firm over a year, and still hadn't seen his offer letter. "They backdate everything," he said. "You'll probably have to fill out your withholdings form the day paychecks are cut."

Unbelievable, Brian thought, sitting back down. He began to read the Malco offering document closely. An S-1 registration document was designed to tell the SEC everything it needed to know about the company: its history, officers, directors and shareholders. It explained the work the investment banking firm would do to sell stock to the public, and what its remuneration would be.

W&T had chosen $20 a share as its target offering price, although that price wouldn't be final until the day the SEC approved the deal and Malco went public. Malco was selling 2 million shares to the public. Before expenses, the deal would give Malco $40 million. Brian turned to the financial reporting section of the S-1, to see what kind of profits Malco had been generating. For a deal this big, he figured he would see a seasoned company, run by veterans in the oil and gas industry, and making steady profits every one of the past few years.

What he saw instead astonished him. Malco, the offering document stated, was a company formed in the last two years, by two men whose experience in the oil business consisted of having owned some royalty interests. One of the owners was actually a former Warren Taylor broker, and amazingly, he had left the firm because his securities license was in jeopardy.

The Securities and Exchange Commission had accused this broker of fraudulently inducing people to invest in securities for which they were not qualified. Brian knew that this usually meant pushing elderly people with lots of money, but little understanding of the market, to invest in high-flyer deals. As a settlement with the SEC, the broker had agreed to leave Warren Taylor and Currant and give up his broker's license.

According to the document Brian was reading, the broker formed Malco less than a month after leaving W&T. The firm had virtually no assets, a lot of liabilities, in the form of loans by various people to keep the company's bills paid until the public offering, and nobody had any experience. Given the extent to which companies were required to disclose everything in an offering document, Brian wondered how in the world W&T could, or would, sell a deal like this to investors. It looked like a good deal for the owners of the shell company, for the brokers who made commission on it, and for a bunch of lawyers who did the paperwork. Brian couldn't see how the new shareholders were going to make anything, given the company's lack of history and prospects.

Brian stood, looking over his cubicle wall. "Jim," he said to the broker next door, "I just read the S-1 on Malco. How in the hell can you get anybody to buy this piece of crap?"

"Hey," Jim replied quickly. "Don't be too quick to judge. We've done forty deals like Malco in the past year, and people have had the chance to make money on all of them. They all went up a lot right after they went public. W&T makes it happen." He went on to explain that people who were astute, watched the stock closely and got out at the right time stood to make money – in some cases, huge profits. "It's not my fault that the stupid ones stay in too long," he laughed. "I'll guarantee you one damn thing. I'm out at the right time!"

"You?" Brian said. "You get stock yourself? I thought we all worked on commissions, selling this stuff."

"That's just part of it," Jim replied. "There's a little pot of stock hidden away on each deal, and those of us who push it the hardest get to share in it. The stock never even ends up in my name; I just get cash money for my share of the profit. And do you want to know the best thing? I don't even have to pay income tax on it!"

Brian sat down, astounded at what he had heard. None of it sounded legal, but surely W&T had figured out a way to make it be above board. This firm wouldn't risk its existence just to do deals . . . would it?

It was the first time Brian Sadler was surprised at the guts of a Warren Taylor deal, but certainly not the last. He had no idea that very soon he would not only be pushing deals like Malco himself, he would someday be yet another ex-broker who owned a public company.

# Chapter Nine

Brian pushed himself to the limit from his first day at W&T. He quickly "unlearned" the techniques he had been so carefully taught at Merrill Lynch, and he found unbelievable exhilaration from cold calling. He learned that W&T charged much higher commissions than other firms, because they weren't competing for the same business. W&T's deals were usually successful, people knew it, and they were willing to pay the price to get into a W&T public offering. Higher commissions from the buyers of stock meant the firm could offer higher commissions to its best performers. And they did, with the percentage increasing exponentially as a person's sales increased.

The firm bought lists of high net worth individuals worldwide who had previously been big investors in risky deals, which often meant the potential for very high returns on investment. Every morning at Warren Taylor and Currant began with "The Push", the name for the 8 am sales meeting nobody wanted to miss.

On Brian's second day, he arrived at the building at 7:45, eager to attend his first meeting of The Push. He was surprised to find the parking garage filled with incoming brokers. Everyone was yelling, laughing or gulping Starbucks as they left their cars and headed for the elevator bank. He and a dozen other brokers, male and female, entered the next car. "You the new guy on Team Bravo?" the guy next to him asked.

"Yes, I'm Brian Sadler."

"Jim Poteet," he said, shaking Brian's hand. "I'm glad you're here. Your team has to get Malco done this week, and they've been short of people. The last guy who occupied your cube took a dive out the window on Thursday. Thirty five stories down. Wow. Just couldn't take the pressure!"

Brian was aware his mouth had dropped open as he stared at the guy. He couldn't think of a response, and the entire elevator car was totally quiet. There was a ding and the door slid open. Suddenly everyone burst out laughing. "Just messin' with ya, pal," Poteet said, slapping Brian on the back. "We're all too damn rich here to take a dive."

Everyone continued laughing as they walked onto the sales floor. Brian forced a laugh too, even though he had to overcome the knot which had formed in the pit of his stomach when he was in the elevator. "I'm the new kid," he thought. "I have to get used to this stuff, and I'm damned sure not at Merrill Lynch any more."

Brian had just dropped into his chair and fired up his computer when he saw Carl Cybola run to the middle of the sales floor and jump on a large round desk. "This is THE PUSH!" he shouted. All around him, people in every cubicle jumped up and began shouting and cheering. Brian had never seen such frenzied enthusiasm. Guys were waving their suit coats around over their heads. Hands were held high in the air. It was like a football game, he thought. These people are crazy about this place!

Carl let the cheering continue for a minute or so, then asked the brokers to quieten down. "This is Tuesday of Malco week," he said to the crowd. Brian was aware he could hear Carl through the overhead speakers used for paging, and saw that Carl was wearing a lapel microphone. "Team Bravo, you have $40 million of Malco to sell and you have three days left to sell it. We're going public on Friday morning, and I want this damned boat floated and on the high seas by then." He told the group that Bravo had pre-sold $31 million in shares by close of business yesterday. "You guys know what happens on the Tuesday of offering week," he yelled to the crowd. More cheering erupted, interrupting the discussion for a full two minutes.

"OK, OK, calm down," he yelled. "Today's the day Team Bravo gets a little competition. Teams Alpha and Charlie, it's your turn to see what you can do. Bravo continues to sell, but you other two teams can make some big bucks pushing this baby cart around the park. Malco's hotter than a dog in heat, folks. This thing sells itself. And here's the kicker. We have nine million bucks to go. The person who sells the most Malco between now and the market close on Thursday gets . . . " He paused, and the crowd again went wild. "Diamonds!!" a girl near Brian yelled. "Trip to Paris! Trip to Paris!" a guy shouted.

Carl once again got the crowd under control. "Here's the deal, kids," he said. "The person who sells the most Malco between right now and 4 pm Thursday gets . . . a brand new Lamborghini!"

This time the yelling and screaming went on for a full five minutes. Carl tried in vain to hush the crowd, and finally he got things back under control. "Here are the game rules," he said. "Your customer's cash has to be in house by Thursday night. The car will be a Lamborghini Gallardo, brand new, worth $189,000. And it'll be yours. No lease, no nothing. Titled in whatever name you wish. Watch out where you title it, guys," Carl yelled, his arms waving wildly. "All together now . . ." and the group in unison shouted, "Everything offshore . . . means no tax man knocking on your door!"

The pandemonium was incredible. Brian wondered how people working on the floor below W&T's offices could hear themselves think. And he wondered how anyone could win a two hundred thousand dollar car and not pay tax on it. But he wanted to find out the secret W&T obviously knew, and he vowed in his mind to be a winner within six months.

The meeting ended with Carl yelling, "Get to work, everyone! You have calls to make, people to separate from their hard-earned money, and a Lamborghini to put in your garage!" Yelling and clapping, everyone sat down in their cubicles.

# Chapter Ten

The week was the most incredible adventure Brian had ever been on. The days were filled with calls, many of which resulted in sales. W&T's intranet had a page where lists of names were posted, and from which the brokers could pull names to call. As he made calls, Brian discovered most of the people he was calling were professionals or executives. All had gatekeepers, like an executive assistant or a front office receptionist, but when he mentioned Warren Taylor and Currant, almost all of the potential clients took his call.

Discussing it later with Jim Palmer, his cube-mate, he was told that W&T had a very well-known reputation for making people money. "Most of our deals are still hot, months and months later," Jim explained. "We do a lot to make sure the price stays up. We make the owners of the company sign in blood that they won't dump stock for a year, even if it's up a thousand percent. The tradeoff for the owners making a shitload of money is that our investors have to make a shitload too. That way, everybody's happy . . . including us brokers!"

Brian's calls went very well, and many people seemed pleased to be offered the chance to invest in a hot W&T deal. Almost no one asked anything in detail about Malco Energy itself, even though Brian had prepared a fact sheet he was ready to use if someone wanted to know something. In reality, he had trouble finding many selling points, since the company had no seasoned management, no business and nothing but hopes and dreams, but he at least could fall back on W&T's success with prior offerings, most of which looked much like Malco when they hit the street.

After the market closed on Tuesday, there was a noticeable quiet which settled on the trading floor. "I wonder if everyone else is as exhausted as I am," Brian thought.

Jim Palmer stuck his head around the wall and said, "How'd you do, newbie?" "I made some sales," Brian replied. "I guess tomorrow morning I'll get a report that shows how I did."

"Is that how they did it at Merrill?" Jim asked. He explained that W&T didn't want people to go home not knowing how their day went. They needed the rush of knowing they did well, or the knowledge they needed to push harder, to get them ready for tomorrow.

He showed Brian how to go on the intranet to a page that had a number of listings and names posted. "This stuff is all in real time," he explained to Brian. "As soon as you post an order, it hits the sales sheet, showing the amount you sold and your commission." Brian saw several lists on the page. At the top was a list of top brokers for the month. There were ten names listed. The top guy had already put a half million bucks in his pocket as commission income. Brian's throat got dry as he scrolled down the list, making himself a promise that he would do anything, anything in the world, to be on that top ten list.

Other "top ten" lists showed the various deals the company was working on. Since this was Malco Week, and the company was set to go public on Friday, Malco's list was at the top. Not surprisingly to Brian, a couple of people who were on the Malco top ten list were also top sellers company-wide. Jim Palmer was on the Malco list, with sales over $4 million and commissions of nearly $25,000 for the month. He knew Jim had other sales than Malco, so he figured Jim's total income for the month had to be way over fifty grand. He suddenly was more impressed with Jim.

"Have you found the Malco list for today?" Jim yelled through the wall.

Brian said he hadn't, and Jim told him to scroll down below the master Malco list. There was a smaller list, showing all of today's sales for Malco, and each salesperson's numbers. Jim explained this sub-list would be posted from now until Thursday, and really was for nothing more than determining who won Carl's contest.

"Speaking of the contest, Jim," Brian asked, scooting his chair back into the aisle so he could see into Jim's space, "W&T must be making big bucks in order to give away a Lamborghini."

"Did you look at the registration statement?" Jim asked him. Brian said he had, but hadn't gotten to the part about fees. "W&T will make millions on the deal," Jim explained, 'but they also will put our chairman on the company's board, and pay him a could hundred grand a year for that, plus signing up to be a client of W&T for investment management. Don't forget, we're handing this company over thirty-five million bucks after expenses, and they don't have a damn thing in mind to do with the money, except look for some oil. It'll take a while to spend that kind of money. And while they're sitting on it, guess who's going to be investing it for them? You got it. Good old W&T. And a bunch of that money we just raised for them will go right back into other new deals of ours, because in our infinite wisdom, we are recommending our own hot stocks as good investments for the company!"

Sliding back into his cube, Brian thought about how all that worked. No wonder these stocks continued to be high flyers after they went public, he thought. People buy Malco, who doesn't really need their money for awhile, and W&T puts that money in the next deal. Malco doesn't need to sell its investments, so when the stock goes up after the public offering, a lot of shareholders, like Malco, just hold on to it, because many of those investors are W&T's own companies, holding all that stock. "This is a dream deal," Brian thought. "Investors can almost be guaranteed to make money, as long as the market stays hot."

Turning back to the screen, Brian saw that a broker named Gillian Jensen was top seller of Malco for today, earning several thousand dollars for her effort. He didn't recognize any of the other names, and saw that only two of them were Team Bravo people. Obviously opening the floodgates to allow the other teams to sell was a good thing. It was working. He also saw his own name, far down the list, showing total sales of fifty thousand dollars and commission under $1000. "Not bad for day one of sales," Brian thought. "If I do this same thing for twenty-two business days in a month, I've made over twenty grand. In a damn month!"

A final Malco screen showed the tally for total sales at $34.5 million, which meant that $3.5 million had been sold today. They had five and a half million bucks left to raise for Malco, and two days left in which to do it.

# Chapter Eleven

Brian went home exhausted. He ordered Chinese food for delivery, popped a beer, and settled back. His mind was racing. The sales calls today had been easy for him. He had really not pushed himself. He thought of himself more in the Merrill vein – calmer, more reassuring to customers, confident about his product, and with a good solid pitch to make. *I don't need to be a hotshot like some of these other guys,* he thought to himself. *I can do this my way, and I can make half a million a year.* At that moment, on day two, he set a personal goal. *I am going to have forty grand in commissions in my third month*, he vowed. *And I won't ever have less than forty grand a month after that, as long as I am a W&T broker.*

If he had known then what the next two years would bring, he would have been astounded at his lack of vision.

# Chapter Twelve

DALLAS, TEXAS

TWO YEARS LATER, JANUARY 2005

In two years, Brian had paid his dues at W&T. The place was a madhouse, and he was one of the madmen. He'd paid a price, but what a reward awaited those who were good at this, he thought as he left the garage of his apartment building and pulled on to Turtle Creek Boulevard. He passed the Mansion on Turtle Creek a block from his place. Brian thought about how far he had come in so short a time. His entire lifestyle had changed. He had gone from paycheck-to-paycheck, to having not a worry in the world about money, ever. His only worry was whether he would be number one in sales or not. He ate the competition for breakfast, he thought satisfyingly. He was the *threat* at W&T.

He only had a few blocks to drive to work; the Porsche 911 convertible made it in less than ten minutes, as usual. Traffic was light before 8 am, and Brian always got to work before The Push started. It was his time of day to shine, to be recognized for the success he always knew he was, and to get energized for the day.

"Hey, Carl," he said to his boss as they both entered the elevator in the parking garage. "Have you tried Usa yet?"

"The new Japanese place?" Carl replied. "No. I hear they have some kind of exotic beef."

"Yeah," Brian responded. "It's Akaushi beef. It puts Kobe beef to shame – they have a New York Strip there that'll set you back a hundred and fifty bucks." Brian went on to explain that he and his girlfriend had drinks and dinner there last night and ended up with a tab of nearly eight hundred dollars.

Some of the newer guys at W&T were in the elevator. Brian saw surprised looks on the faces of some of them. "Hey guys," he said. "I was where you are two years ago next month. I was wondering whether my next meal would be McDonald's or Burger King. You guys have the world at your feet. If you can sell, you can make a fortune. If you can't, you're in the wrong elevator!" Everyone laughed, and the opening of the door ushered in a new day at Warren Taylor and Currant.

# Chapter Thirteen

Brian's first sales effort, the Malco Energy deal, had given him something far greater than the few thousand dollars he had made in commissions. He hadn't made the top ten list for Malco. He hadn't made the top anything list. He was just one of the guys, selling some stock to some people. But the gift he got from Malco was the knowledge, deep inside, that Warren Taylor and Currant would make him a star – a success in everyone's eyes – and he was ready to grasp it. At whatever cost.

He watched from the sidelines as a girl he'd never met won the Lamborghini and got over fifty thousand in commissions besides, for being top Malco salesperson for the final week. Malco went public, the former W&T broker who owned most of it was an instant multi-millionaire with an annual salary of nearly a million dollars, and he had to do not much of anything, since the company didn't have any business. All he really had to do, Brian knew, was let W&T handle his company's investment portfolio. *Nice work if you can get it,* he thought.

W&T had invested most of Malco's money in new hot deals, and Malco's stock skyrocketed, reflecting the increase in its investment portfolio of W&T companies. There were a few losers, sure. There always were. But, Brian thought, nine out of ten ain't bad, on average.

The Push that morning started with Carl Cybola's usual frenzied announcements, followed by the usual screaming session, and ending with discussions of the deals the company had working that week. Now W&T was taking fifty companies public a year – about one a week. The firm had nearly two thousand employees, 70 % of which were brokers. The rest spent their time pushing paperwork for the salespeople. The firm occupied five floors of The Strand, and things were absolutely going crazy, every single day.

# Chapter Fourteen

## SIX MONTHS LATER

The day the Feds walked in was a gorgeous one. It was the middle of June, and already nearly 80 degrees. Brian had lowered the top of his convertible so he could enjoy the breeze during his brief drive to work. The Push that morning was just like always. There had been a contest, and a young hotshot who'd only been there a month won a thousand bucks just for correctly spelling the name of the latest hot deal's CEO. At least it *was* a contest, Brian thought; the guy's name turned out to be Khalim Salamandi.

Brian had known there were a few things going on that weren't all rosy. There had been several investigations into the marketing techniques of W&T's salespeople. The Securities and Exchange Commission had even fined the firm $25,000 for allowing its people to be overly aggressive, in the SEC's opinion. That news was greeted with guffaws at The Push the morning after it was announced. "Twenty five grand they fine us," Carl yelled through the overhead intercom system that now piped his meeting to three of the company's floors. "Twenty five grand is what I wipe with in the morning!" People went nuts; they were laughing, yelling and clapping. And Brian Sadler was clapping right along with them, giving and receiving high-fives from the people around him.

A bigger concern was the SEC's investigation into a couple of public offerings W&T had done in the past six months. There was beginning to be pressure for the firm to stop doing so many "blind pool" offerings, which was the term used for companies that raised money but didn't have any immediate use for it. W&T's logic was, all of the firm's public deals ended up doing one thing or another, mostly in the fields they were supposed to be doing it in, and everybody made money, so what was the big issue?

W&T's biggest problem at the moment was a major issue indeed. It seemed investors were a little upset when Bellicose Holdings, one of W&T's offerings, turned out to be headed by Francois Rochefort, a Canadian who was both a coke addict and who had served ten years for fraud in a French prison.

Investment banks are expected to do an incredible amount of due diligence on the companies they're bringing to the public market, Brian knew. He also knew when a company like W&T did an offering a week, and was so lax in paperwork they hadn't yet even provided him an employment letter, something had to eventually blow up. The firm had done limited checking on the background of this joker, Brian decided, and it had blown up in their faces.

The blowup had come very quickly. Within a week after the company went public, W&T was awaiting the customary very large check from Bellicose, to do its usual investment of the company's funds. About three days late, a company check for twenty two million dollars had arrived at W&T, but when the firm deposited it, Warren Taylor's Chief Financial Officer got a call from the company's bank. "The check is no good," he was told. "There are not sufficient funds to cash it."

Investigating further, it developed that Bellicose Holdings

had less than ten thousand dollars in the bank. Two days before, virtually all of its assets, nearly twenty four million dollars, had been wire transferred to an account at a large New York bank, then transferred again to a bank in the Caribbean.

Reading the financial news each day on his laptop, Brian had read in a news release that two subsequent transfers had been made, ending up finally in a dead-end account in the European country of Andorra. From there the money had been withdrawn by a woman who had presented false identity to the bank and had since disappeared, as had the company's majority shareholder. That was all anyone was going to find out from Andorra, a country whose secrecy laws were legendary.

Brian was particularly interested in this company, because it had been his first big success. He had been hailed as Bellicose's Numero Uno – the top salesperson at W&T on this thirty million dollar stock sale. Brian had gotten in the groove, calling doctors, film stars, TV actors and real estate investors. All of them were his current clients, and all of them had made millions on W&T deals. It was easy to raise money when you'd been successfully doing it for a long time, and Brian rose to the top with over $6 million in personal sales to his clients on this deal. Including bonuses but not counting the Porsche he was given, he made over six hundred thousand dollars in six weeks.

Now the SEC and the United States Attorney's office were both looking into Bellicose. As sloppy as things were at W&T, Brian felt certain that at least there must be sufficient records and information to keep the firm in compliance with the complex securities laws. Small violations had occurred in the past. When a firm's doing this much business, Brian figured, lots of little things can fall through the cracks. Bellicose wasn't a little thing, though. Someone was going to end up in jail over this one. And lots of investigation was going to occur before it was over.

Brian himself didn't waste much time crying over Bellicose. He'd gotten his commissions, and after the company nosedived, he made calls to all his big investors, assuring them that the big tax writeoff they'd get now that Bellicose was cratering, would help them lower their tax bills for the home runs they'd had just prior to that one. Not a single one was upset. Everyone talked about how you win some, you lose some – and at W&T they'd all won a lot more than they'd lost.

As a precaution, Brian talked to Carl Cybola and got the OK to guarantee each of the Bellicose investors preferential treatment on the next public offering. They'd get the chance to invest more than usual, to hopefully gain a greater return than usual after the price rose.

"That's a no-brainer," Carl had said as he gave the approval. "Allowing these putzes to increase their purchases only makes it easier for us to sell the next one. Nothing like having a loser to make the winners do even better!"

After The Push that day, Brian had sat at his desk and made an online payment to a shell company in Aruba that owned his Porsche. About a week after he'd won the car, a mousy looking girl showed up at his cubicle after the close of business one day, took him in a nearby conference room, and handed him a packet of information along with the keys to his new 911 convertible.

She had told him that Warren Taylor had a number of shell companies set up to do things like own cars for star salespeople. "It's actually your company," she had said. "There's just no paper trail to ever tie it to you." She showed him documents which would demonstrate that he had located the leasing company online, signed a lease agreement, and would make monthly payments. "Since the car is used by you to come to work," the girl had said, "if I were you

I'd take a tax writeoff for your lease payments. That way, you own the car, but you also get to write off payments on it!" She had told Brian that's how all the other people did it at W&T. So he did too.

On that fateful morning, Brian had attended The Push like he had done several hundred times before, gotten some recognition for his sales this week, heard the latest deal being explained, and gone back to his desk. Around 11 am, he became aware that the place suddenly was a lot quieter than usual. There were no loud catcalls, no music from cubicles, no light banter between people. He stood and looked toward the front of the sales floor. One of the receptionists was backing into the room. It looked like she was trying to keep three men from following her – she had her hands up in a halting gesture. But they pushed by, and Brian could see badges hanging from lanyards around their necks. This was serious.

The guys stopped at Carl Cybola's office door. From where he sat, Brian could hear them ask if he was Cybola, then he heard, "Mr. Cybola, you're under arrest." They moved inside the room then, and he couldn't hear anything more.

Brian's heart rate skyrocketed. He got a sinking feeling in the pit of his stomach, and he sat down in his cubicle. "What the hell's going on?" Jim Palmer asked him. Brian's mouth was so dry, he could hardly respond.

"I . . . I bet they're from the SEC," he replied. Just as he did, one of the cops, or whatever they were, showed up at his cube.

"Brian Sadler?" he asked. "Yes," Brian said, standing. He could see the other two guys moving Carl toward the front door, his hands cuffed behind him. As they opened the door into the lobby, he could see camera flashes. Brian knew the FBI often tipped the newspapers that an arrest was coming down, so they would get press to put fear into people who were considering breaking the law themselves. There's nothing like being arrested and getting your picture on the front page of the Dallas Morning News to halt your career, Brian thought as his heart rate skyrocketed.

"Mr. Sadler," the man said, flashing an ID card in a wallet holder. "I'm Special Agent Myron Callender with the FBI."

Brian's knees almost buckled. He grabbed the cube wall to maintain his balance. "FBI?" he said. "What do you want with me?"

The agent replied that Brian was not under arrest, but there was an ongoing investigation of a company called Bellicose Holdings, and Brian was considered a person of interest. "Do you have a passport, Mr. Sadler?" the agent asked.

"Yes, of course," Brian stammered, feeling sweat running in a bead down his back.

"Don't use it," the agent told him harshly. "We'll be seeing a lot of each other over the next few weeks. We'd better be able to find you; if we can't, we'll have no problem issuing a warrant."

Brian assured the agent he neither had plans to leave the United States, nor would he do so without talking to him. The agent gave Brian his card. "Here are subpoena papers," he said, handing Brian a few documents. "You need to be in my office next Monday with everything you can get your hands on about Bellicose Holdings. And Mr. Sadler," he agent paused, "I mean everything. No funny business. No shredding, no nothing. You don't want to end up being the next guy walking out of here in cuffs."

As the agent walked away, Brian collapsed into his chair. He was stunned, speechless. Jim Palmer looked at him as he walked by, but said nothing. For the first time in his life, Brian felt terror. He felt as though he were about to jump out of an airplane without a parachute.

He made it through the rest of the trading day, but with no

sales success. Brian found himself continually coming back to the thought that he might be leaving here in handcuffs next. But he also knew the Feds were targeting the wrong guy. He had to convince them of that.

Before leaving his apartment the next morning, Brian checked the internet for any information about yesterday's events at W&T. There was a brief story on the Dallas Morning News website's financial section. It referred to a Federal raid on the offices of W&T and the arrest of the firm's sales manager. Carl's name did not appear. The story implied that a much more detailed account was being prepared for the paper. The charges, the story related, revolved around money laundering for organized crime. Brian was shocked. He had been there for two years and had never seen, overheard or been told a single thing that would indicate the firm had anything to do with the mob.

Brian left his place and headed in to work. When he arrived, he saw that Carl Cybola was sitting in his office as usual. It looked like many of the brokers in the office were avoiding contact with him, and The Push that morning was run by someone else. It was much more subdued than usual. An element of fear permeated the office.

Brian emailed Carl, asking him to join him for lunch. Taking time off the floor during the trading day was a rare occasion at W&T, but both the offer and acceptance showed how much things were changing in the lives and minds of these two men. They left the floor around noon, walked around the corner to Zen, the area's most popular night spot, and went straight to the bar.

The place had customers, but most of them were in the dining area, so the bar wasn't crowded. A couple of tables were occupied by people eating lunch. Brian glanced across the room and saw two drop-dead gorgeous girls chatting over their meals. Any other time, Brian would try to find out more. Today, he wasn't in the mood to work on his pick-up lines.

The bartender looked up as they entered, surprised to see them here during the day. "Brian, Carl," he said. "Good to see you guys. Market closed early today?"

"Hey, Jason," Brian replied. "The market's open. We just need a break."

"The usuals?" Jason asked them. When they responded affirmatively, he went to work fixing two martinis, one with Bombay Sapphire gin and one with XO Vodka. When the drinks arrived, Brian raised his glass in a toast and said, "Here's to luck, Carl. Looks like we're going to need some."

"Right back at ya, buddy," Carl responded morosely. "You don't know the half of it."

# Chapter Fifteen

Carl began by saying that no one would tell him anything during the ride downtown. He discussed the humiliation of their arrival at the Lew Sterrett Justice Center, his booking, photo and fingerprinting. "It was like I was a damned criminal," he said. "They pushed me around, stuck me in a cell, and treated me like shit."

Carl said that a desk clerk called him to a window and told him he was under arrest for fraud, conspiracy and money laundering.

"I saw something about that on the news this morning," Brian said. "What the hell is that all about? We're not money launderers!"

Carl looked at him and raised his eyebrows. "Brian," he said slowly, looking him in the eyes. "The Feds told me I was treading on thin ice, and if I talked about this to anyone in the office, they would know about it. They said I might be charged with interfering with a Federal investigation. So what you hear about the charges you are going to have to find out from somebody else. I'm scared shitless. I've never been in jail before. They had me crying like a girl. I'll admit it."

Carl told Brian he had hired Andrew Sweeney, one of Dallas' premier, and most expensive, white collar criminal lawyers. Sweeney had arrived at the Justice Center, stopped the discussions between the Federal agents and Carl, and arranged his $100,000 bail. Carl said he had gotten out after about four hours split between the interrogation room and a holding cell.

"You have to help me out a little here," Brian pleaded. "Are these guys going to come after the rest of us? They talked to me yesterday while one of them was taking you out. They said they're looking at Bellicose Holdings. They gave me a subpoena and told me to be in their office Monday. Carl, you have to help me figure this out!"

Brian was practically begging at this point. He knew the firm had lots of dealings that were, to say the least, on the edge. He just wondered which thing had triggered the investigation which had led to Carl's arrest, and if he too was going to end up under arrest when he showed up on Monday.

Carl looked at Brian intently. "I don't know anything about the specifics of what they want. All I know is I'm charged with a shitload of felonies and if Warren Taylor and Currant thinks I'm taking a fall for Johnny Spedino, they have another think coming. My recommendation to you, buddy, is to hire the best damned criminal lawyer you can find."

"Johnny Speed?" Brian said. "What the hell does a New York mafia guy have to do with us?" Carl just looked at him, saying nothing more.

As he had felt in the office, Brian again found himself losing control. He began to shake, and felt clammy. His heart rate spiked once again.

"I'm not a criminal!" Brian suddenly shouted. Jason, the bartender, looked up from behind the bar, as did a couple of people sitting at tables nearby. When Brian returned their looks, everyone immediately averted his or her eyes.

"Neither am I, Brian," Carl said quietly. "All that matters right now is whether some FBI agent thinks you are. He can screw up your life, at least for awhile, even if you're lily white, and nobody's lily white. Get a lawyer, Brian. You damn sure don't want to show up there holding your balls in your hand, so they can put them on the table and cut them off for you.

"I gotta get back," Carl said, rising from his chair. "I'll pick up the tab on the way out. See you at the office." Without a further word, he turned and went to the bar, leaving Brian dazed at the table. As Carl paid the bill, Brian saw him glance up at the CNN broadcast on the television hung above the bar. The exterior of The Strand, W&T's building was being shown. As Carl watched, his picture flashed on the screen, with the word "INDICTED" below it. Carl looked down, finished paying his bill, and left.

Brian watched Carl leave the restaurant. He slumped as he walked. *He shuffles along like an old man,* Brian thought. That observation scared Brian as much as anything Carl had told him. *Carl's giving up on this,* he thought. *And that means it's every man for himself.*

As he rose from his chair, Brian remembered something Carl had said. He wasn't taking a fall for Johnny Spedino. What the hell did some New York gangster have to do with Carl's arrest? He knew he wouldn't find out from Carl. He had to figure this one out himself, and fast.

# Chapter Sixteen

As Brian left his table, he became aware someone was right behind him. Looking around, he saw one of the girls he had spotted earlier from across the room. "Sorry to interrupt," she said, smiling. "I couldn't help but overhear your comment earlier. I don't judge whether anyone's a criminal or not. I just help out the people who don't know what to do next." She handed him a business card, smiled again, turned and left the room with her friend, who was waiting by the front door.

He walked to the bar. "Jason," he said, "do you know those girls?" Jason replied that they worked nearby on McKinney, and came in for lunch every week or so. "I think she's a lawyer," he said. "I *know* she's a looker."

Walking outside, Brian looked at her card. It gave her name, Nicole Farber, and showed she was an attorney with Carter and Wells, a firm so big its name was a household word in north Texas. If not the biggest law firm in the metroplex, it was certainly in the top three.

Standing on the sidewalk in front of Zen, Brian sent a text message from his phone to Carl, saying he was taking the afternoon off. He walked back to the garage, retrieved his car and drove home, heading straight for his computer. He was determined not to let his fear overcome his reasoning. *This is America, dammit,* he thought. *You're innocent until proven guilty, and I haven't done anything at W&T that a hundred other guys haven't done.*

First he went to Carter and Wells' website. Scrolling down a list of several hundred names, he clicked on Nicole Farber's. Her webpage appeared, with a picture of her that was great, but really didn't do her justice, Brian thought. This girl was truly one of the most beautiful people he had ever seen – long blond hair, green eyes, maybe five foot five . . . he found his mind drifting, and forced himself back on the subject, but glad for a brief interruption from the serious business he knew he faced.

He checked the year Nicole Farber graduated from Southern Methodist University Law School, and calculated her age at around thirty. Her specialty at the firm was corporate criminal defense – exactly the specialty Brian figured he was going to need. And she had served as an intern for the Federal Prosecutor's office while she was in college. That might help too, although Brian wasn't sure. He just didn't even know what to look for.

Brian switched gears, Googling John Spedino's name. There were several pages of results. Spedino was a well-known man, who often had been referred to as Teflon Two, a takeoff on the "Teflon Don" title associated with the late mobster John Gotti.

Brian read several news articles from the New York papers about John "Johnny Speed" Spedino. The man was Brooklyn-born, in his mid-sixties and had been charged with more crimes than one could count. The government's success rate in prosecuting Johnny Speed was zero at this point. He had never served a day in prison, although the charges against him at various times in the past had included murder, assault and battery, running a prostitution ring and jury-rigging.

An interesting story in the *New York Observer* noted that Spedino seemed to be immune from successful prosecution mostly because anyone who was slated to testify against him either changed their mind, or failed to appear . . . ever again. The story said although Spedino was viewed by law enforcement insiders as the top guy to catch, his record remained clean.

Brian searched more articles, trying to find some association with any deal W&T had done. He got nowhere, even after looking at Warren Taylor and Currant's own list of shareholder owners. Having never done this before, he did find it interesting, but seemingly of no value to him in his present situation. The SEC required that brokerage firm ownership be public information. W&T's shareholder list consisted of seven names – three corporations and four individuals, none of which Brian had ever heard of before, and all located in New England.

Since W&T was not itself a public corporation, Brian couldn't get more details about the shareholders other than the list of names, which he printed off in case he might need it in the future. Then he glanced down at the business card lying next to his keyboard. He picked up his cell phone and called Nicole Farber.

# Chapter Seventeen

Brian slept very little that night. Several times he awoke in a start, aware that he had been dreaming. Once he recalled that his dream involved being locked in a cage like an animal. He was sweating profusely after that episode. Around five a.m., he gave up and arose, turning on the TV. Channel Four Sunrise News had a brief report on the arrest of Carl Cybola at W&T, and said the FBI was looking for several other people to whom they wished to talk about the incident. The announcer said at least one subpoena had been issued for the production of documents by an employee of the firm, and that the FBI had issued an arrest warrant for a Canadian whose whereabouts were presently unknown, and who was CEO of a company recently taken public by W&T. Brian knew that company was Bellicose Holdings. He also knew they'd been unsuccessfully looking for Rochefort for awhile.

Nothing Brian saw, heard or thought gave him the slightest comfort. He had no idea what the Feds had on him, or even wanted with him, for that matter. He thought about what they might find – the car leased from an overseas shell corporation, the expense accounts he'd turned in when, instead of clients, the diners and drinkers had been girls he and his friends had picked up. All this seemed like peanuts compared to taking a guy out of the office in handcuffs, but Brian had absolutely no idea how all this worked. Feeling himself spiraling out of control again, he fought to calm himself down.

The workday began quietly at W&T. Again, the morning sales meeting was not run by Carl, and to say it was subdued would be a gross understatement. Brian tried to concentrate, but could think of nothing else but what faced him at the FBI meeting on Monday. He began to make notes of what files and other information he should give them about Bellicose. Having signed a confidentiality agreement at W&T, one of the few pieces of paper apparently deemed important enough for a new hire to complete, Brian knew he couldn't just take the information. It belonged to the firm, and he made a note to find out who could tell him what he could and could not produce for the Feds.

Around eleven, Brian stuck his head in Carl's office. Cybola looked up and Brian said, "Taking your advice, Chief. I'm heading to my lawyer's. Out for a few hours, I guess."

Carl wished him well, and Brian took the elevator to street level, hit the sidewalk and walked three blocks north on McKinney to the mirrored tower that housed the offices of Carter and Wells. Entering the building, he headed toward the building directory but an attractive lady behind a reception desk in the lobby said, "May I help you, sir?"

She advised Brian that Carter and Wells' reception area was on the fortieth floor. Glancing at the directory as he headed to the elevator, he saw that the firm's lawyer listing took up several columns, and it appeared the firm occupied a number of floors of the building.

Arriving on the fortieth floor, Brian announced himself to the receptionist and took a seat. After a brief wait, a man in his early twenties and dressed in a conservative pinstripe suit entered the lobby and called Brian's name. "I'm Ms. Farber's assistant, Ryan Coleman," he said. "Come right this way, please." Following the young man, Brian snaked through cubicle farms, not unlike those at W&T, but he was struck by how quiet everything was. There was an underlying buzz of activity, certainly, but nothing loud.

They arrived at another, smaller reception area which was tastefully decorated in old wood. It reminded Brian of a finely decorated men's club. Six office doors encircled the room, and there were two desks. Brian figured one of them was Ryan's – a girl about the same age as Ryan sat at the other one, and smiled as he glanced at her. Ryan opened one of the office doors and stood back to allow Brian to enter, closing the door behind him.

Nicole Farber's office was about fifteen feet square. Her desk sat in the middle, and a window behind her reached from floor to ceiling. The day was clear, and he could see the buildings comprising The Galleria several miles to the north. "Hi, Brian Sadler," she said as she came around her desk. She had a big, sincere smile on her face as she gestured to a small sitting area with a coffee table, couch and chair. "Let's talk here, where it's not so formal," she said. Coffee was offered, accepted and ordered through Ryan, who brought a silver pot, two china cups and saucers on a tray, which he sat on the coffee table. After pouring for them, he left the office.

"So I know something about you already," Nicole said, touching his sleeve gently.

*A toucher,* he thought. *Well, if she and I don't hit it off as lawyer and client, maybe I'll ask her out* – the thought briefly ran though his mind as he switched back and concentrated on the subject at hand. "What's that?" he replied.

"You're not a criminal," she said, laughing.

Brian remembered his outburst in the bar at Zen the day before, and smiled himself. "I'm really not," he said.

"OK," she responded. Tell me what's going on in your life that made you say that, and let's work backward from the day the FBI agents came to your office. I'm all ears." She sat back in her chair, folded her arms and looked intently in his face.

Brian began by giving Nicole every detail he could recall of the day the Feds came to W&T, and handed her Myron Callender's card and the subpoena papers. He related what he had heard from Carl Cybola at lunch, but also what the agent had told him. He also told her a lot about Warren Taylor and Currant, and mentioned most of the specifics he could remember about Bellicose Holdings. He told her about the principal shareholder, who had disappeared after receiving the net proceeds from W&T's public offering. Although she said nothing while he spoke, apparently content merely to make notes on a legal pad now and then, he got the feeling Nicole knew more about both W&T and Bellicose than he would have thought. Her body language, however, told him nothing. She never nodded her head or smiled knowingly. She just listened.

He told her about Johnny Spedino, and asked her if she had any idea what link he might have with W&T.

She smiled and said, "It's your turn to talk now. I'm making notes about things we'll talk more about later. Just keep going."

After about an hour, Brian was finished. Nicole looked at her notes and said, "OK. You have a decision to make, after which I may have a lot of work to do. I'm busy as hell right now, but I'm willing to take your case. I'm really good at criminal defense. My track record the last three years for acquittals is ninety percent, and I'm pleased to say none of the other ten percent ever served a day of jail time."

"Jail time!" Brian exclaimed. "I've never so much as gotten a traffic ticket. Do you seriously think I might be facing jail time?"

"I don't want to scare you, Brian, so let me just tell you this. These guys live to make examples out of rich guys who prey on the little man, in their eyes. They will try to bankrupt you with legal fees first, then take away a chunk of your life by putting you in jail. Even Club Feds aren't a country club. Are you seriously facing jail time? Who knows? I don't even know what kind of case they may have against you. For that matter, I don't even know if you've told me the whole story up to this point."

"So what's the decision I have to make?" Brian asked her.

Nicole replied, "I charge $450 an hour. I need fifty thousand dollars up front as a retainer, and I promise you we'll burn through that within a few weeks, so be ready to pony up more. You haven't told me much about yourself personally, but I gather fifty grand now and then won't be a problem for you."

"Money's not the issue. The issue is, are you the best I can find? I can't take a chance and I can't have a big blemish on my life, which might cause me not to be able to work in securities, or finance, or somewhere else. I need to skate this deal and come out without a hitch." Brian paused and looked at her. God, she was beautiful, he thought. She smiled at him and he glanced for the first time at her left hand. No ring. That didn't always mean anything, but it was a start. *Focus, Brian,* he thought to himself. *You don't need good looks right now. You need brains.*

Nicole said, "I'm good, Brian. The track record I mentioned is the best in town. I interned in the Federal Prosecutor's office when I was in law school at SMU. I handle mostly white collar securities criminal defense, and I'll put in the time and effort to provide you the best defense possible, given the facts we have to work with. In return, you'll have to work closely with me. I know you have a job, so we can meet after the market closes. Don't plan to have much of a night life for awhile if you hire me. We'll be burning the midnight oil on this one."

She told Brian to think about it, but not for long. The deposition with the FBI was set for Monday. "I can get that meeting moved out a week or so," she said, "but not more than that. I need to know what you have to show them, and we'll talk about what you plan to say, so you are totally ready for that deposition."

Brian looked at her. He had never put his life, his future, in the hands of a stranger before. Somehow he felt Nicole could be the person to get him out of a situation he didn't even understand in the first place. He trusted his gut every day in the marketplace. It was a big part of what made him the confident, successful person he was today. "Done," he said to Nicole. "We have a deal."

She walked to her desk, buzzed Ryan and asked him for new client papers. Within minutes, Ryan opened the door, laid two documents on the coffee table, and stood nearby, awaiting instructions.

"Take these with you," she said, "and bring them back tomorrow afternoon after the market closes, around 3:15. One of these is an agreement for representation. The other is the firm's wire transfer instructions. Wire the retainer tomorrow before you come. Ryan, clear my appointments after 3:15 every day the rest of this week, and put in a call to Myron Callender at the FBI."

"Ms. Farber," Ryan said. "You have the mayor's dinner tomorrow night at the Art Museum, and you're scheduled to be going with Mr. Carter." Brian figured Carter was the name partner of the firm. He was impressed with how far this girl lawyer had come in so short a time.

"I can't do it, Ryan," she said. "Of all people, Randall Carter will understand. Just advise him. It won't be an issue." Ryan turned and left the room.

Nicole stood, extending her hand. Brian took it, and she clasped his hand with both of hers. "You're in the best hands possible. No one will work harder to make this come out well for you. I'm not intimidated by the FBI, and you won't be either. You'll know your rights and if you're really not a criminal, I'll help make sure they don't make you out to be one."

As Brian rode the elevator down, he thought about the whole situation. Nicole's aggressively positive attitude had him convinced she really was the best he could get, and he didn't know anyone else anyway. *So I'll put my future in the hands of a beautiful girl I met in a bar, one I'd like to end up in bed with, and give up control while I let her drive the train which either exonerates me or puts me in a cell.*

He continued to think as he walked back to Warren Taylor's building. One thing was certain at this point. Brian Sadler felt a lot better now that he had someone on his side who obviously had done this before.

# Chapter Eighteen

Brian had intended to return to work after leaving Nicole's office but since it was already 3:30 p.m, the market had closed for the day. He wasn't in the mood to call customers and push stocks. He had a gnawing in his gut that made him scared to do anything the same way he had done things up to now – he had no idea what he was in trouble for, or even if he was in trouble, regarding the Bellicose Holdings deal. *After all, I was only a salesman,* he thought. *I didn't create the terms of the deal, I've never met the guy who skipped out with all the dough, and I didn't price the offering. I know nothing about this deal except the documents W&T provided me.*

He retrieved his car and drove home. It was a beautiful June afternoon, and he had the top down. *I've got to start pulling documents together,* Brian thought. *I need to start making a list of things I can give the FBI on Monday. The more I give, the more they'll see how much I'm trying to cooperate.*

He began a list in his mind of things he could give the FBI about Bellicose. He had a lot of notes he had written, mostly to use as selling points for people who generally bought with nothing more than a gentle nudge anyway. And on that deal, there wasn't much positive news to generate. All he could tell people was that this was just another W&T deal. Hold on for the ride, and get off when you've made enough profit. He had known that this deal, like all the others, would be pumped up, and stay inflated, by the investments of previous W&T public offerings. It was really a no-brainer for him. He just had to decide which of the high net worth clients he had so carefully cultivated would be the recipients of this latest offering of manna from heaven.

One thing nagged at Brian. There was a nasty little secret behind all of W&T's offerings. Everybody knew about it, but nobody talked about it. He had to figure out how to keep The Millionaire's Club from becoming an issue, Brian decided.

Every morning saw a little more news being created about Warren Taylor and Currant. There were brief stories on the local online news, and as he showered, Brian could hear the sound from the TV mounted in his bathroom. The newscaster indicated that unnamed sources close to the matter revealed that one of W&T's recent public offerings was the target of the entire investigation. The company's name wasn't given, but Brian knew it was Bellicose.

When he got to work, he saw an urgent email in his account from the firm's corporate office. The entire staff got it. It instructed everyone to say nothing to the media, and advise the legal department of any contact from outsiders seeking information on anything. The email referenced the confidentiality document each new hire had signed. That reminded Brian to get it out; he dropped it into a portfolio to take to Nicole's office that afternoon.

Brian went online and checked his bank account. He had almost twenty grand in his checking account and another hundred thousand in the money market. He initiated a wire transfer for $50,000 to Carter and Wells and saw his balance reduce instantaneously. He read over the documents Nicole had given him. They seemed to be fairly straightforward. One interesting paragraph in the retainer letter was highlighted in bold, so no one could miss it. It said, "If at any time, in Carter and Wells' sole opinion, Client fails to be forthright in every respect, including disclosure of all information requested and required by his or her attorney, Carter and Wells may terminate this relationship immediately, refunding the balance of Client's retainer, if any. Client acknowledges that termination of representation, if at a critical point in the timeline of Client's defense, may cause Client to require new representation quickly. Such new Counsel may not have the same level of knowledge and expertise about Client's situation."

Brian thought about that. It seemed fair – if he failed to tell Nicole things she needed to know, she should have the right to dump him as a client. Then he thought about a movie he'd recently rented. On the witness stand, the defendant was exposed by the other side's attorney to have been lying all along. His own attorney stood, pointed a finger at the witness stand and yelled, "You lied to me!"

*What if I accidentally forgot something, and Nicole dumped me as a client right there in the courtroom?* Mulling it over, he decided he would deal as openly as possible with her, and this would all work out. Brian was basically an optimist. He always saw the glass as half full. I can do this, he said to himself, turning to his computer screen and trying to concentrate on work for a change. He signed the retainer documents and stuck them in his portfolio.

# Chapter Nineteen

Around 2 p.m., Carl sent Brian an instant message asking if he'd come by when he had a minute. Brian had noticed all day long that Carl had been sitting at his desk with his office door closed, staring out at the trading floor. He looked like a defeated man. When Brian opened the door, Carl said, "Sit down, Brian, and shut the door."

"What's up?" Brian asked. "You doing OK? You really don't look so hot."

"The firm is putting me on leave," Carl said. "Apparently they got a call from the SEC. Since I'm facing Federal charges involving securities fraud, the SEC very strongly suggested I wasn't the kind of person who ought to be running an investment bank's sales division. So much for innocent until proven guilty."

Brian was surprised. "They can't fire you, can they? Like you say – you haven't been convicted of anything!"

Carl explained that he had gone through all that with the firm's legal guy downstairs. The firm couldn't afford any more negative press than it was already getting, and they were going to put Carl on paid leave until this matter was settled.

"At least you're getting paid," Brian responded.

"I make forty thousand a year base pay. Everything else I make is commissions on sales. All I'm going to get is base - $3400 a month. That's my *car payment,* Brian. Thirty four hundred a month."

"I don't know your personal business, but I know you've made a shitload of money over the past year or so. You may have to live on savings for awhile, but you can beat this deal."

"Easy for you to say," Carl replied. He was sweating profusely at this point. "I live pretty high. You know how it always seems to work out that whatever money you make, you need just a little more? That's how it's been with me. I bought crap I didn't need. I have an apartment that costs me ten grand a month, and I bought a condo in Belize about two months ago. Paid cash for it – four hundred grand – so I'm really in a bind. I'll owe the IRS about six hundred thousand next April, and my lawyer's saying I'll need at least two hundred grand over the next sixty days so he can prepare for my defense. I don't have eight hundred thousand dollars. I was planning on continuing to work, and paying the IRS out of the money I made in the future."

Brian sat in the chair, speechless. "I . . . I don't know what to say," he replied.

Carl looked at him, leaning across the desk. *A desperate man,* Brian thought.

"You gotta help me, Brian," he said, staring him in the eye. "We have to stick together on this deal. I have no desire to hurt anybody, and I don't think you want to see me hurt either. I need some money, Brian."

"Hey, Carl," Brian said. "Are you trying to blackmail me?" He stood and opened the door. "I don't know what the hell just happened, but you better figure out somebody else to push around, buddy. As you well know, I have my own set of expensive problems right now. And hurt me? What do you mean, Carl? You think you can hurt me?" He turned and left Carl's office, slamming the door behind him. People in nearby cubicles looked up, then quickly down again as Brian walked by them.

Brian went back to his desk. He suddenly felt dizzy and nauseated. He felt the mantle of terror creeping over him again. His world was changing in a microsecond, right before his eyes. He quickly pulled all his notes on the Bellicose deal and put them in his portfolio. Brian saw no need to make copies of any of the offering documents. All that information was on file with the SEC and available to anyone with a computer. He figured the FBI had all that stuff already.

Unable to concentrate, he left the office and walked to Zen. He sat down at the bar. Looking around, he saw that he was the only customer in the place – it was almost 3 p.m. and the rest of the world, Brian thought, was going about its mundane set of tasks and responsibilities, blissfully unaware that people like him had problems that were about to swallow him whole. He felt nausea sweeping him again. Jason, the bartender, came out from behind the bar and said, "Hey man, what's up?"

"I need a quick drink," Brian replied. "Give me the usual, straight up." As Jason worked on Brian's martini, he said, "Brian, if it's none of my business just tell me so. I hear the news like everyone else about W&T and Carl. Are you going to be OK over there?"

Brian thought for a minute. He wondered that very thing himself. "Sure," he smiled and responded with a bravado he didn't really feel. "Sure I am. I'm bulletproof and invisible." As he said the words, he hoped and prayed they would be true.

# Chapter Twenty

As he made the short trek from Zen to Carter and Wells' building on McKinney, Brian thought how unusual his life had become. He hadn't had a drink before five p.m. in years – except on weekends and vacation, of course. And this week he'd had a martini, or two, twice during the workday.

He arrived at the law firm right on time at 3:15 p.m. Ryan met him in the lobby as usual and took him to Nicole's office. As he was ushered in, she was in front of her desk, leaning back on it slightly. *An incredibly sexy pose,* Brian thought, a*nd an incredibly sexy outfit.* She was dressed in a St. John suit and looked as though she had just stepped out of a Nordstrom show window.

"You look absolutely terrific." Brian felt the words come out as though he couldn't help himself. He was like a kid in school, instantly infatuated.

"Why, thank you, sir," she laughed. "You don't look so bad yourself. And now that we have boosted each other's egos, let's get down to business. Do you have the retainer document?"

Brian handed the executed document to her. She laid it on her desk, grabbed a yellow pad and gestured for Brian to sit where they had been last time. Taking a seat, she said, "OK, I have some good news and some not so good news. The good news is that I spoke to Special Agent Callender and got your deposition moved. I need more time to get you prepared for this. I don't know if you realize what a deposition's all about, Brian, but you're pretty much on your own. I can be in the room, but I can't discuss each answer with you. However, with my help and the time we have to prepare, you'll be ready to go."

She told him they now had two weeks before the deposition, and gave him the date and time. "Put this on your calendar," she said. "It's one of the biggest dates in your life so far."

"OK," Brian responded. "But I'm more interested in hearing the bad news."

Nicole looked at him and said, "We don't often see the FBI involved in cases like this so early. What I mean is, the SEC usually comes in first and noses around, gathers information, and that sort of thing. The SEC is an enforcement agency on its own. It can issue subpoenas, perform depositions, and recommend charges be filed against individuals and corporations. And it's definitely involved in this case – right up to its eyeballs. But so is the FBI, which is highly unusual. So I asked Agent Callender exactly why they were involved. I hope the answer surprises you."

She told Brian that the disappearance of Francois Rochefort from Bellicose Holdings was reported by that company's Chief Financial Officer to the police as a possible kidnapping. Since the man was known to have been a citizen and resident of Canada, the FBI was brought into the picture, since a crime could have been committed across international borders. "And Brian," she said, leaning in toward him and taking a much more serious tone, "Francois Rochefort, as you know, has a less than stellar past. He has a prison record. So how, you ask, did he become the beneficiary of over $25 million through W&T's generosity in doing a public offering for his little shell company, which had no business, no prospects, no hopes or dreams or anything at all? Well, here's how. Hold on to your seat and if I'm telling you something you already know, then honey, you and I may be finished before we've even gotten started!"

Brian sat up in his chair, amazed at what she was saying. He knew all that she had told him about Rochefort. Now he also knew why the FBI was involved. But what the hell was she talking about now?

"Here's the rest of the story," she said. "Rochefort is a shill. He's never had an independent thought in his life. His actions are directed by a puppeteer who pulls his strings. Everything he does, every shady deal, even the crime for which he went to prison . . . everything was directed by someone else."

"Johnny Speed," Brian blurted out. Since Brian knew John Spedino fit into the picture somehow, he figured this had to be the way.

"Yep," Nicole said. "Johnny Speed runs Francois Rochefort. He always has. So the FBI tells me they're interested in all this because, for once, they're going to make a case that is going to nail Johnny Speed and put him in prison."

"Level with me right now, Brian," she said. "Did you know there was a connection between John Spedino and your firm before I told you?"

Brian replied that his only knowledge of Johnny Speed had come from the conversation with Carl Cybola, which he had told her about yesterday.

"So that's all you know?" she said. "That's OK, then. I'm really glad you mentioned Spedino's name to me before the Feds did. If it had been the other way around, it would have made me nervous as hell, frankly, and I would have suggested we completely change our course. I've represented lots of criminals in my time, and done a damned good job keeping them out of jail. But with you, my tactic is that you're an innocent bystander. If that's not true, I want to know it now."

# Chapter Twenty One

"So how . . . " Brian began. Nicole interrupted him. "If you're wondering how Rochefort got to W&T and ended up with millions of your clients' money, that's the big question. As you well know, every deal your firm does has to have due diligence. What the hell happened this time?"

She was referring to the stringent investigation required by the Securities and Exchange Commission on every new public offering. An independent law firm, not otherwise affiliated with the investment banker, would be hired to look into backgrounds, verify facts in the offering documents, and generally give a thumbs-up to the public offering being what it appeared to be. It was not a guarantee that things were as they appeared, but after the due diligence, there should be no surprises either. Tens of thousands of dollars were spent on the due diligence for each new stock offering. Those funds were paid out of the offering itself, so they reduced the amount the newly public company would receive from its offering. The investment banking firm therefore hired the law firm, which had not previously been the primary lawyer either for the broker or for the company, but was independent.

Brian knew that sometimes the company itself recommended the law firm. Since the company ultimately paid the substantial bill, it was sometimes in its interest to steer a big piece of business to a firm which could be helpful to the newly public company in the future. Maybe a side deal would be cut where the company would receive a discounted service fee down the road, or perhaps a promise from the lawyers to somehow help the company push its products or services. These side deals were never agreed to in writing, because both parties had to certify to the SEC that the due diligence law firm was truly arms length, with no business or other ties to the company. But Brian had heard that certain companies sometimes picked certain law firms, who magically turned up later, doing substantial business with the new public entity.

"One of my first steps," Nicole said, "is to find out who did the due diligence on this deal, what it turned up about Francois Rochefort, and if it was bad news, who at W&T agreed to let the deal continue anyway. This is a big deal, Brian. As long as you're not a criminal, like you told everyone in the bar last week, then it's news to you like it is to me. Now it's your turn to talk. What do you know about all this?"

Brian looked her with an ashen face. "I knew bits and pieces about this, Nicole," he said. "You have to realize my role in this entire Bellicose scenario. I got information from W&T, passed that information on to my client base, and happened to sell more Bellicose stock than any other broker. I read some of the S-1, the public offering document, but not all of it."

"Help me understand how this works, Brian. You have a client base who will buy stock from you even though, by your own admission, you, the selling broker, only know 'bits and pieces' about the deal? How much money are these people investing, on average?"

Brian thought a moment. "Some invest over a hundred grand, many invest around fifty grand, a few invest a little bit. You have to realize something, Nicole. These people are rich bastards. Really rich. I have heart surgeons, the guy who invented the latest laser surgery techniques, chairmen of oil companies, three women who run their own public technology companies, and at least two dozen Hollywood stars. They don't need to know a lot. They need someone with a track record telling them this is a deal they should invest in."

"And they usually make money, don't they?" Nicole looked at him. "Even though you know only 'bits and pieces' about a company that has no track record, no plans for using the money, a president with no experience running a company, and nothing else you normally would see with a company going public, you felt comfortable pushing a million dollars of stock off on these rich bastards, as you call them? Explain to me, Brian, with a company like this, what made you confident that this stock would make money? What made you feel sure you could pitch your existing client base on this stock? Explain that to me."

Suddenly he realized that her entire demeanor had changed. Up to this point, Brian had seen a smiling face, a calm assurance, and total control of her actions. Now Nicole was angry. "I . . . I guess my clients know they're going to be OK overall if they stick with me on deals." Brian stumbled for words. "Sometimes they win, sometimes they lose. W&T has made money for its clients more often than not."

"What are you not telling me, Brian?" she asked pointedly. "Something's missing here. What makes these people so loyal, to buy stocks in shitty little companies that no one else would take public in a million years? And how do these stock prices manage to stay above the offering price, so the original investors make money, like you said, more often than not?"

Brian told her he was a sales guy – he didn't know what went on behind the scenes to keep stocks propped up. He had wondered the same thing sometimes, he told Nicole, and Carl Cybola had told him to shut up and enjoy the ride. "I'm not an officer of W&T," Brian said. "I'm a stockbroker. I'm selling deals. I don't know why you or the FBI, would expect me to know so much."

"Because you're a smart guy, Brian. Too smart to just do deals and take the money without wondering why things are how they are, and thinking about the consequences attached to your actions. You either know, or think you know, a lot more than you're telling me. So let's hear it. I want it all."

*Man, you're beautiful when you're mad,* Brian thought, involuntarily smiling at her. That didn't help a thing.

She got up, slammed her note pad on the table and said, "Listen, hotshot. I don't know what you've done in this deal, but you are about an inch away from needing another lawyer. No secrets, Brian. By the time you're deposed by the FBI, I have to know every single thing you know. And you're spending four hundred and fifty bucks an hour sitting here smiling at me like a goofy schoolboy. Get it together and start talking." She sat down, folded her arms across her chest and glared at him.

A quiet buzz from the phone on an end table next to Nicole interrupted them. *Saved by the bell,* Brian thought for a second. She picked up the phone, listened and then said, "Nothing more tonight, Ryan. Have a good evening." She put the phone down and said, "You were saying?"

"OK, OK," Brian said. "Here's how it works." He told her that once brokers had been at W&T awhile, and had proven themselves both to be loyal to the firm and successful at what they did, they were invited to join the Millionaire's Club. Nobody ever talked about it, and Brian had never even heard it mentioned until one day after the market had closed. "Carl asked me to stop by his office and when I did, he shut the door and said, 'You're a player, Brian. From what I see, I think you're in this to make big bucks for yourself, and to be a major success. Am I right?"

Brian had responded affirmatively, and Carl had talked obliquely for awhile about how many different ways there were to make money without breaking the law.

Brian recalled that Carl had said, "Think how many people go through life making thousands of dollars, or even hundreds of thousands, and never realizing their potential. That's a shame, Brian. Guys like you have to take advantage of every means available to you if you want to realize what you can really do, and see what kind of sales guy you really can be."

Nicole sat immobile, continuing to listen to him, her eyes never leaving his. *She's studying me to see if I'm lying.* He continued, "Then Carl told me he wanted to make me an offer – to take me to the next level. 'I'm going to tell you something not a dozen people have ever heard, Brian', he told me." Brian went on; he told how Carl had offered to let Brian join the Millionaire's Club, explaining that it was nothing more than a stock trading concept Carl and some others in the firm had developed, which was a foolproof way to make profits. He first swore Brian to secrecy, telling him he was going to make him a millionaire within thirty days.

Carl also told him if he ever told another living soul what he was being said today, Brian would discover problems in his life from places he didn't even know existed. "What do you mean?" Brian had asked. "Maybe I don't want to be in the Millionaire's Club." Carl had laughed and said, "You want to be a millionaire, Brian. I can see it in everything you do. You're a lot like I was a few years ago. You want it all. And I can help you get it."

He told Brian that a few brokers in the firm who worked for Carl were involved in a program whereby their customers *couldn't* lose money. "The way it works," Brian told Nicole, "is that certain clients get orders filled for them only after the outcome of a transaction is known."

Nicole leaned forward, a surprised look on her face. "Brian," she said. "are you saying they backdate fill orders to buy and sell stock for customers at a guaranteed profit?"

"That's the deal in a nutshell," he said.

"And you're a member of this neat little fraud club?" she said, standing up. "Party's over, Brian. You were wrong. You ARE a criminal."

"Hey, wait a minute!" Brian retorted, also standing. "I never told you I was a member of the Club. I didn't join. I mean, to be perfectly honest, nothing's been done about it yet."

"You expect me to believe that?" Nicole asked him. "You were the top salesperson on Bellicose Holdings' offering. And that happened just because you were that good, all by your little old self?" She walked to her desk. He turned and followed her.

"Not exactly," he said. "All of W&T clients usually make money. That's because the firm has so many blind pool offerings." He was referring to the companies which went public with no immediate plans to use the proceeds.

"And blind pools make people money?" she responded. "In my experience, it takes profits, and real business operations, and solid management to make company stocks rise. How do W&T's companies do it with none of that? Does your Millionaire's Club also have a crystal ball?"

# Chapter Twenty Two

Brian explained the way W&T's reinvestment program worked. He told her that the firm took these companies public, then managed their portfolios of newly acquired cash for them, putting almost all the money right back into the next W&T deal. "I've given it a lot of thought, Nicole," he said, sitting in a chair in front of her desk. "I have no doubt it's legal, as long as it's fully disclosed. And it is."

Outside the window behind Nicole, Brian could see the sun setting in the west. He glanced at his watch. It was 7:30 p.m. "Got something else to do?" Nicole asked him.

*Damn, she doesn't miss a thing, he thought.* "No, just getting a little hungry."

"We're not finished," she replied. "Don't start drifting away just yet."

She spent another hour asking him question after question about the reinvestment plan W&T had created. He told her he knew of more than two dozen companies that had gone public and had their funds invested in each other.

Finally she closed her notebook. "Here's what I think, Brian.

It's like a Ponzi scheme, but legal so long as it works." She was referring to the classic scam created in the early twentieth century by Charles Ponzi, where people were guaranteed high returns by investing with him. Instead of generating true returns, he used money from future investors to pay interest to the earlier ones. As long as he had new investors from whom to generate dollars, his scheme stayed afloat. Once he couldn't pay interest any more, however, it all collapsed and Ponzi went to prison.

"It's not a Ponzi scheme," Brian responded fervently. "First of all, everything that's being done is clearly spelled out in the offering documents. The SEC approves the offerings. It's just a series of blind pools, one after another."

"I know what it is. But it's like a Ponzi scheme in one respect. If the flow of new deals ever stops, there won't be anything to continue to prop up the older ones. They'll all collapse like a house of cards. And I'll bet then the SEC won't be looking favorably on these deals. And you already know that, Brian. You're a smart guy."

She stopped taking notes. It was almost dark outside. "Let's call it a day," she said, standing and stretching.

Brian stood and said, "Want to grab a bite to eat?" She smiled and said, "Thanks, but no thanks tonight. I have plans."

The surprise must have shown on Brian's face. *Plans?* He had never considered that she might be involved with someone. She started laughing. "Wow," she said. "I rarely have that effect on people!" He stammered, trying to think of a save. "I got here at six a.m.," she said. "I had Ryan bring in lunch so I could work through. Moving my day around to accommodate you didn't mean I could drop my other stuff. I put in a normal workday and added time for you too. So I'm heading home to a martini and a good book in my pajamas."

"None of my business," Brian managed to blurt out. "I'm sorry . . ."

She smiled at him. "No problem, Brian. I'd love to have dinner with you sometime. In fact, we need to do it. I want to learn more about Brian Sadler the person, instead of just Brian Sadler the stockbroker. It'll happen, just not tonight."

She told him that the next two days would be devoted to Bellicose Holdings. Together they would look at everything they could find about the company and its elusive founder. She grabbed a briefcase and they walked toward the reception area. Only a few people remained at work in their cubicles or offices. Riding down together in the elevator, she touched his sleeve. "Brian, I can help you even if you are a criminal. That's what I do best. But it's much more rewarding for me to exonerate people who don't deserve the treatment they're getting.

"At this minute, I'm fairly certain you truly don't think you're a criminal. I'm also fairly certain the government thinks you might be. I'm also totally certain you are in the middle of a bunch of deals that, to put it really mildly, can't pass the smell test. Do the SEC or the FBI have something on you already? Only time will tell. But if you tell me absolutely everything, I can at least know which direction we're heading, and spend my time and your money the way I should be."

They exited the building. "Can I walk you to your car?" Brian asked.

"I'm in the garage next door," she said. She touched his hand. "Have a good night, Brian. See you tomorrow afternoon. Get some rest." She turned and walked away.

He stood for a minute, watching her go, not wanting to let the reality of her fade into a memory. Then he turned and walked to his car.

# Chapter Twenty Three

It was the Saturday before deposition day. The evening before, she had told Brian they needed to spend several hours wrapping up all the loose ends. They would role-play. She would ask him questions and he would answer, using techniques and ideas she had drilled into his head.

She had told him she wanted to run some errands and go to the gym, and she would meet him in front of her building at 2:30 p.m. "I'm coming from a workout," she said. "So don't plan to dress up for our meeting. It'll be a workout too. Count on it."

Brian was able to park on the street since it was a weekend afternoon. A few strollers were on the Uptown sidewalks, window-shopping or sipping lattes in front of Starbucks. She came over from the garage, looking incredible in a tank top and a pair of gym shorts. Her hair was wet and she wore a Red Sox baseball cap. She was stunning, he thought. Brian had gone to the gym too, and wore a t-shirt and shorts.

They worked all afternoon and, as usual, it was dark when she called it a wrap. "You're ready," she told him. "You'll be fine."

"And you're great at this," Brian said to her, leaning back in the armchair.

"I'm great at a number of things," she replied. "I can cook like a master chef. I'm a marathon runner, when I take time to do it. And . . ." she smiled at him. "Well, let's just say in bed I think I'm pretty good too."

Brian looked at her. They had never even had the dinner she had promised him. "That last part sounds interesting," he said. She stood and pulled her tank top over her head. She wore no bra. Her breasts were small but perfectly round. Her nipples stood erect. She walked to the office door and locked it, turning off the light. There was a full moon and the half-light in her office clearly illuminated her as, putting her thumbs in the waistband of her shorts, she dropped them to the floor. Now she wore only a thong.

She went to her desk, leaning back on it so that her hips were thrust forward. Brian leaned down and took off his gym shoes and socks. He pulled off his t-shirt and stood up. He went over to her, his erection clearly outlined through his shorts.

"Well, what have we here?" she said, smiling. She pulled down his shorts and briefs, taking him in her hands and moving up and down slowly. He uttered a groan as he reached to cup her breasts in his hands. He played with her rock-hard nipples as she gently rubbed the tip of his penis. He moved his hands down to her thong. She raised her hips to allow him to take it off.

Moonbeams played over her naked body as she leaned further back on the desk. "I want to feel you inside me," she said. He moved closer and she guided him into her. She was totally ready and he began to thrust slowly, in and out. She panted, her hands on her breasts, pinching her nipples. "Give it to me," she said hoarsely. As he moved deeper inside her, his cell phone suddenly rang.

Not wanting to break the rhythm, he ignored the ringing until .. .. he woke up. His cell phone rang once again, next to the bed. He shook his head, not wanting to lose the momentum of the dream he had just experienced. He had a massive erection, but was all alone in his apartment. It was 3:30 a.m.

He answered the phone, and a raspy, gravelly man's voice he had never heard before said, "Listen closely, Brian. I know you'll do well in your deposition. You help us, we'll help you. You hurt us, and well, it'll work the same way. I hope you clearly understand me. You've never done anything as serious as you will do a week from Monday. Don't screw up the rest of your life, Brian. Be as smart then as you've been up to now and you'll be healthy, wealthy and wise." The caller hung up.

Brian lay in his bed, his heart racing. All thoughts of the dream were erased as his adrenalin flowed. His heart was beating so fast, he thought he might be having a heart attack. *What the hell am I in the middle of?* he thought. There was a lot of cold sweat, but no more sleep for Brian Sadler that night.

# Chapter Twenty Four

The days at Warren Taylor and Currant went by quickly for Brian as he anticipated the close of the market each afternoon. The firm was working on deals and although his mind was always on the upcoming deposition, Brian continued to place stock in the hands of his clients, generating thousands of dollars a day in commissions for his own account.

Each day's closing bell marked the beginning of his next meeting with Nicole Farber, who was quickly becoming an obsession. He couldn't stop thinking about her. All day long he found himself recalling how she smelled, how she smiled, how she walked, how her naked body glistened in the moonlight. *I'm like a kid in high school,* Brian thought as he walked to her office the Friday afternoon before his Monday deposition. *But I have to concentrate. I can't let my fantasies about her fog my thinking about the reason we're meeting.*

He had decided not to mention the phone call he had gotten during the night. Once he had calmed himself down and thought about it, he decided that it was best to keep this to himself, at least for now. Brian wasn't sure what the man had meant about his helping them, or who "they" were. He wasn't sure what it all meant, but he knew both from the tone of voice and what the man had said, that it was dead serious stuff. He had looked at the call record on his phone to see the caller's number. The call originated in the 212 area code. Online, he Googled the number, which showed as unknown. So the call came from somewhere in New York City. No real help there, he thought.

Yesterday he and Nicole had gone into great detail about Bellicose. She had a computer-generated list of over a hundred questions, most of which arose from reviewing the S-1 offering document. "When did you have time to do all this research?" Brian had asked her.

"It wasn't me, babe," she replied. "I have two paralegals dedicated to nothing but Brian Sadler right now. We're spending your hard-earned cash like it's going out of style, but we're making sure we're fully prepared for deposition day."

The next few days' meetings with her were spent going over all the records Brian could produce. He showed her his confidentiality agreement. She placed a call to the FBI, telling Special Agent Callender if he wanted documents subject to the confidentiality agreement, he should subpoena them directly from the brokerage firm. She knew it was a long shot – a judge would likely force Brian to turn over the records, agreement or not, but she wanted to keep Brian out of a fight with his employer if possible.

Nicole had told Brian to bring all records to her, even if they were not going to be shown to the FBI because of the confidentiality agreement. He brought cold call scripts, client lists, all of his written notes, and copies of a few emails he had gotten from the company about Bellicose during the offering. She looked at everything, made extensive notes and gave them back to him to return to W&T.

# Chapter Twenty Five

Things moved along quickly. Nicole and Brian reviewed everything once, twice and a third time. Except for the few things Brian had chosen not to reveal to her, she had covered it all, and in his opinion, she had done a masterful job of preparing him.

They sat in her office on the Friday evening before his deposition on Monday. "We're almost ready," she told Brian. "You're going to do fine, because you know exactly what to expect. Let's meet here tomorrow afternoon and do some role-playing; I'll ask the questions and you can get used to the style of questioning, and the answers you need to give. I'm going to the gym before we meet . . . want to meet here around 3?"

Brian's mouth fell open. It was the dream taking the form of reality.

"What's wrong?" she asked.

"Nothing, nothing at all," he stammered a reply. "I . . . uh, I'm going to the gym tomorrow too. I'll see you here at 3. Gym clothes OK?" She said yes, and that she would meet him in the lobby, since the elevator required special access on weekends.

He walked out of her office, a déjà vu experience having unfolded before him. He went straight to Zen, where the evening crowd on a Friday night was noisy. The bar was jammed. He saw Jeff Spivey and Sam Cooper, the two brokers who had first told him about W&T, at a bar table nearby. They waved him over.

"How are you guys?" he said, taking a chair. "Haven't seen you in ages."

"Let's cut the small talk, Sadler," Jeff said. "Everyone in the firm's about to shit bricks waiting to find out what the hell the FBI is looking at you for. What's going on?"

Brian told them he didn't know much except that Bellicose Holdings seemed to be the focus of their attention, and that was all he had been asked to produce records about.

"You going to be OK?" Sam asked. "I feel a little bad since I think that night at Martini Park is what got you interested in coming to W&T in the first place. And you made a hell of a success, no doubt about it. But how's this going to turn out, do you think?"

Brian smiled at them. "I'm OK, guys. First place, I didn't do anything wrong. All I did is sell a deal the bosses told me to sell. I sold it to people whose names I got from W&T, and I used techniques I learned from watching other people at W&T. There's nothing they can accuse me of that everyone in the firm didn't do. Now let me buy a round and let's talk about the Cowboys. I'm sick of talking about Bellicose."

The trio had dinner in the bar, and continued to drink and talk until after 11. During the evening, Brian had gotten a number of calls on his cell phone, all from Carl Cybola. Brian had his phone on vibrate, and he chose not to take the calls. He wouldn't let Carl ruin his evening with the guys. He needed the break.

"Gotta go, guys," Brian finally said, signaling for the tab.

"This one's on me." He considered the irony of his paying the $400 tab this time, compared to his concern the last time they'd met as to whether he had enough room on his credit card to even buy his own drink. Things had certainly changed, Brian thought. He wanted to keep it this way.

# Chapter Twenty Six

As Brian retrieved his car from the garage, he called Carl's number. Carl answered immediately. "Where the hell are you?" he almost yelled.

"Hey, Carl," Brian said. "Lighten up, buddy. I've been out for a few drinks and now I'm headed home. What's up?"

"I'll tell you what's up, Brian," Carl said. "My time's up. I've agreed to cooperate with the U.S. Attorney's office. I'm not supposed to be calling you or anyone else, but after I acted like a shit at the office and tried to threaten you, I thought it was the least I could do, to tell you before your deposition on Monday."

"How do you know I have a deposition?" Brian asked.

"You think the U.S. Attorney's not in the middle of this whole thing?" Carl responded. He went on to say he had a lot of information on the firm's involvement with Bellicose, and had agreed to testify against several people at W&T whom he could tie to Francois Rochefort. "And Brian," he said. "Let me give you a little tip. I told you awhile back I wasn't taking a fall for John Spedino. And I'm not. He WAS Bellicose. It was his deal from the start. And you know how he got W&T to take the company public,

Brian?" Carl paused. "I know, but I'm not telling you now, before your deposition. You don't need to hear that from me. On Tuesday I'll be telling everything I know to the U.S. Attorney, and I'll be a free man. No worries, no problems, no Feds on my back."

Wishing Brian good luck, Carl hung up. Brian thought he sounded upbeat for the first time since all this had begun. He decided he'd tell Nicole all this tomorrow. It was undoubtedly important and could have a bearing somehow on his own situation.

# Chapter Twenty Seven

When he awoke on Saturday morning, sunlight was streaming through the window. It was 7:30 a.m. Before he got out of bed, Brian thought about what this afternoon would bring. How close to reality would his dream turn out to be? Deciding to do nothing to change it, he went to the gym, timing his arrival at her building for 2:20 p.m. even though she had told him to meet her at 3. In the dream, he had gotten a parking spot on the street at 2:30 p.m. Today there was nothing available. He circled the block three times, then saw a couple heading toward a car parked in front of Nicole's building.

He waited patiently while they backed out their car, then took the space. He had a half hour to kill, so he went across the street to Starbucks, sitting outside where he had a clear view of Nicole's parking garage. *I don't even know what kind of car she drives, he thought, and yet I've had sex with her.* Well, not real sex. But it had seemed like it at the time, until his rude awakening with the phone call from his mystery man.

About five minutes before three, he saw her drive by Starbucks in front of him. She was at the wheel of a white Mercedes convertible, and was wearing a ball cap! As she drove into the garage, he walked across the street and was standing in front of her building as she walked toward him on the sidewalk.

He had made fun of himself this morning as he dressed in exactly the outfit he had been wearing in his dream. She wasn't in her tank top and shorts, however. She wore a polo shirt tucked into a pair of yellow cotton shorts. He saw that she was also wearing gym socks and yellow tennis shoes. She looked color-coordinated, but somehow when you looked at her, it didn't make you think she had actually given that any thought when she was getting dressed. It was just as though it was how she was *supposed* to look.

"Hey there," she said, smiling. "I've been thinking about you all day."

Brian involuntarily shuddered for a second. Recovering, he said, "Me too!" There were a lot of people in the office as they walked to her area. Everyone was working; no one looked up as they passed down the hallway. Reaching her office, she told Brian to sit down while she got some water. He sat in the armchair, as in the dream, hoping she'd sit on the couch and not in the other chair.

Arriving back with two bottles of water, she handed him one, kicked off her shoes and sat on the couch, curling her feet under her.

"Before we get started," Brian said, "I want to tell you something that happened last night after I left here." He told her everything he could remember about Carl Cybola's phone call.

She took notes as he spoke. When he finished, she said, "Is there anything you've told me about Carl Cybola, his relationship to you or the firm, or anything about Bellicose, that you want to change now that you've heard what he told you? I'm not saying there should be, Brian, but if there is, for God's sake now's the time to tell me."

Brian assured her there was nothing Carl was going to say to the U.S. Attorney that would be harmful to Brian's situation in any way. "I've told you the entire truth," he said. "Carl knew a lot of inside stuff, but I didn't. And I never participated in it. I was about to, but I hadn't yet."

The afternoon and early evening were spent much like the dream. She asked pointed questions to which he gave direct answers. She asked him things about the firm which he couldn't have known. As he had been taught, instead of answering with things he thought might be happening, he said, "I have no knowledge of that."

It was dark when she closed her notebook and said, "I don't think there's anything more I can do for you, Brian. I want to tell you a few rules and I want you to remember them very closely." She picked up a yellow pad. "First, you'll be sworn in like you're in court, and a court reporter will be in the room just like in court. My job will be to object, but only rarely, which is not like in court. In a deposition, a judge will decide later whether most of your testimony will be allowed in court, if this ever gets to that point, which I think it won't." She told him that she also could be a resource for him. If he was asked something and wasn't sure how to respond, he could whisper to her and she would help him if she could.

"Don't volunteer information. If they ask you a question, answer the question. Don't give them more information than they asked you. If they ask you something close to the truth, don't help them get where they want to be. If they ask you if Carol did it, and it was Mary, don't say 'No, Mary did it.' Instead, you just say, 'No, Carol didn't do it.' See what I mean?"

He nodded, trying to concentrate on this important last information, while wondering what was going to happen next.

"If you don't know something for sure, say 'I don't recall.' You should never be reluctant to say that if you aren't sure. And Brian, you can *never* be certain what someone said *exactly,* even if it just happened. They can't kill you, they can't touch you, they can't beat you up. If they ask you about a conversation, and they say, 'What did Carl say next?' your answer should be what?"

"I don't recall," Brian replied.

"Right," she said, "but even better, say 'I don't recall specifically.' Because even if the conversation happened this morning, there is no way you can recall it word for word. If you say 'I don't recall specifically,' you'll make them have to say, 'Can you relate it in words or in substance?' That'll take a lot of time and frustrate the hell out of them. Just keep your cool and you'll be fine."

"You're really great at this," Brian said. He felt himself blushing as he attempted to steer the conversation as it had happened in his dream.

"You're paying enough to get the best, Brian," she said, "and I'm good at what I do. I can't think of anything else I'd rather do." She stood, putting on her shoes. "Want to grab a bite to eat?" she asked.

He stood, resigned to the fact that the dream now was nothing more than that. He agreed that dinner was a good idea, and they soon ended up in Papa's, a casual Italian place a couple of blocks down the street just off McKinney Avenue. She had a pasta salad, he had a calzone, and they drank a couple of beers each.

As they walked back to their cars, she said, "Get some rest tomorrow, Brian. Come to my office Monday at nine and we'll ride over to the FBI's field office together."

# Chapter Twenty Eight

On Sunday Brian bought groceries, worked out for an hour at the gym and read the Dallas paper by the pool at the Mansion on Turtle Creek. Since his apartment building was next door, the tenants had rights to use the facilities at the Mansion. Brian didn't eat there much, but he met people in the bar for drinks fairly often, and on warm weekends, he enjoyed the scenery at the pool.

Around six p.m. he went back to his place, starting a DVD he'd ordered online. It described the new archaeological finds at Petra in Jordan. Several mummies had been unearthed there, and there was speculation that one of Jesus' disciples might have been buried in the area. He found it difficult to concentrate. His mind was racing not about Nicole, but about the deposition. He found challenge invigorating and he felt confident he could do a good job tomorrow. *After all,* he thought, *I really can't help them much if they're trying to hang the Bellicose deal on somebody. For sure they can't hang it on me.* Around eleven, he called it a day and went to bed.

He was in a dead sleep when the cell phone rang. Awaking suddenly, he glanced at the clock. 3:30 a.m. Same time as the last call, he thought. He picked up the phone and saw the caller

ID said "unknown." The same gravelly voice as last time started talking before he said anything. "Listen closely, Brian. You have an important job to do tomorrow. You have to help us, so we can help you. We take good care of our friends. Don't hurt us, Brian. You don't want us to be angry. Do well tomorrow. Your future may depend on it."

He was gone before Brian had even fully grasped what he said. He lay in his bed, thinking of what he was involved in. How could he help? He didn't even know what these people wanted from him. It was over an hour before he fell asleep again, tossing and turning the rest of the night.

# Chapter Twenty Nine

At six a.m. he arose, turned on the bathroom TV as he usually did, then stepped into the shower. He could hear the newscast in the background as the water ran down his body. Suddenly he stopped, turning off the spigot. He had heard Carl's name.

He opened the shower door so he could see the TV. Carl's picture was on the screen, then a cutaway to a street scene where a reporter stood, emergency lights flashing in the background.

"Cybola was arrested at Warren Taylor and Currant only a few weeks ago, and was under indictment by the U.S. Attorney for a number of crimes, including fraud," the newscaster was saying. "It appears he was out for an early morning run when he was struck and killed by a hit-and-run driver. The vehicle was found about a mile away, and turns out to have been stolen. Police have no clues about the driver. Anyone who may have information about this crime is urged to call Crimefighters."

Brian started shaking. He dropped the towel, then sank to the floor as his legs gave way. *No way was Carl Cybola out for a morning run,* Brian thought. *This guy hated exercise. Carl was killed because he was about to cut a deal with the Feds.*

For over an hour, Brian sat at his kitchen table in a pair of briefs. He took a sip of coffee now and then, but mostly he stared into the air. The guy on the phone had said, "do well – your future may depend on it." Was that why Carl no longer had a future? What the hell was he involved in? Brian didn't know what to think, what to do. He knew he had to concentrate on the deposition, but couldn't think of anything but the veiled threats he had received and how Carl was now dead, probably because of what he was about to tell the Feds.

His cell phone rang. He started to ignore it, then saw Carter and Wells, Nicole Farber's firm, on the ID. He thought for a second that he didn't even know her cell number, but obviously she knew his.

"Hey," he said.

"You've seen the news?" she asked.

He said he had, and she asked him how he was doing.

"The truth?" he said too loudly. "I'm scared to death, Nicole. I think somebody killed him."

"It looks that way," she said. "But you don't know what he knew. And you really don't know how much he knew. And you don't know it wasn't an accident, at this point. So I want you to settle down, pull yourself together, and let's get through this morning and on with your life."

# Chapter Thirty

Dressed conservatively in a dark suit and tie, he arrived at her office at nine and she met him in the firm's reception area herself. They went to her office. He nodded to Ryan as they passed his desk. They had a cup of coffee and she said, "Brian, you're ready for this. You're an honest guy, not a criminal. You said so yourself, and you've got me believing you now. So you're going to go in there and be nothing more than the honest, straightforward, sincere guy you are. There's nothing like the truth to make things right."

She had arranged a sedan and driver to take them to One Justice Way, the offices of the FBI a few miles west of them near Stemmons Freeway. "I want you relaxed, not worrying about traffic," she said when she told him she was spending some of his money on a limo.

Arriving at the FBI's office, Brian was surprised at the high security. Thick, heavy glass separated the receptionist from the waiting room. A carrier like the one in a drive-in bank was used to deliver documents back and forth. They were told to take a seat, and shortly Special Agent Myron Callender opened a door, inviting them in.

They were taken to a conference room, where a court reporter sat at one end of a large table with her machine in front of her. Two men dressed in dark suits sat at the table as they entered the room. They rose, and Agent Callender introduced them as field agents who were working on this case. He explained that their role would be strictly as observers and they would ask no direct questions, although it would be possible from time to time they might pose a question for Agent Callender to ask.

Nicole established her position as Brian's attorney. They were served coffee, then asked if they were ready to begin. Brian was told to raise his right hand, and swore to tell the truth, and nothing but the truth, so help him God.

The deposition started with nearly an hour of incredibly routine background questions. The agent made detailed inquiries about Brian's college days, his degree, his time at Merrill Lynch, and then turned to Warren Taylor and Currant. He began a series of questions aimed at determining how Brian had found out about the position he had taken. He asked some specific questions about dates, and Brian answered, "I don't recall specifically." He glanced at Nicole, whose face remained impassive.

Callender rephrased the question, making it more general as to timeframe, and Brian said, "I really don't recall."

Callender hesitated for a moment and said, "Do you even recall the month to which I'm referring, or what year it was, Mr. Sadler?"

"I'm afraid not," Brian responded. "I do a pretty poor job at recall."

Nicole sat up in her chair. "May I have a word with my client?" she asked.

"Of course," Callender said. "Let's take a fifteen minute break."

The agents and the court reporter left the room. Nicole whispered to Brian, "This room is bugged; talk quietly. Want to explain just what you think you're doing?"

"I really don't remember much," he answered quietly.

"Don't screw around with these people, Brian. They won't take well to games."

"Believe me," he replied. "This is no game." He stood and walked down the hall to a restroom, leaving her sitting in the conference room alone.

The deposition began again and, except for a few questions of little significance, Brian's lack of recall was total. He didn't recall anything that had happened, and the more Callender asked, the more he couldn't tell them. Finally the agent said, "May we go off the record?"

Nicole responded, "OK with me."

Callender looked at Brian. "Mr. Sadler, I really thought you had nothing to do with any of this, that you were nothing more than some guy who happened to sell a lot of this crap and made some money, but you weren't part of the fraud itself. Now I don't believe that. You're deliberately refusing to answer my questions, and this outcome isn't going to be something you're going to be happy with, I'm afraid. I'm going to ask you point blank, right now. Do you intend to give us any more information, or is this deposition effectively finished?"

Brian looked at him. "I don't know what other questions you have, so obviously I don't know whether I will recall anything or not," he responded. "So far you haven't hit on subjects I remember much about. I'm sorry that my answers aren't as helpful as you had hoped."

"Ms. Farber," Callender said, turning to her. "Have you advised your client to respond to my questions this way?"

"Absolutely not," she responded, anger apparent on her face. "But in fairness, if he has no recollection, he can't answer your questions."

The agent turned to the court reporter, asking her to take the proceedings back on the record. "For the record, the client is unable to respond to my line of questioning with any answer except that he cannot recall. For this reason, I am now considering this deposition finished."

The reporter began to dismantle her machine, and the two agents in the room stood. One of them looked across the table at Brian and said, "I hope your lack of recall is not a serious tactical error, Mr. Sadler. We will undoubtedly see you again. Perhaps it will be in a deposition room like this. Maybe it'll be in the booking room of a jail. Who knows?" The three agents left the room.

Neither of them spoke as the car headed back to Nicole's office. Brian stared out the window. Nicole sat with her arms crossed, an angry expression on her face. Brian's cell phone rang. He pulled it out of his pocket, glad for the distraction. The caller ID showed a number in the 305 area code, which he knew to be Dade County, Florida. "Hello," he said.

"Good job today, Mr. Sadler," the gravelly voice said. "Now we'll help you." The call ended abruptly.

As Brian pocketed his phone, Nicole said, "Do you get calls often where you only listen?"

Brian looked at her. "Pardon me if I seem abrupt, Nicole," he responded. "I don't think my calls are your concern."

"Your *life* is my concern at the moment, Brian. I don't know what you think you were doing in there today. I'm not sure if you thought it was the smart thing to do, or a cute idea to snub your nose at the FBI. These guys can make your life miserable just because they're pissed off at you. They can sic the IRS on you for no reason at all, and you'll end up getting audited. They can show up often enough at your office that your boss finally gets nervous and fires you, just to keep them from taking a look at him. But you – after all our meetings, you chose the high road. You decided to be a smartass with the damned Federal Bureau of Investigation. You just didn't recall anything." She sat back in the seat, arms folded.

Nicole turned again to him. "I'll say one thing; I've never had a client do that before. Most of my clients at least respected the power the government has. But I'm sure you have a good reason for giving the finger to the FBI. And once we get to the office, I absolutely can't wait to hear what it is."

# Chapter Thirty One

The sedan dropped them in front of Nicole's building. As the driver opened the back door for Nicole, Brian hopped out the other side. They stood on the sidewalk. "Come on up," she said.

"You know what, Nicole," he responded. "I'm not a kid in school. I paid you a lot of money to get me ready for today, and I probably owe you even more than I've already paid. I chose a course of action today for reasons you don't know, and I'll live with the consequences of my actions. I'm not a kid whose mom has caught him doing something bad, and I'm not interested in your review of how things went today. So at this point, I hope you'll continue to represent me going forward, and if either of us finds a reason we need to talk, let's talk."

"I'll think it over," she said, turning and going into the building.

# Chapter Thirty Two

SIX MONTHS LATER
DECEMBER 2005

It was a blustery, cold winter afternoon in Dallas. The rain pelted the window of the apartment, making streaks down the glass. Thunder rumbled occasionally. The forecast called for snow showers later as the temperature would drop into the thirties after dark.

Brian Sadler, dressed in sweat pants and shirt, sat in his favorite oversize leather chair, his feet propped up on the matching ottoman. He'd been reading the most recent draft of the Bijan Rarities offering document all that Sunday afternoon in his apartment. The New York law firm he'd hired to prepare the registration statement had been working on the project for nearly six weeks. Now they were on draft number four, and they had emailed him the latest version late yesterday. He had gone to W&T this morning and printed the document; he found it easier to proofread in hard copy format.

Although he had gone garage-to-garage from his apartment to the office, he was glad he didn't have to get outside in the weather. It was damp and chilly, and the sky had settled into a gray pallor that hung over the city.

Back at the apartment, his pen and yellow highlighter were close at hand, along with a mug of coffee. He'd painstakingly read each draft the firm had prepared, after which he generated a spreadsheet with his comments, emailing it each time to Samuel Lowe, the attorney at the Karr Dandridge law firm who was handling this project for him. Today would be no exception. He needed to get finished with the proofing so he could generate his list of changes and get it sent off. Tomorrow promised to be a busy one at W&T and he didn't have time to work on this stuff at the office anyway.

His mind ached from having read nearly three hundred single spaced pages and making yet another round of corrections, additions, deletions and changes. At this point most of them were minor, but all of them were critical. Within two weeks, W&T expected to submit the offering documents to the Securities and Exchange Commission and have yet another public offering pop out of the oven a few weeks afterwards.

It had been an eventful six months since the last time he saw Nicole Farber on the sidewalk in front of her office. The FBI had advised the U.S. Attorney, who had advised Nicole, who had advised him, that he was no longer a person of interest in the Bellicose case. From what Brian could piece together, once Carl decided to become a witness for the government, he had turned over every document he could get his hands on, including hundreds of pages of highly confidential information which belonged to W&T. If Carl had been alive, he would have faced a lawsuit of immense proportion from his firm. He had stolen much of the information and at that point, nothing really mattered except that the U.S. Attorney and the FBI had evidence which allowed them to issue arrest warrants for W&T's two top executives.

The word around the office was that one of these two men was an associate of the mobster John Spedino. That connection had allowed W&T to be used as a conduit for the laundering of tens of millions of dollars of mob money through the blind pool public offerings. It probably would have continued, Brian thought at the time, if someone hadn't decided it was time for a little payoff.

When Spedino decided to make a withdrawal from his W&T deals, he apparently did it through Bellicose Holdings. On the surface, it had looked like just another blind pool offering, with one exception no one knew about. As soon as the proceeds, which as usual contained a lot of laundered money of Spedino's, made it to the company's coffers, the criminal president, Francois Rochefort, withdrew the funds and disappeared. Everyone presumed he was in hiding under Johnny Speed's protection and that Spedino himself had received back twenty-five million of his dollars.

When the Chief Executive Officer and Chief Financial Officer at Warren Taylor and Currant were arrested, it sent shock waves throughout the company. The firm's principal shareholders were three hedge fund managers from Boston. Each had been in the securities business for twenty years or more without so much as a hiccup. They appointed Chief Operating Officer Robert Overton to the post of CEO. Overton also had many years in the business and his integrity appeared above reproach. The SEC had sent a team to Dallas to monitor the transition, and they stayed on premises at W&T for over a month, until things began to settle down.

Six months later, it appeared that W&T was going to live to fight another day. It was questionable for awhile whether enough people in the firm were involved with the money laundering scheme that the investment bank itself might collapse. Only through full disclosure to the SEC and calm assurances to customers had it managed to continue in business.

Things were different, though. Looking out the window at the steady rain, Brian thought of how much more conservative the firm was today. Two blind pool offerings in the works had been withdrawn in the days immediately following the arrests, and in half a year, only six deals had been done by W&T.

Six new public companies, and not one of them a blind pool. Each of the offerings now was a real operating company, with real people and real substance behind it. Each company had plans for using the money it got in its offering, and so far it looked as though each company had done exactly what it was supposed to.

The first company after the fall of W&T's top executives had been the test case. No one knew if the firm could successfully bring another deal to the market. Would the SEC over-scrutinize the offering until it just dried up and died? Would W&T's previous client base still support the firm's salespeople by investing in deals? And once the company went public, would its stock price go right in the tank with all the negativity surrounding the firm that took it public?

Everyone held their collective breaths at Warren Taylor and Currant that day in September when EvenGlow Cosmetics hit the market. The deal was small by W&T standards – only $5 million – and the SEC had given its approval without delay. The Houston-based company was a fledgling multi-level cosmetics company that had hopes to be the next Mary Kay. It planned to use its public money to expand its existing product line and recruit salespeople to buy and sell its products through downlines of individuals.

Brian and the other salespeople had found it more difficult to sell - there were far more people who didn't return his calls – but with a smaller deal and a solid business idea, the company's stock finally ended up all pre-sold. On offering day, things all went off without a hitch.

He reflected on how it had seemed that day. It was far more subdued at W&T. Nobody made a hundred thousand bucks in commissions. No Lamborghinis were won. It was, he decided, more like the offering days at Merrill Lynch. Much calmer and much more professional.

# Chapter Thirty Three

As far as Brian knew, John Spedino remained free and charged with no crime. The two W&T executives had been released on $500,000 bail each but had immediately disappeared. No trial date had yet been set on the numerous laws they had been accused of breaking. At both W&T and in the press, everyone assumed the Feds were diligently trying to work a deal that would put Spedino in the slammer in exchange for the two execs going free, and everyone assumed the Feds had these guys in a secret place, hidden away from Johnny Speed's friends.

Brian had thought how difficult a choice it might be to turn state's evidence and rat out a guy like Johnny Speed. He was Teflon Two all right, but people around him sometimes ended up hurt or dead for no apparent reason. This time Spedino might have had all the reason in the world to keep these guys quiet. That was why, according to the rumor mill, they were in a safe house somewhere far away, for their own good.

The most important thing for Brian had happened within a week after W&T got the word he was no longer going to be pursued by the FBI or the U.S. Attorney. It was October - the same month that

W&T had successfully taken their second company public under the "new plan," where companies actually were real operating entities.

One morning the mail clerk made his way from cube to cube on the sales floor, dropping off packages and mail to each desk. A thick Fedex package landed on Brian's desk. "Probably a big deal for ya, Brian," the mail guy said.

Brian could never remember the kid's name, but had made small talk with him about Rangers baseball a few times. Thanking him, Brian ripped open the envelope, shaking the contents out onto his desk.

There was a nicely bound investment banking proposal for a company called Bijan Rarities Limited in New York. Brian looked at the envelope and saw that it was addressed to him and sent from New York. He wondered why someone had sent it directly to him, since there were people in the firm who got these things every day from companies needing money. It was those peoples' jobs to make the decision which ones W&T would look at and which would go in the trash. Guys like Brian never saw a deal on the front end like this.

He had just decided to send it downstairs to the corporate guys, then he opened the front cover to see how much money these Bijan guys were looking for. There was a yellow sticky note inside. It said, "For Brian Sadler. Payback time."

# PART TWO

## Chapter One

JANUARY 2006

Thinking back on it, Brian was surprised it had taken him two days to link the word "payback" to the phone call in the limo that day after the deposition. The voice had said, "Good job. Now we'll help you." He had forgotten about it, since nothing had happened for months.

Brian had taken the Bijan investment banking proposal home with him the night it arrived. It was well done and very thorough. It discussed the company's current operations, its need for $4 million, and its prospects for the future with the infusion of new capital. It included three years of audited financial statements and the most recent six months' unaudited numbers. As he read, he learned about the world of acquiring archaeological wonders, and it fascinated him.

Bijan was on the tips of everyone's tongues in the world of ancient relics at the moment, because of the upcoming sale of the sarcophagus of Inkharaton, a pharaoh who had been missing from the line of kings for thousands of years until the discovery of his tomb in 2005. Because of Brian's interest in the subject, he knew that the sale would put Bijan on the map as one of the best-known names in the rarity auction field.

Within three days, Brian had devoured the Bijan document, spent hours poring over Bijan's website, and had placed a call to Darius Nazir, the owner of Bijan Rarities. Early the next week, Brian put in for three days off and headed to New York City to talk to Nazir himself.

Bijan Rarities fascinated Brian. His love of ancient things, his interest in reading archaeological adventure fiction, his secret fantasy to be the twenty-first century Howard Carter, unearthing the next King Tut tomb in Egypt – all these things came to the forefront as he had immersed himself in this company. From a Fifth Avenue storefront, Bijan sold some of the greatest and most interesting rarities of the ancient world to discerning collectors everywhere.

Throughout the document, reference was made to Darius Nazir's contacts. In this business, Brian surmised, it was who you knew. You had to be on top of discoveries in order to be the one who got to broker their disposition. You had to be there virtually from the discovery itself, to beat out the other firms who would do whatever they could to land a hot piece of history, with the attendant publicity for the selling firm, not to mention hundreds of thousands of dollars of potential commissions on the sale itself. It was fascinating stuff to Brian Sadler, the armchair archaeologist.

Brian was not a frequent flyer and didn't feel like paying a thousand bucks each way for the privilege of sitting in the front of the American Airlines 767. He therefore sat in a cramped aisle seat in coach, all six feet of his frame trying to balance between knees stuck in the seat in front, and the kid behind kicking the back of Brian's seat. He thought how much flying had become a hassle in the years since 9/11. Not that he used to fly so much before then. It was just easier, before the Transportation Security Administration hired a bunch of people with no tact, no interest in being helpful and a bored attitude, who moved people through lines like cattle going to the slaughter.

Reaching into his briefcase, he pulled out some web pages he had printed before he left. Brian had copied Bijan's announcement of the firm's handling of the sale of the sarcophagus of Inkharaton, along with a lengthy article from *Archaeology* magazine, giving details of the amazing discovery of Inkharaton's long-forgotten tomb. Although he had read it before, the story of how this tomb was discovered, and how the priceless sarcophagus came to be offered for sale by a New York rarities dealer, still fascinated him.

# Chapter Two

In mid-2005, the announcement was made that a new tomb had been discovered in the Valley of the Kings, the first since Howard Carter had found Tutankhamen's tomb in 1922. For a brief period, the press had given a lot of attention to the find, because such things tended to grab the attention of mainstream people everywhere. It was a chance to read about a time long gone, to hear about a man who walked the earth and ruled a nation, three thousand years ago.

Inkharaton was the forgotten pharoah. His name had been obliterated from hieroglyphs by jealous successors, and even the lists of kings which scholars had developed had a hole where Inharakton's name belonged. For all this time, it was known only that a nameless pharoah ruled Egypt shortly before King Tutankhamen, around 3500 years ago. Archaeologists had looked for the tomb of this missing individual for forty years. Not having a name to help them, they were virtually at a standstill until that day in 2005 when a workman's donkey shied away from a snake and pawed the ground.

The man was helping dig a new roadbed for the tour buses

that brought needed dollars to bolster Egypt's economy. The government had decided to create a roadway which snaked among the tombs, to be used to lure tourists who wanted to see the locations of long-dead pharaohs without braving hundred degree heat. Buses could traverse the new road and tour guides could point out tomb entrances as people watched from the air conditioned comfort of the bus. It was a plan that horrified the Director of Antiquities and many scholars, but one which the President, in his desire to generate revenue, pushed through the legislature.

A side effect of excavating anywhere in Egypt was the distinct possibility that something would turn up. Ancient inhabitants of this land had possessed almost unfathomable abilities in architecture, government and art. While much of the world was in the twilight of emerging civilization, the dwellers of this barren country ruled democratically, built monuments which lasted longer than any other thing on earth, and used a beautiful language of pictures called hieroglyphs to record for posterity what they did during the days of their lives.

The excavation of the Valley Tourway was no exception. As men moved rocks and rubble by donkey, a base was created which would be smoothed and covered with asphalt. On that fateful day, the worker led his donkey toward a dumping ground. Large baskets on both sides of the donkey's back were loaded with stones so that walking was difficult for the burdened animal. As the man pulled him along with a rope, a snake suddenly twisted across the path in front of the beast, causing it to try to rise up. With the weight on its back, it could not do so, and instead it pawed at the snake.

The reptile moved on, but a small hole appeared in the ground where the donkey had struck it with his hoof. By chance, the worker had turned to see what was causing the problem, and noticed the hole. He knelt and picked up a rock, using it to enlarge the size of the hole. The man grew excited. He stood within eyesight of the tombs of Seti I and Ramses X. "What should I do?" he thought to himself.

By then, however, another man had moved up behind him, pulling his own donkey along toward the dumping ground. "What is it?" he called to the first worker. And the rest, as they say, was history.

Brian read how the worker had stayed at the site while the second man informed the team leader. As is required in the Valley, the Department of Antiquities was immediately notified. Given the location and potential importance of the hole, the Director himself had shown up about two hours later. By chance, he had been in Luxor for a meeting and was therefore close by.

All work had stopped on the roadway. The workers, smoking cigarettes and milling about, watched as the Director's driver pulled his SUV close to the site. "It's here, Director," pointed the man who worked for the official as overseer of the Valley of the Kings.

# Chapter Three

Within a week, excavation had begun in earnest. The road project was put on hold and a wooden fence erected, to keep prying eyes and sticky fingers away from the site. Armed guards patrolled the area at night. No one ever knew what to expect from a new tomb. Usually the looters had gotten there first, thousands of years ago, and what was left was in total disarray. Rarely, as in Tut's tomb, treasure of inestimable value was found. Always however, artifacts, hieroglyphs and pictures gave a stunning glimpse into the lives of the ancestors of today's Egyptians, and excitement was in the air.

The small hole led to a stairway mostly filled with rubble. It was painstakingly cleared, stone by stone, in the stifling heat. At the bottom of thirteen steps was a stone doorway, encased by a lintel made of three enormous blocks. Carvings were literally everywhere on the lintel and work again stopped as interpreters were called from Cairo to come to the scene.

Within days there were front page headlines. *USA Today* reported that interpreters read the words written nearly fifteen hundred years before Christ. They said, "An eternal curse will befall he who defiles the death temple of the great Inkharaton, ruler of Upper and Lower Egypt, brother to the gods, pharaoh of the people." The curses placed on tombs always grabbed the reader's attention, but in reality many tombs had them. Researchers believed they were used in hopes to ward off tomb robbers, who usually arrived within a year or so after the burial of the pharaoh. Sadly, most defiled tombs bore witness to the fact that robbers were more greedy than superstitious.

The Director of Antiquities looked closely at the door. All the pictures had been taken, all inscriptions carefully recopied to paper by hand, and it was time to open the tomb. To him, the lintel and doorway appeared intact. There were no telltale holes where a grave robber might have sneaked into the tomb and brought out gold and jewels. But the Director also knew the chances of finding another Tut treasure were a million to one. "Let us open this tomb," he said to the head of the workmen. He gave detailed instructions on how to remove the door with as little damage as possible to the carvings and the lintel.

For a week the work continued on the stone door. The Director of Antiquities nabbed a room at the Nile Sheraton in Luxor, no small feat during the height of tourist season. Each morning he made the trip across the river, where a driver with a Jeep met him to take him along the west bank to the Valley of the Kings. He interviewed the four armed guards who were stationed at the site each night, making sure nothing out of the ordinary had happened. Those guards were replaced with a new set, whose job was to keep tourists, reporters and other busybodies away from the staircase and the door at its bottom.

On the seventh day, the door had been loosened and small hooks were placed on its four sides. A cable was attached to the hooks and strung up the stairway, where it was connected to a winch on the front of the Director's Jeep. At his signal, the driver began to very slowly draw in the cable. It stiffened as it pulled all four hooks taut, then the winch ground noisily as it struggled to move several tons of solid rock.

The winch broke, after which the decision was made to connect the cable to a backhoe. The machine was then slowly moved backwards as it pulled the giant stone forward into the area at the foot of the stairway. The rock was over two feet thick and it took several hours to move it sufficiently to offer a chance to peer into the black opening behind it. While the work progressed, the Director asked that three reporters who were outside be allowed in. The first was from Al-Ahram, Cairo's oldest newspaper. He then asked for the BBC reporter and one from CNN. He wanted complete coverage worldwide. He told the reporters to stand aside, which was somewhat difficult in the cramped area at the bottom of the stairway. To make more room, he sent the workmen away who had helped prepare the stone to be moved.

As the senior man present, the Director had the right to be the first to see inside. He motioned to the workman whose donkey had created the hole. "You found it," he said. "You may have the privilege of being first to view the tomb. Please look inside and tell me what you see." He handed the poor man a flashlight as a ladder was propped up against the door, which filled the stairway almost completely, except for a couple of feet at the top.

Shaking, the workman climbed the ladder until he reached the top of the rock door. He leaned forward across it, stretched the hand holding the light in front, and stuck his head into the inky darkness. He switched on the light.

# Chapter Four

Sahib . . ." he stuttered. "Speak up, man!" the Director said loudly. "We cannot hear you!"

"Sahib," the man said again. "There is a small room here, full of furnishings, with another door beyond. All the furnishings appear to be upright. Nothing seems to be disturbed."

As the workman came down the ladder, the Director could hardly contain his excitement. He wanted to appear professional before the world's news agencies, but his imagination raced as he prepared to see the interior himself.

Peering into the darkness, the Director turned on his flashlight and shined it around the room. The area was about six feet square, and another door indeed stood at the rear wall, just opposite his current position. Two large statues of Anubis, the canine-like God of the Dead, flanked the next doorway. The lintels and door itself did not appear to be made of heavy stone as the entrance was. Instead, they looked to be carved from the sandstone which surrounded the tomb.

As the workman had described, the room was full of furnishings and pottery. Things were sitting in no particular order, but were all upright and intact. The Director recalled that the first sign that Tut's tomb had been desecrated was the disarray in which the robbers had left the furniture, which had held no interest for them. They had turned things over, pushed them aside and cleared a path to the next doorway. In the room before him, the Director could plainly see that the items of furniture sat just as they had been positioned by priests who put them in place as the men backed out of the room.

His heart raced as he moved down the ladder, making way for the news reporters to climb up, take pictures and prepare a story which would interest the entire planet.

# Chapter Five

Over the next couple of months the excavation team had worked feverishly to open rooms, catalog items and bring the findings to the world through the internet. The tomb had never been entered before – a first in Egyptian archaeology – and although its finery was not the magnitude of King Tutankhamen's, the historic significance of the find was unparalleled. The hieroglyphs revealed that the pharaoh Inkharaton had held the title Pharoah of the People. In stark contrast to any other tomb ever discovered, he was shown pictorially walking among his people, sitting by the Nile and talking to them. He was a god among men.

Although many hoped for the gilded treasures seen in Tut's tomb, the items chosen by the priests for burial with Inkharaton were things people used in their daily lives. Instead of gilded chaise longues, there were beautifully painted wooden chairs, arranged around a table. Tack for horses was ornate but not excessive. It was as though even the things which surrounded him in death, to accompany him to the afterlife, displayed his desire to be a man like other men around him, instead of a god, hidden away in a palace-prison, insulated from his subjects.

At last the burial chamber itself was opened. Inside a stone coffin there was an ornately painted wooden sarcophagus, depicting the countenance of the god-king, but with almost no gold. All the colors of the rainbow were used in the incredibly beautiful artwork which adorned every square inch of the seven-foot casket. In its own right it was as beautiful as Tut's. Like everything else, it was a tomb for a man the people revered. It was a casket for one of the people, made of wood, not gold.

The mummy itself was tightly wrapped in linens as usual, and the Director ordered a portable x-ray machine to be brought to the burial chamber. Electric lines snaked up the stairway as everything was readied, the mummy carefully removed and laid on the smooth surface of the machine. Befitting this modest pharaoh, under the linens were only a few items of jewelry. Both arms had bracelets and there were earrings. All were probably made of gold, although the Director did not intend to cut into the wrappings and examine the mummy, so they would remain where they were.

As the beautifully decorated walls in the funerary chamber were photographed and cataloged, one of the workers noticed a small door cut into the wall. It was only about four feet square and bore no seal or markings. It was like a door to a storage closet, and the supervisor wasted no time in ordering it to be opened. When the supervisor peered into the long chamber, he stopped all work and again called the Director of Antiquities. "Sir," he said. "You must come quickly. We have found a second sarcophagus!"

For the first time in history, a second burial casket was found, and this one was lavishly decorated in sheets of gold, lapis lazuli stones and a lifelike depiction of the pharaoh Inkharaton. An inscription on the wall of the burial chamber, next to the door behind which the golden casket had been stored, explained the unusual situation.

Two sarcophagi had indeed been made for Inkharaton. The high priests intended for him to be buried in the one befitting his status as a god. They were unhappy, the hieroglyphs said, when before his death the pharaoh chose the less impressive one, denoting his love for his common people and his desire to be more like them than the gods. So the beautiful golden casket, emblazoned with Inkharaton's likeness, was relegated to a storage chamber in the burial vault itself, to play second fiddle for eternity.

# Chapter Six

Once everything had been cataloged, photographed in situ, checked and double-checked, the Director of the Department of Antiquities came up with a novel plan. He took it to the President of Egypt, who saw no flaw in it, so the Director moved to put his remarkable idea into place.

The Director knew that there were collectors and institutions who would pay an enormous sum to be the rightful owner of a sarcophagus from 3500 B.C. He also knew that Egypt didn't have a lot of extra cash to fund his department, the new Valley Tourway project and to dig for undiscovered sites and tombs. Finally, he knew that Egypt should and would be the rightful resting place for Inkharaton's gilded sarcophagus, even though his body had never lain in it.

An announcement was made that the golden sarcophagus of Inkharaton would be offered for sale at auction to the highest bidder. While the new owner would hold title to the relic, a stipulation was put on the sale. For a period of one hundred years, the object must remain in Egypt, on display in the tomb, at the Museum of Antiquities or at any other place designated by the then-current

Director of Antiquities. After that time, so long as Egypt continued to display the casket half of the year or more, the requirement continued. If Egypt decided to remove it from display for more than half the time, the owner was free to take possession and move it, but only to another museum, where it would continue to be enjoyed by the world.

To fuel the ego of the new owner, all information about Inkharaton's sarcophagus would state that it was owned by the person or entity, if they wished. Therefore, among many other things, a plaque in the display area would stand next to the casket, and would say, "The sarcophagus of Inkharaton displayed here is owned by . . . and is on permanent loan to this museum."

The Department of Antiquities had created a list of firms who were qualified to act as agents to sell such an object. The usual names – Sotheby's, Christie's and the like – were there. The Director's former second-in-command, a man named Darius Nazir, also made the list. And, a rarity in Egypt, it was not a political favor that had allowed his firm, Bijan Rarities, to be included with the giants of the auction industry. Nazir was a genius at marketing rarities. He had a sixth sense which allowed him to pair an object with the perfect potential owners, create a frenzy of bidding among them, and realize the greatest return for his sellers. Since leaving Egypt for New York, Nazir had quietly become one of the power brokers in the ancient relic auction field.

After allowing the submission of proposals for a short time, Nazir's firm was selected by a committee from the Antiquities board and the museum. His commission charge was five percent of the sale price – right in the middle of the group of bidders. The government would pay all marketing costs, which in this case could run over a half million dollars. This sale would be advertised in all the right places, even though it might end up being a museum that paid the price that brought the final rap of the auctioneer's gavel. The idea here was to advertise the concept the Director had dreamed up. It was unique, it could create a win-win situation, and it was fair for all.

# Chapter Seven

Brian stopped reading. Looking at his watch, he figured he had about 45 minutes before landing at La Guardia Airport. Putting his reading materials back in the briefcase, he glanced to the back of the plane. One person was in line for the restroom. He knew that post-9/11 rules prohibited people from congregating anywhere on the plane, so he waited until that person went inside the tiny bathroom before he rose and strode to the back.

A flight attendant was dumping trash into a plastic bag and closing down the galley's food service trolleys, preparing for landing shortly. Brian saw that she was younger than he was, and also really attractive. She smiled at him and said, "Heading home?" He told her he was from Dallas and in town for only a day or so on business. "I hope you have a great time," she said. "Have you been to Quo?"

Brian hadn't, and she told him it was one of the city's hottest nightspots. "You should stop by," she told him. "It's on 28th Street in Chelsea. If you're in midtown, grab a cab. It's worth the trip." He promised to give it a try if he had time. She smiled at him and he glanced at her left hand. No ring. He decided to go to Quo if he could, just to see if she might be there.

Back in his seat, Brian thought about Bijan and how everything fit together. The firm had landed the biggest sale of an ancient relic since Schliemann's discoveries at Troy had hit the auction market seventy years ago. From the material he had found online, he knew the opening bid for the sarcophagus of Inkharaton was set at ten million dollars. He also knew that the auction, set for just a month from now, was being held in a tent which was being erected in the roadbed immediately outside of Inkharaton's tomb.

This decision had been a mastery of marketing. Discovery Channel had paid the Department of Antiquities a half million dollars for the privilege of filming the event, which would be held at night, and preceded by a tour of the tomb itself. Only qualified bidders who had posted a good-faith deposit of one million dollars were allowed on the scene, so the live television show would be watched by literally millions of people around the globe, most of whom could never otherwise hoped to have seen the tomb and its contents.

The captain's voice came through the overhead speakers, announcing landing in about twenty minutes. People around Brian began shutting down laptops, stowing carry-on luggage above their seats, and retrieving jackets. Brian stood and pulled a topcoat out of the storage bin. He'd need it in the December weather after he landed.

# Chapter Eight

Luggage came through more quickly than usual, and Brian was in a cab headed for Manhattan within thirty minutes after landing. It was noon, and snow was falling steadily. The roadways were a slushy mess and the cab driver complained in broken English about how lousy the weather was in New York.

Truth was, Brian loved cold weather. Dallas summers made him irritable and he hated the sticky feeling you had all the time when it was a hundred degrees in the shade. He looked outside at the dark day and watched the snow fall as the cab made its way from Queens into the Midtown Tunnel, then out on Manhattan island. Turning north on Third Avenue, they moved slowly uptown to the mid-fifties, winding over to Fifth Avenue and stopping at the address Brian had given the driver. It had taken nearly an hour to get to town from the airport.

He paid the driver and stepped from the cab, retrieving his briefcase and a rolling suitcase. Crossing the sidewalk, he followed instructions on a small sign and pressed a button to request entrance to Bijan Rarities.

Within seconds, a buzzer sounded and the door opened slightly.

Brian entered the room and was immediately enraptured. Directly in front of him was a full-size replica of the sarcophagus of the lost pharaoh Inkharaton. It was incredibly beautiful. He paused, setting down his cases and staring at it. A young lady came up to him and said, "Good afternoon. May I help you?"

He gave her his business card and asked for Darius Nazir, telling her he was a little early for his appointment. She advised him that Nazir was still at lunch and the weather was slowing everything down, but he was certainly expecting Brian and would be back shortly. She directed him to Nazir's cramped office, where he dropped off his coat and luggage. She locked the door behind him as Brian returned to the showroom.

He was like a kid at the circus. The place was tastefully decorated and only thirty or so objects were displayed. It looked much like a museum. Each thing was in its own Plexiglas case, the smaller ones on pedestals. A discreet card by each item gave its description and selling price. Besides the girl who had greeted him, a man in his twenties sat at a desk toward the back of the showroom, working. Both of them were obviously of Middle Eastern descent. *Probably Egyptian like Nazir,* Brian thought.

He stood before a beautiful silver knife which dated from the third century B.C., the time of Alexander the Great. It had been found in a cache of treasures at Alexandria, Egypt, the city founded by the hero. Although nothing had ever been successfully linked to Alexander himself, Brian liked the way Bijan created the mystique and possibility that this very relic could have been held in the hand of Alexander. He glanced at the card for a price. In small letters at the bottom were the letters P.O.R. Price on request. *If you can afford to come in here,* Brian thought, *the price is not likely to be an issue.*

A quiet bell rang and Brian turned to see a man standing at the entrance. He was buzzed in by the young man at the desk. The newcomer, a man in his mid-sixties and dressed in a dark three-piece suit and overcoat, strode purposefully to Brian and said, "I'm Darius Nazir. It's nice to see you."

"Thank you," he responded. "How did you know who I was?"

"Oh," Nazir laughed. "Collette called me on my mobile to let me know you'd arrived, and hopefully to rush me up a bit!" The girl smiled from across the room.

"Come, come," Nazir told him, removing his coat. "Meet Jason, my other assistant." The young man shook hands with Brian, took Nazir's coat and his umbrella, whisking them away. "Pardon the mess in my office," Nazir told Brian. "You may have heard we have an auction coming up shortly," he said, smiling. "I'm spending a lot of time working on it." Brian tried to place his accent. His English was flawless but with a definite highly educated flavor. *Maybe Oxford or Cambridge.*

They talked for awhile about the Inkharaton sarcophagus. Nazir said he was impressed by Brian's research, and Brian responded that it was as much an interest in ancient relics in general as it was research for this project that had caused him to read the lengthy article about Inkharaton.

Collette opened the door, stuck in her head and said, "Coffee, anyone?"

"I need to warn you, Mr. Sadler, that the coffee is Turkish," Nazir said. "It's very strong but it's perfect on a cold day like this."

Soon they were both enjoying coffee in small cups. They had dispensed with formalities, and were Brian and Darius. "I'd like to know the level of interest Warren Taylor and Currant has in my proposal," Darius Nazir said at last.

"If I may be so bold, may I ask one question before we begin?" Brian said. "How did you find our firm, and what other investment banks are you working with? The reason I ask is that we certainly are not well known in the northeast, nor have we ever done an offering for a firm remotely like yours."

"Two fair questions," Nazir responded, sitting back in his chair and folding his hands across his vest. "Although part of what I do for a living is auctions, I don't believe personally in having too many people in a deal at one time. What may work for selling the Greek vase out on the floor doesn't necessarily work for selling Inkharaton's sarcophagus. I think you must gear the deal toward the situation you're facing."

In the next hour, Nazir explained that he had a close friend, a man who knew one of W&T's hedge fund owners. Nazir's friend had mentioned that W&T was an aggressive firm, had just come through an ordeal and had been certified as reputable, and was looking for business.

Brian's radar went up at once. "May I ask the name of your friend?" he said to Nazir.

"I doubt you would know him, and in his position, his name usually isn't in the forefront of conversations," Nazir replied casually. "His involvement really isn't important in considering the proposal I sent you."

Brian replied that although that was true, the firm had an obligation to ensure its dealings were with honest individuals whose backgrounds and histories would not create issues down the road, either for W&T or for the public offering itself. There was nothing as bad as a deal on which hundreds of thousands of dollars had been spent, then one secret became public – one untruth in the offering document came to light – and the deal fell apart in a wave of negative publicity.

Darius Nazir looked at Brian intently. "The man is a client of mine, whom I have known for twenty years. He is an American who lives in my native Egypt."

The stress level Brian was feeling must have decreased visibly as Nazir made that admission. "Are you all right, Brian?" he asked.

"I'm fine," Brian replied. Brian knew that the "payback" had to involve John Spedino in some way. Nazir's admission that his friend was living in Egypt helped ease Brian's tension. At least it wasn't Johnny Speed himself.

"Did you send the proposal yourself?" Brian asked, fishing for an answer to the "payback" sticky note on its cover. Spedino had to be in the picture somewhere, Brian knew, because the investment banking proposal had the note attached.

"No," Nazir responded. "My friend was in town and agreed to send the proposal to you and a couple of others. Why do you ask?"

Brian hedged his answer, preferring not to continue down this path at the moment. For now, this whole meeting could turn out to be a once in a lifetime experience.

Brian settled into the chair and told Nazir the reason for his visit. "To be perfectly honest with you, Darius," he said, "I am not one of the people at W&T who makes a decision on proposals like yours. I'm in the sales department, but somehow your document was sent to me. I think it was a fortuitous event. I'm inclined to believe there are no coincidences. I'm probably the most interested layman in Texas in the concepts of your business, and specifically in the relics you handle. I hope you will take this as it's intended. I'd be honored to discuss the possibility of my personally becoming a shareholder with you."

They took a break at 4 p.m. Walking into the showroom, they saw through the tinted front windows that the snow was falling much harder now. Darius asked Brian if he had checked into his hotel. Finding that he hadn't, Darius suggested he should do so as soon as possible. "When the weather is like this, people get stranded in Manhattan, and desk clerks have been known to let a room go to a man with a hundred dollar tip in his hand." Darius offered to send his young associate to the Inter-Continental Hotel a few blocks away to firm up Brian's reservation. In a half hour the deed was done and the young man was back, room key in hand.

Meanwhile, Brian and Darius talked. Brian explained that he was certain he and the firm could and would do the Bijan Rarities public offering, but that he himself had been considering a change in his personal life. "I've never had such a feeling as I had when I read your proposal," Brian admitted. "I must admit I'm fascinated by your business." Brian explained that he was willing to help Darius Nazir raise the money he wanted regardless. However, he hoped Nazir would at least talk to him about the possibility of Brian's also investing his own money in the firm and becoming a shareholder.

Snowy afternoon turned into wintry evening as the men talked. At 6 p.m. Collette opened the door and told them she and Jason were leaving for the day. Nazir stepped out of his office, saw them off and dimmed the lights in the showroom. A series of spotlights continued to brightly illuminate the imitation sarcophagus so that it could clearly be see by passersby on the sidewalk. *There won't be many of those tonight,* Brian thought to himself.

# Chapter Nine

"Would you join me for dinner, so we may continue our conversation?" Darius asked. Brian agreed enthusiastically. They decided to walk the few blocks to the hotel, since there was little chance of getting a cab as the snow intensified. Darius loaned Brian a pair of rubber galoshes. "You'll need these for sure," he said.

As they stepped from the building onto the sidewalk, Darius turned, locked the door and set an alarm. Brian looked down the street at St. Patrick's Cathedral. He couldn't see the top of the spires in the swirling snow. *It's like a wonderland,* he thought.

As they began the trek to East 48th Street, Darius apologized for the walk.

"It's no problem at all," Brian responded. "I'm a big fan both of snow and New York City. So I'd rather be out here than in a cab any day!" Traffic was light and they made the trip in less than twenty minutes. Darius sat in the lobby bar while Brian dropped his things in his room.

"First things first," Darius said as Brian joined him and ordered a martini. "I don't know what foods you like, but my favorite restaurant in Manhattan is a Chinese place not far from here." Brian enthusiastically agreed. Chinese was one of his favorites as well. They settled in on their martinis as Darius returned to the discussion they had been having at the office.

He told Brian that the timing actually was good to consider bringing a partner into Bijan Rarities. Darius said he wanted to travel for pleasure more, and his adult children lived in California. His wife, he said, had died ten years before, not long after he founded Bijan. "There are a lot more things we need to know about each other before we can determine if it's a fit," Darius told Brian, "but I'm open to the concept of having a minority partner."

"I read in the proposal that you previously worked for the Antiquities Department in Egypt," Brian said.

They talked about the interesting work Darius had done for twenty five years, and the digs he had been privileged to be involved in. He fascinated Brian with stories of ancient ruins uncovered as infrastructure improvement projects caused streets to be dug up in Cairo. "The ancients built literally everywhere in northern Egypt," he said. "It's difficult to dig very deep without uncovering evidence of their presence."

He related how, as a bachelor in his late thirties, he had vacationed in London and met a beautiful Syrian girl. They had fallen in love and for several years maintained a long distance relationship. She worked for a large American bank and told him one day she was being transferred to New York. Devastated, he spent days calculating how he might get a job in America himself, and marry this girl he had come to love.

The Director of Antiquities at the time was very well connected. He made some calls to a wealthy New Yorker who had been a benefactor of the Museum in Cairo. He was also an archaeology buff, and the Director had allowed him behind the scenes at a number of excavations on the man's trips to Egypt.

A few months later, Darius was placed at the Carlyle Museum, a privately funded institution where the Director's friend served as a board member. Darius married his Syrian sweetheart and settled in to his work, remaining at the museum for ten years. He arranged acquisitions, helped prepare exhibits and guided the fund-raisers the museum regularly held. One day, he said, the man who'd helped him get his job came to him and said that a rare opportunity had opened up. A storefront had become vacant in a Fifth Avenue building the man owned, and he offered to back Darius in a rarities gallery.

Art galleries abounded in New York, but the concept of a store selling antiquities was something novel. Darius said he had jumped at the opportunity. The man had provided sufficient capital to allow them to purchase a number of interesting pieces, and some friends of Darius' benefactor had put other objects in the store on consignment. All together, Bijan Rarities opened with a black tie event, a string quartet from the Met, and that night he sold four pieces for over a hundred thousand total.

"I've had a wonderful time ever since," he told Brian. "Five years ago, my backer told me he wanted to get his money out. Although the place was worth many times what it was the day we opened, he always treated his investment as nothing more than a loan, and I paid him interest every year. So I used the company's bank line of credit, borrowed a couple of million dollars, and paid him off in full." He continued. "That was a good feeling, owning my own very successful business. But at that time, I was already over sixty years old, and I knew I had to eventually think of a succession plan of my own."

His children, Darius said, were professionals. One was a doctor, another a dentist, in San Francisco and La Jolla respectively. They visited New York regularly, but neither had any interest in the gallery or in living in the city where they grew up.

They continued to talk as they walked in the intensifying snow. They went five blocks north to 53rd Street, then a couple of blocks east to Peking Duck House. Once inside, they were glad for the warmth, and Brian found himself really hungry as he smelled the aromas wafting from the kitchen. Another martini later, they were enjoying dumplings and a wonderful meal.

That first evening, the men became good friends. It was as though a bond was formed which was forged in destiny. Brian's exuberance and enthusiasm for the subject balanced his lack of knowledge of the business itself. He could raise money while Darius taught him the ropes and ran the gallery's successful auction and sales business. By the time dinner and coffee were finished, the two had created a friendship.

Darius was heading north on the subway while Brian was going back to the hotel. They parted ways in the subway station, agreeing to meet the next morning at 10 a.m. at the gallery.

Once Darius boarded his northbound subway car, Brian thought about finding out how to get to Quo and the flight attendant who might be waiting there. He decided he had had enough excitement for one evening. His head was spinning with possibilities. He boarded the southbound train and exited at Grand Central, walking the few blocks back to his hotel and a night dreaming of Inkharaton and the upcoming auction of his sarcophagus.

# Chapter Ten

THE JUDEAN HILLS NEAR BETHLEHEM
LATE MARCH, 3 B.C

Benjamin sat in his room, quill in hand, carefully writing on a piece of parchment. He shivered involuntarily as he recalled the events of last night. He could hear his father in the other room, telling his mother what had happened to the small band of shepherds.

Benjamin's mother asked Joab if he was going to talk to the priests about what he and Benjamin had seen. "I don't know," he heard his father reply. "There is no doubt the story will be told everywhere in a very short time. Not only did we see the event, but dozens of others did as well. It may be better that they hear it from another."

In truth, Joab feared telling the priests. He knew it would be viewed as blasphemy or worse. Many times last night he had heard the baby proclaimed as the Messiah. He even knew the child's name – Yeshua. What if the priests chose to take action against the parents of this child? They could be imprisoned for the words they had spoken. Or the baby could be hunted down and killed. Joab did not wish to tell a story which could result in such drastic retaliation against this poor family. And to relate what they had seen . . . it was such a fantastic story it would likely be believed by no one who had not also witnessed it.

"I will ponder these things," Joab said to Rachel.

She rose and walked to Benjamin's room. She hugged her son tightly and said, "I am so proud of you. I believe every word your father told me, and I only wish I had also been chosen by God to be part of the miracle you witnessed."

Benjamin was glad she believed the story, but was also certain there were many who would be greatly angered by it. He continued recounting the events on his parchment until he was finished. He lay down on his cot and fell into a deep, dreamless sleep.

# Chapter Eleven

## NEW YORK CITY

Brian Sadler slept fitfully. Although his mind was filled with the excitement of his discussion with Darius Nazir, he could not ignore the knowledge that all this had been orchestrated by someone, and that this payback might come with significant strings attached. John Spedino was involved somehow, Brian was certain. However, he chose the high road which was fueled by his eternal optimism. He chose to ignore the nagging doubt, and focus instead on how to make a deal with Nazir for Bijan Rarities. *If this happens,* Brian said to himself, *I can deal with Spedino or whomever it is, when or if it ever comes up.*

He looked out the window. The snow had stopped and the morning sun's first rays appeared over the East River. Six inches or more of snow had fallen in total. It was a winter wonderland on the streets outside. New Yorkers being what they were, people were already going about their morning chores. He could see a grocery store across Lexington Avenue from the hotel. The shopkeeper was sweeping his sidewalk free of snow as best he could. Some people were actually jogging. It was slow going, given the combination of heavy clothing and deep snowdrifts, but they were slogging it out anyway.

Brian spent the day at Bijan Rarities. He had a 7 p.m. plane back to Dallas, and he cut it so close he almost didn't make it through security at LaGuardia in time to catch the plane.

Flying home, he thought about everything that had transpired. The day had begun with a discussion of Bijan's financing needs. Darius wanted $4 million from a public offering to supplement the company's $5 million line of credit. Bijan also had a net worth of over $3 million – most of that was tied up in inventory, store fixtures and the cash the company had on hand to buy and sell items as they came in.

Brian admitted he didn't bring expertise to the deal. Darius countered that he had plenty of that himself. What he needed was a partner who knew how to finance acquisitions and sales, how to deal with banks, lines of credit, and all the alternative sources of financing that a company might be able to tap if a truly monumental, once-in-a-lifetime opportunity came along. From college through Merrill to W&T, Brian knew enough about these subjects to be an asset to the company.

"What I also want," Nazir had said, "is a partner who can be my acquisitions man. And with your burning interest in rarities, you'd be a natural."

Before noon, Brian and Darius had put together the outline of a deal whereby Brian would become a 40% shareholder and have the option to buy Darius out if he ever decided to sell. For this investment, Brian was prepared to put $1 million of his own money in the company. Darius asked for more. If the company's net worth was $3 million, he suggested 40% was at a minimum worth $1.2 million, and in reality the company's value was far higher than its net worth. It was profitable, well-established in its field and virtually unique in the types of ancient rarities it sold. All of those intangibles made it more valuable.

Darius therefore countered at two and a half million, and they settled on $1.5 million, plus Brian's guarantee that the $4 million public offering would be accomplished by W&T in the next 90 days. They also set Brian's annual salary at four hundred thousand dollars plus ten percent of the net proceeds on any deal he brought to the gallery himself. Darius made everything contingent on a background check he would order up on Brian. Brian figured it would be no problem, hoping the FBI inquiry had truly gone away as it appeared to have done.

Darius was obviously excited about this deal. Likewise, Brian was visibly pleased about the arrangement they'd hammered out. It was his ticket out of the investment banking business and most importantly, working at Bijan would be more like enjoying a hobby than actually putting in hours at a job.

The two spent the afternoon working on the upcoming Inkharaton sale. Darius showed Brian all the things he had been doing to get things ready. If a bidder wished to remain in New York instead of traveling to Egypt where the sale would take place, he or she could attend by closed circuit satellite feed in Bijan's gallery. Although Darius thought there would be a very limited bidder list, and every bidder would probably want to have a representative at the site in the Valley of the Kings, it never hurt to have an alternative venue for a potential multi-million dollar participant.

In a few short hours, Brian had learned a lot about what made a gallery run seamlessly. And he and Darius Nazir learned about each other. At the end of the day, they seemed to have the mutual respect that made a natural fit for two partners.

# Chapter Twelve

## DALLAS

Brian's first move the next morning was to go to the CEO's office two floors below the trading floor. Robert Overton's assistant, a girl named Julie whom Brian had occasionally seen in the elevator, smiled at him. "I'm Brian Sadler, and I'm a trader upstairs," he said. "I'd like to get an appointment with Robert sometime today if I might."

Julie promised to get with Robert when he arrived and let Brian know. He thanked her, turned and went upstairs. Not ten minutes later, Julie emailed him with an appointment in a couple of hours. Brian used the time to get his thoughts together. He outlined bullet points on a legal pad and photocopied the Bijan investment banking proposal for himself. The original would go to Robert Overton.

Arriving in Robert's anteroom right on time, Brian stood while Julie opened the door and ushered him into the spacious wood-paneled office. Like Nicole's, this office also had commanding views, but to the south. Dallas' architectural marvels, some of the most beautiful office buildings in the world, stood like soldiers in formation only a couple of miles away.

Brian had not met Robert Overton previously. Introductions were made, then Brian launched into his discussion. He told Robert that he was ready for a change. He had done well at W&T, gotten scared like everyone else in the recent tough times, but had emerged a team player who continued to support the firm in whatever form it took. Robert glanced at a file on his desk. Brian figured it was his personnel folder.

He continued, explaining that he had inadvertently received an investment proposal from a company whose business interested him. Brian laid out the entire story to Robert – his quick visit to New York, his immediate interest in working with the company and its founder, and his belief that this company deserved the proceeds from a public offering. He outlined the company's strengths, gave highlights of its strong financial position and laid Bijan's proposal on Robert's desk. "I'd like to help sell this deal as my last one at W&T," Brian concluded, "and hopefully, if you're on board, I can leave on good enough terms that W&T can help Bijan Rarities with our investment banking needs in the future."

Robert asked a number of questions, each of which Brian had anticipated. He had studied the company's proposal so well he virtually knew it by heart. Finally Robert said, "A group decides which deals we do, Brian. I'll take this to the investment committee next Monday. If they like it, we'll do it. It's as simple as that, and you'll have an answer by 3 p.m. Monday. Good enough?"

Brian answered affirmatively. The men discussed Brian's tenure and success at Warren Taylor and Currant, and Robert seemed genuinely interested that Brian do well in his future endeavors. "However things turn out, I wish you good luck in the future, Brian," he said, standing and extending his hand over his desk. "You've done well for the firm and yourself during your time here, and I personally appreciate the contribution you've made."

Riding the elevator upstairs, Brian felt a sense of exhilaration. *This will work out,* he thought. *I'm going to be a partner at Bijan Rarities.*

# Chapter Thirteen

THE JUDEAN HILLS NEAR BETHLEHEM
LATE MARCH, 3 B.C

The next day, Benjamin finished writing his first-hand account of what the shepherds had seen. He carefully rolled the two parchments and tied them with a string. His father was gone all day. When he returned that evening, Benjamin asked what he should do with the parchments.

"I too have wondered that very thing," Joab told his son. "At first, I thought of asking the Sanhedrin where we should place this account for safekeeping. Then I decided against mentioning our adventure in the synagogue." He told Benjamin that in the past two days alone, some rumors had begun to arise, and people were murmuring that a band of shepherds had had an unusual experience. Nothing was tied to them yet, and he didn't intend to be the one who brought it up.

"I worry that they will take it out on you, my son," he said, as he tousled the boy's hair with his hand. If the priests think we are heretics, they will surely stop your education. It's best that we say nothing. And as far as the parchments go, I will think of a plan." Joab took the scroll into the other room with him.

Benjamin went to synagogue school the next day, and things

went exactly as they had every day before. He was practically bursting inside. When school was dismissed that afternoon and he was walking home with his friend Saul, he felt he could wait no longer. "Saul," he said, "can you keep a big secret?" His friend made an oath after Benjamin told him this was the biggest secret he had ever known.

The boys sat under a tree in the shade beside the dusty road that led to their homes. Saul lived about a half mile further down this road than Benjamin's family. His father was also a shepherd. Benjamin told him the entire story, omitting nothing. Saul sat in rapt astonishment.

When Benjamin finished, Saul asked if he could have been dreaming.

"I was there, doing all those things," Benjamin replied. "It was no dream!"

He told Saul that his father had cautioned against telling the priests, because they would probably think his family were heretics and blasphemers. Benjamin even thought they might put his father in jail if word got out. He again made Saul promise not to tell a single person, and Saul repeated his oath. The boys continued their journey home.

Saying their goodbyes, Benjamin turned into his yard. His mother greeted him with a smile and said, "Your father is feeding the animals behind the house. I think you and he are going on an adventure tomorrow!" Excited, Benjamin pressed his mother for more information. She told him Joab had come home after spending the day in the village, and announced that he was going to Qumran to talk to the Essenes about what to do with the scroll. "And he's taking you with him."

"And here he comes now," Rachel said as Joab turned the corner from the side of the house. He hugged Benjamin and said, "Did your mother tell you we are going on a mission tomorrow?"

*"Yes!"* replied Benjamin. "But what kind of *mission?"*

"Wait and see," Joab responded, smiling. "We'll have plenty of time to talk on the trip tomorrow, since we are traveling almost twenty miles, and I'll tell you everything. Now come with me. We have to finish preparing our donkeys for the trip, then pack our bedrolls. We may be sleeping under the stars tomorrow night in Qumran."

# Chapter Fourteen

Shortly after the sun rose, Joab and Benjamin put blankets on their donkeys and began their journey. Rachel had given them dates, flat bread and dried meat so they would not go hungry, and there were skins with water and wine. Not knowing what to expect when they arrived, they were prepared to eat and sleep alone, although Joab thought it was likely the Essenes would offer them food and lodging, however meager each of those might be.

Benjamin was excited. He had never ventured this far before, and he looked forward to making a trip of this magnitude, and being trusted by his father to join him in his visit to the Essenes.

As they trod the dusty road, Joab told Benjamin of his discussion with the priests yesterday at the synagogue. Careful not to mention the event the shepherds had witnessed the other night, he had inquired in general about the Essenes, who were known to be compilers of Biblical information. The priests with whom he spoke did not act surprised or inquisitive about the discussion. Joab had told them he was thinking of visiting the Sea of Arabah, and had heard of Qumran nearby, so wanted to know more about it.

The priests had told him that the Essenes were a strange lot, living in a dusty town in the Judean hills. It was a rather desolate place, the priests had said, and it was said that once the Essenes had inscribed Biblical writings on parchment, they secreted them in caves which dotted the landscape around their community, Qumran.

Benjamin had heard of this place only in tales. The stories said that a sect of odd but very well respected Jews, who called themselves Essenes, lived in isolation in this desolate village near the Sea of Arabah *(author's note: today it is called the Dead Sea)*. The group was known for its righteous behavior in a time of unrest and turmoil. In synagogue school Benjamin had been taught that the Essenes sought to keep Moses' laws from being corrupted by foreign influences. Judea was a mixture of ethnic groups today. Each of them brought different interpretations of the laws of Moses. The Essenes strived for purity in teaching, in acts and particularly in the written word, which in their opinion could not be allowed to be modified.

The Qumran sect of Essenes spent their days copying the Holy books onto scrolls, their particular goal being to ensure no man or popular religion of the day would or could usurp the very words of God as handed down to His prophet Moses. They accomplished this goal by copying ancient, crumbling texts onto modern parchment, sealing the finished works into earthen jars, and secreting them away in nearby caves. Someday, whether soon or hundreds of years into the future, men would gaze upon the scrolls of Qumran and know how the law was truly written, without man's intervention.

Joab told Benjamin that he had brought his parchment and hoped that the Essenes would add it to their trove of historical documents, to be kept and read by people of the future. "It is important, Benjamin, that the chronicle not be lost. You may be the only person who both saw it and wrote about it. It is our duty to preserve your words."

They stopped for lunch near a small lake. The donkeys drank the cool water while Joab and Benjamin sat on a blanket, shaded by a grove of trees. "Since that night," Joab said, "we haven't talked much about what we all saw. You have had time to think about it since then, and you have even written it on parchment. What thoughts do you have?"

Lying on his back in the shade, Benjamin thought for a moment, then told his father that the events of that night formed part of his dreams every single night thereafter. "Do you believe, father, that the baby was truly the Messiah we have been awaiting?"

Joab said, "Yes, son, I do. If it had been a man and woman claiming their son was the son of God, that would be one thing. But we were given a sign by angels, led to the place by a heavenly light, and we saw for ourselves the unearthly events that happened. Do you remember that figure in the back of the stable?"

Benjamin nodded and said, "That was another angel, father. He was the herald angel, telling us of the Messiah's arrival. He even told us to bow down and worship Him whom God has sent."

"I believe just as you do, son," Joab said. "And I am ashamed that I cannot spread the word to everyone I see. But I am afraid. Not for myself, but for you and your mother. The Sanhedrin are powerful men. The news you have written on your parchment would threaten their very existence. And they would strike out. I am certain of it. Your education would end. We would be persecuted, perhaps even having to leave our home and settle where we would not be known. For now, therefore, I think it is best that we keep in our hearts the things we have seen, and make sure your record of the events is maintained for generations to come."

They rose and made their way to Qumran, arriving in the early afternoon. Joab introduced themselves to a man who met them at the gate, and said he wanted to talk to the leader of their group. As they walked through a courtyard, Benjamin was struck by how dusty and brown everything was. It was as though nothing had any color. A thick layer of sand covered everything. Other men took their donkeys away to be fed and watered. Their meager packs were laid in a corner of the walled yard.

Their guide ushered them into a large room, where men sat on stools at high desks, copying documents onto parchment with large quills. Each desk was positioned in front of a window to afford maximum light to the scribes. At the end of a room sat a man dressed in a brown robe identical to the others. He stood as they approached him and said, "I am Onias, called 'the younger'", the man said. "It is my great fortune to oversee the important work of our brothers here."

Onias ushered them outside to the courtyard. They selected a cool place in the shade and a young man brought fruit to them. He also served steaming hot coffee to the men, and offered a fruit drink in a cup to Benjamin, who gratefully accepted it. Once they were settled, the Essene said, "I am pleased to welcome you here, and I am interested to know what brings you to our community."

# Chapter Fifteen

Joab explained to the man that his words might sound heretical, and he wished no ill will toward anyone. "I tell what I saw," he said, "and God's hand was everywhere that night. I can only believe He wanted the events of that night made known." Joab related the story. Several times Benjamin wanted to add a comment, but it would have been very improper for him to do so. Most Jews believed children's opinions were worth less than those of their elders. Benjamin was glad his mother and father always were interested in what he thought, and his father had spent a long time on the trip to Qumran listening to Benjamin relate his thoughts about that evening on the hill and at the Inn.

Joab's story took two hours. Onias sat quietly, having said nothing, moving only to gesture for more coffee and some sweet cakes. When Joab finished, the Essene looked at Benjamin and said, "You were with your father throughout this entire time, child. Is your account the same as his?"

The boy was pleased to have been asked. He nodded his head and asked, "Do you believe us?"

"Pardon the boy's impertinence," Joab said quickly.

Benjamin looked down, rebuked, but Onias replied, "He is worried, and rightly so. Both of you should be. If your story is true, you have seen events that will change the world forever."

He went on to explain that two things made him believe the fantastic story Joab had told. "First, I have already heard news that this event happened, and I hoped someone would bring a first-hand account. Many, many people saw some or all of what you experienced. Their stories are spreading throughout our lands, as eager men find themselves unable to contain the wonder of what they experienced."

"If I may ask, how would you have heard so quickly, here in this remote community?" Joab asked.

Onias laughed. "We are not as isolated as one might think. Members of our sect, and outsiders such as yourselves, visit Qumran daily. They bring us materials to translate or rewrite for posterity. Some stay with us while on a journey. Either way, we are always anxious to know the events happening outside our walls."

Benjamin spoke. "You said that two things made you believe our story. What is the second one?"

Onias looked at him with a warm smile. "My father was Onias the Righteous," he said. "He was the best man I ever knew. He earned his title because he was upstanding and fair in everything he did. This was unusual in a world of turmoil. He prayed constantly, and many things he prayed for came to pass. This enraged the Jewish leaders of the time and, when I was a young boy, he was stoned to death for making it rain by praying."

Onias' eyes misted as he spoke of his father. He said that Onias the Righteous had set a prediction onto a scroll seventy years before. "I located that scroll three days ago when I first heard of the events in Bethlehem with the child. I have read it many times since. The scroll is a prediction by my father, given to him in a dream. It speaks of a baby who will be born within a century, who will become the savior of mankind. It speaks of God's son coming as a child in a stable. It speaks of an earthly mother and a heavenly father. And it speaks of you."

"It . . . it speaks of *me*?" Benjamin said. "A scroll written seventy years ago speaks of me?"

"Not just you," laughed Onias. "The most exciting thing about your visit today was when you told me you were shepherds. The scroll of my father says that shepherds in the hills outside Bethlehem would be visited by messengers from God and would be shown where the newborn King lay."

No one spoke for several minutes. Joab dropped his head and began to pray. His eyes closed, he took his son's hand and held it tightly. Tears fell from Joab's eyes.

The moment passed. Joab asked the Essene what they should do.

"Why did you come here?" Onias responded.

"I was in hopes that you would believe us and would put our scroll with the ones you have hidden away for future generations to see and know."

"You were right to do this, Joab. I believe you saw and heard everything you have told me, and it was good to have your son commit the events to parchment. Your scroll deserves to be part of the historic records."

Night was falling quickly. "You must be very hungry," Onias told them. He took them to a room off the courtyard and asked one of the Essenes to bring their packs. "You may stay here tonight, and tomorrow we will place your scroll in hiding. But first, come. We must eat."

They walked into a large room where perhaps fifty men were eating. There were heaping plates of hot food on a long table and the men sat on benches on either side. "Sit here," Onias guided them. He moved to the head of the table. Joab and Benjamin were offered lamb and chicken, chickpeas, fava beans and many other vegetables, and flat brown bread. There was wine with which to wash everything down. Benjamin hadn't realized how hungry he was. The food tasted absolutely wonderful.

The men sitting around them asked where they were from, then inquired about the political climate in Bethlehem. Everyone knew of the census, of course. Even the Essenes were not exempt from making the journey to their birth cities, although none had yet gone. "We will wait until the last moment," one man said, laughing, "until perhaps the Romans will have decided there's some new way to kill us besides taxing us to death." Several others laughed.

The talk continued for nearly an hour. It was obvious to Joab and Benjamin that these men were glad to have word from the outside whenever possible, and it was a pleasant evening talking with them. No one questioned the reason for their visit to Qumran. Joab imagined that many visitors, like themselves, had secrets of one type or another to entrust to this sect of Holy scribes of priceless information.

At last the men began to disperse. Stars shone brightly overhead as Joab and Benjamin made their ways across the courtyard. Onias had left the dining hall at some point and was nowhere to be seen. The two travelers fell onto their cots, suddenly exhausted. They slept a dreamless sleep.

# Chapter Sixteen

A rooster's crowing was the first thing Benjamin heard as he woke. He sat up on his pallet, noticing that his father had already left the room. He could hear voices in the courtyard, and the sun's light was already well up. He went to a water bowl in the corner, splashed his face and donned his robe.

Joab and Onias the Younger were sitting in the courtyard near a small fire. They were drinking coffee. Joab waved to his son and Onias greeted Benjamin as he sat by his father. Onias told them that he had given their situation much thought during the night. Benjamin saw that Onias held the parchments on which he had written. Onias called to a man walking by and said something to him in a quiet voice. "We will prepare your scroll now," he said to the boy. "Come with me."

They entered the room where the scribes were working on transcriptions. The man to whom Onias had spoken had an earthen jar on a table in front of him, and he was carefully wiping it with a cloth to remove any dust. Onias handed Benjamin the scroll. "It would be my honor for you to place it in its resting place," he said.

Benjamin inserted the rolled-up parchments into the jar's

narrow neck. Then he reached into his pocket. "I would like to place something else in the jar," he said. From his pocket he took a small piece of parchment on which he had written a number of words, and a coin.

"So what do we have here?" Onias asked.

"This is the coin the Messiah child held in his hand," Benjamin replied. "I wrote a short description of it on this parchment. The coin belongs with the scroll."

"Indeed it does," Onias responded, smiling. "Some day this coin and this scroll will have an impact of unbelievable proportions. It will not be in my lifetime, or yours. Maybe not that of your grandchildren or great-grandchildren. But someday, what you have written will shake the world."

The man sealed the top of the jar with a plug of mud and smoothed it out with a small knife. Onias then took the jar and said, "Your donkeys are readied. Let us make a short journey to place your jar."

Benjamin was excited. He hadn't known this was going to happen. "It's your privilege, my boy," Joab said. "You may place the jar in its safe place."

For over an hour the trio rode their donkeys up into the hills which surrounded the community of Qumran. Onias led them to a rocky mesa, where he dismounted. "We must walk from here," he said, pointing to a narrow path which wound downhill from the place where they were. They had to be careful not to lose their footing; at last Onias stopped. He pointed to a clump of shrubs clinging to the side of the hill. Benjamin saw nothing until Onias moved the scrubby plants aside, to reveal the entrance to a cave.

"Ever since my father knew that the Messiah was coming, he kept this place prepared for the document that would reveal it to the world. He passed to me the responsibility of putting the scroll into this cave. And now, Benjamin, you must place the jar."

The boy crawled into the tight space. He felt very cramped. He could not stand. At the back of the room he saw a small entrance into an anteroom of the cave. He crawled through, and saw an indentation in the back wall, with two stones lying on the floor of the cave in the sand. He carefully placed the jar in the area at the rear of the second room. His small hands trembled as he sat the jar on the ledge. He noticed that the two stones almost perfectly covered the hiding place. Obviously, long ago, someone truly had prepared this place for this very day.

His task complete, Benjamin backed out of the cave. Emerging from the coolness back into the harsh sunlight, Onias said, "Let us pray." They held hands, praying that God would bless the depositing of this jar, and thanking God for the baby He had sent. "May this scroll remain safe until *it is time* . . . time for the world to see it," the Essene closed. Then they returned to Qumran.

# Chapter Seventeen

DALLAS

The next few days moved slowly for Brian Sadler. Although he had to wait until Monday afternoon for the investment committee's decision on Bijan's proposed public offering, he wasted no time working on the details of his personal investment in the gallery. He prepared a memorandum outlining his proposed deal with Darius Nazir – 40% of Bijan Rarities Limited for $1.5 million and a guarantee that $4 million would be raised in a public offering no later than 90 days from the date of signing. He called Nicole Farber. Reaching her assistant, Ryan, he left a message that he needed to speak with her.

It was nearly six p.m. when his cell phone rang and he saw Carter and Wells' name on the display. "Nicole," he answered.

"Mr. Sadler, it's Ryan Coleman," was the reply. "Ms. Farber apologizes that she can't return your call today and asked that you email whatever you need, and she'll get back with you when she can."

Brian asked if she was in the office.

Ryan hesitated a moment, then said, "Do you need her email address or do you have it?" Obviously she wasn't talking to him at this point. He responded and ended the call.

He emailed the memorandum to Nicole, asking if she would prepare a Letter of Intent to send to Nazir. He wasn't sure, given her specialty, if she would do something like this. He hoped if not, that she would shuffle the project off to someone else in the firm. Having not received a bill for more money, he figured he had funds left from his initial payment and decided it was worth a try.

On Friday Nicole called him at work. "Glad to see you're planning a move to make an honest living," she quipped.

"How are you?" Brian asked.

"Not bad, but busy. But back to business. I've put together your Letter of Intent and I'll email it in a few minutes. Your proposal sounds exciting. Is W&T going to do an offering for Bijan?"

He told her about his discussion with Robert Overton and that he was waiting for an answer. "Want to meet for a drink tonight after work?"

"I'm working late tonight," she replied. Fueling his hopes slightly, she said, "But I would like to see you again sometime. Bye." She hung up.

# Chapter Eighteen

On Monday Brian had trouble concentrating as he awaited word from the investment committee meeting. He wasn't worried. He knew from experience that the Bijan deal had merit, and was something that another firm would take even if W&T didn't. But he had a nagging thought that his involvement with the FBI might come back to haunt him, even though he had done nothing to hurt W&T.

At 4 p.m. the phone rang at his desk. Robert Overton told him that the committee had approved his deal and work would begin the next day on preparing for a public offering. Overton congratulated Brian and again thanked him for a good run at W&T.

Brian left the office. In his car, he called Darius Nazir on his cell phone. He told him the letter of intent would be emailed tonight, and W&T would be preparing agreements to represent the company as its investment banker in an upcoming public offering. Nothing was set in stone. All investment banks had out-clauses that would allow them to exit a deal at any time, for any reason, or for no reason whatsoever. However, when this stage was reached, a deal was all but done, save any major catastrophe no one had considered.

Darius was thrilled, and told Brian the background check was finished and everything was ready to proceed from his side. He told Brian how much he looked forward to working with him and promised to read the letter of intent, sign and return it immediately. "When will you join the gallery?" he said.

"I should stay here for at least a few weeks," Brian responded. "I can keep things moving forward better if I'm still at W&T than if I'm an outsider."

They set a timetable to have a contract in place for Brian's $1.5 million investment by the end of the week, and to have his funds wired to Bijan in 30 days or less.

# Chapter Nineteen

Brian was not concerned about the Bijan public offering not happening, except for one thing which was out of everyone's control. If the stock market took a major tumble between now and the offering day, W&T had the option to pull the plug on the offering. And they would. If investors were in a panic mode, people who had agreed to buy Bijan stock would back out, and W&T would be left having to spend millions of its own money to pay Bijan the offering proceeds. There was nothing anyone could do about that possibility, so Brian, the optimist, refused to consider it as a possibility.

And in fact the market, fueled by continuing success in the oil and energy sectors, steadily rose over the weeks before Bijan's offering date, which had tentatively been set by the firm for mid-May. Meanwhile, their contract finished and signed, Brian prepared to buy his shares of Bijan.

He converted almost all his investments into cash, used a line of credit he had established at Chase to finish things up, and wired $1.5 million to Bijan Rarities' bank account in New York. He and Darius spoke daily. Nazir was working feverishly to finish the auction of the sarcophagus, which was set for the next weekend. He was leaving for Egypt in a few days, and asked Brian to join him there. It was tough for Brian to turn down such an offer, but he knew his time was better spent keeping the offering on track. Every day at the office meant dozens of questions to answer, drafts of documents to read and forward on to Darius, and all the small things that were part of the process.

"Come to New York, then," Darius offered. "As an owner of Bijan, and its new acquisitions man, you should be here to represent the gallery." "Acquisitions man?" Brian responded. Darius explained that he had given much thought to the roles each of them should play and, if Brian was agreeable, Darius wanted to slow down his constant travel schedule and spend more time in the gallery. Darius would run the store and oversee all auctions, while Brian handled the financial side and traveled the globe chasing leads, bringing home the antiquities which would fuel sales at Bijan.

Brian thought it sounded great, and promised to try to come to New York for the simulcast of the Discovery Channel broadcast a week from Friday. The auction was set for 1 p.m. New York time, which was nine in the evening in the Valley of the Kings.

# Chapter Twenty

Brian was in touch daily with Sam Lowe, the New York attorney representing him on the Bijan offering. They had finalized the offering document and sent it to the Dallas lawyers hired by W&T. Everything was moving along. W&T was negotiating with Brian at this point over stock options. They wanted options, which gave them the right to buy Bijan stock at a fixed price for a period of time. If the stock went up during that period, W&T would make a bunch of extra money. Usually deals that W&T thought might be tough to sell commanded a lot of options, which acted as an incentive for the investment bank, and a way to make money even if things didn't go exactly as planned.

Brian argued with his colleagues at W&T, who were putting together the finishing touches, that Bijan was a jewel, a company any broker would be proud to take public, and one that didn't need options tied to it. W&T resisted. Time was on their side, because Brian wanted the offering finished and done with sooner rather than later, so he could get on with the new aspects of his life. He agreed to a reduced number and the deal moved ahead.

"I'll join you for a drink at 7 p.m.," Nicole told him. They agreed on Steel, one of Dallas' hip new establishments, and the call ended. Brian had called her, ostensibly to advise that the letter of intent and contract she had prepared were now signed and finished. His ulterior motive was to have dinner with her. She had declined the dinner offer, saying she had a big case the next morning and had to be fresh. But at least she had agreed to drinks.

Most of the guys in the bar noticed Nicole as she walked in. She was dressed in a red suit. With her blond hair it was impossible not to see her. He stood as she approached the bar. She took his hand, squeezed it and said, "Hi, Brian Sadler, who is NOT a criminal."

"Get over that," he laughed.

An hour later, they had caught up. From news reports, Brian knew that Nicole was defending the Chief Operating Officer of a pharmaceutical company in Fort Worth who, among others, was the subject of an investigation by the Securities and Exchange Commission. The SEC claimed her client had masterminded a plot to hide poor earnings. There was basis to their claim.

They talked about how, like Brian's situation, Nicole had to prove her client wasn't part of the problem. In this case, he had instead tried to formulate a solution. Finally she said she had told as much as she could without violating attorney-client privilege, and ordered another drink as the subject changed to Brian's work.

"I got the invitation to Bijan's simulcast of the auction," she said. "Thanks for inviting me." Brian had put her name on the invitation list after Darius asked him to submit names of people he wanted to invite. He only offered a couple.

Brian told her about his trip to New York, the visit to Bijan and his immediate infatuation with the business and its prospects.

"It sounds like love at first sight," Nicole commented. He looked into her eyes and responded,

"Love at first sight. That pretty well sums it up." There was a long pause as neither of them looked away.

"Ahem," Brian cleared his throat. "Well, I am now the acquisitions officer and minority shareholder of Bijan, and W&T is going to bring the company to the public market in a couple of months." He asked if she had heard much about the auction of the sarcophagus of Inkharaton.

She said she had first learned of it from the memorandum Brian had sent her, which allowed her to create the letter of intent he signed with Darius Nazir. She recently saw advertisements in the Wall Street Journal and the New York Times, and said that the sale seemed to have generated a lot of interest in ancient things and Egypt in particular.

He mentioned the Discovery Channel broadcast and said he was going to New York to be at the gallery when the simulcast happened. "Why don't you come with me?" he asked her.

She laughed. "My goodness, sir," she deadpanned in a Scarlett O'Hara voice, "I feel I hardly know you!"

They both laughed and he said, "Really. I'm serious. That invitation is your pass to an incredible event. It's strictly by invitation only, and there are people who would pay a lot of money for that pass. And, to be honest, I'd love to have you come to New York and see the gallery."

"Brian," she said, "there was a time in our professional relationship when I'd have bet money we could really click together, personally. I have to tell you something. What you did that morning in your deposition felt like a slap in the face to me. I was blindsided. I was your counsel, and I looked like a fool. I've tried to let it go, but what it said to me was, 'Brian Sadler's not at all what you think he is. There's a side to him that may show itself at any time, and you have no idea what it'll do to you.'"

He tried to apologize for not telling her in advance what his plans were. "My entire decision on this was because of what Carl Cybola did," he said. "I knew you wouldn't walk in that room and represent me if you knew what I was going to do, and I needed your help."

"Really?" she responded sarcastically. "Which parts of 'I don't recall' did you need help with?"

"You've got to understand that I did what I thought I had to do to survive. I had no intention of pissing you off, or causing you any grief at all. It was a matter of living to fight another day. And apparently it worked."

She conceded that his strategy had, in fact, worked that time, but he should consider himself forever on the FBI's radar screen. "One step in the wrong direction," she said, "and they'll be all over you. Don't ever forget it. The Feds have long memories, and you're indelibly etched in their bureaucratic minds."

She told him she had to go. "Please consider coming to New York," he said.

"I don't know where this is all going," she replied. "I don't know if there'll be anything between you and me. I do know there's a lot of work to do before I'll feel I know you well enough to spend much time with you." She stood, leaned over and kissed his cheek, turned and said, "But that doesn't mean I don't think you're a sexy guy." She walked out of the bar.

# Chapter Twenty One

Brian talked to Darius four or five times a day as the week of the auction arrived. He made reservations for an arrival on Thursday around noon. Darius would already be in Egypt getting final preparations made for the sale on Friday night. "Collette will handle everything you need," Darius told Brian. "She's extremely bright and very capable. I know you're new to all this, but with her help you'll be fine."

Brian could hardly contain his excitement as he walked off the plane at LaGuardia Airport. This was truly the beginning of a new life – a chapter closing and a new one opening in the book that was Brian Sadler. As he walked to the baggage claim area, he saw a man holding a sign that said "Sadler." He stopped and the man said, "Brian Sadler?"

He acknowledged and learned that Darius had sent a car and driver to pick him up.

"I took Mr. Nazir to Kennedy Airport earlier this week for his trip to Cairo," the driver said to Brian as they waited for luggage. "He told me you're his new partner. I'm pleased to be assisting you, Mr. Sadler."

*Truly a new chapter in my life,* Brian thought. *A driver picking up Brian Sadler, the new partner in Bijan Rarities.*

The driver dropped Brian at the Inter-Continental, where he checked in and stowed his luggage in his room. He walked up to Fifth Avenue. It was a gorgeous spring day – the time of year when one day might be cold and dreary, and the next sunny and warm. This was one of the latter, and Brian found himself gazing upward at the skyscrapers like a tourist as he walked along 48th Street.

Arriving at the gallery, he saw a large sign in the window announcing Discovery Channel's broadcast tomorrow afternoon. There were over twenty people in the gallery, looking not only at the sarcophagus, but also at the other items Darius had selected for display. Collette smiled when she saw him, broke away from a customer and walked to him. "Just in time," she said. "Things have been crazy all week. Mr. Nazir prepared this for you." She handed Brian a series of printed sheets. At the top of each was a picture of one of the antiquities on display. Below it was a lengthy description, and at the bottom a set of numbers and a price.

"Those numbers shown above the price," Collette explained, "are our cost code." She taught him quickly how to interpret it. Although I'm sure the rules don't apply to you, Jason and I are not allowed to sell anything for less than a fifty percent markup over cost. We get a 10% bonus if we sell anything at 90% of its listed price on the sheet or more."

Brian thanked Collette, waved to Jason across the room, and went to the office. In the middle of Darius Nazir's desk was a brown envelope with Brian's name on it. Inside was a note from Darius telling Brian to make himself at home, use the office as his, and to get ready for an interesting auction. Other papers in the packet gave detailed information about the auction, including a timetable of events in Egyptian and New York time. There was also a corporate credit card with his name on it. Attached was a note from Darius asking Brian, as his first official use of his new card, to take any of the gallery's invited guests to dinner after the simulcast, if it worked out.

The phone on the desk buzzed quietly and Collette's voice came over the intercom. "Mr. Sadler," she said. "Mr. Nazir is on line six for you. Just press the blinking light."

Brian did so, and Darius welcomed him to New York. He expressed his appreciation to Brian for coming, and his assurance that Brian would do fine, even though he was receiving a trial by fire, since the auction was his first official duty as a shareholder in the gallery.

"As you know," Darius said, "bidders had to be pre-qualified. There are only six bidders; they are listed on a sheet in the packet I left for you. Have you seen it?"

Brian acknowledged and turned to that sheet. Darius said that two of the bidders, whose names were highlighted in yellow, would be at the New York gallery. The others would be in Egypt with him.

Brian looked at the names. One was a representative of the National Museum of Canada; the other represented Marilyn Lukonen, a New Yorker who was one of the wealthiest people in America. Lukonen had founded the wildly successful magazine "In Touch," and now hosted her own television show. Products bearing the "Marilyn" logo were in upscale boutiques across North America.

Darius explained that Lukonen was a collector of Egyptian art. She had expressed an interest in the sarcophagus as soon as Bijan got the rights to sell it. "She's a really reasonable person," he told Brian, "and not one of these people who wants to accumulate everything just because she's wealthy. Her stated goal is to provide this piece for the world to see, in its original tomb, for generations to come."

# Chapter Twenty Two

They finished the call after Darius explained a number of other things to Brian about how things would go. "I want to let you know that there will likely be several reporters at the gallery. I sent invitations to both the newspapers and the trade press. But have no worries. Collette and Jason are fully prepared to handle everything," he said. "I'm just glad you're there representing Bijan."

Brian made a quick call to Karr and Dandridge, the law firm handling the offering on his side, and arranged to meet Sam Lowe for a drink at 7. Sam's office was in midtown as was Bijan's gallery, so they chose the Oak Bar at the Plaza.

The rest of the afternoon went quickly. Brian stayed on the floor as much as possible. Occasionally Collette or Jason would ask him to meet one of the firm's clients who had come into the store. "This is Brian Sadler, Mr. Nazir's new partner in the gallery," they said to each client. Brian was proud to be representing Bijan and was thoroughly enjoying his first day at his new profession.

That evening, he and Sam caught up on the progress of Bijan's public offering. From the lawyer's standpoint, everything was ready to go. They chatted a few more minutes, finished their drinks and Brian paid the check. "Sorry to cut it short," he told his attorney, "but I have to be at the gallery tomorrow at 5 a.m. and I better get some sleep first!"

# Chapter Twenty Three

Around midnight, a tractor pulling a semi-trailer parked just off Fifth Avenue on 53rd Street, the closest intersection to Bijan Rarities. Emblazoned on the sides of the trailer were the name and logo of the Discovery Channel. Two men exited the cab, opened the trailer and began to raise a satellite dish which extended from panels which were in the top of the trailer. Once they had the dish raised about twenty feet, one of the men sat at a console in the trailer. His job was to test the satellite reception in the concrete canyons of Manhattan. If a satisfactory link to Discovery Channel's satellite couldn't be achieved, the truck would have to be moved.

The other man began to snake thick cables along the curb from the truck to just in front of Bijan's front door. He then pulled the cables across the sidewalk and covered them with a metal arch that would allow pedestrians to cross over the cables without tripping on them. He also set out four large yellow signs which cautioned walkers to watch their steps.

The man in the truck yelled a confirmation that he had a good signal, which meant the truck was now in place for the broadcast. For the rest of the night, the two men sat inside the trailer, communicating with their counterparts in the Valley of the Kings near Luxor, Egypt, making sure that the simulcast scheduled for 1 p.m. New York time would come off without a hitch.

# Chapter Twenty Four

Brian's 4:15 a.m. wakeup call jolted him from a deep sleep. He sat straight up in bed and forced himself to immediately get up, avoiding any chance of falling back to sleep. He dressed in slacks and a sweater, taking a complete change of clothes for later in the day, before the gallery would open for the invited guests and bidders.

There were only a few people on the streets at this time of morning. Brian quickly walked to the gallery. Collette had made a sign the evening before, which was posted on Bijan's front window, saying that the gallery was closed for the morning and would open for invited guests only at 12 noon.

Lights were on in the gallery showroom. Brian knocked on the door and Collette waved to him from the back, running to unlock the front door for him. As she did, two uniformed police officers also arrived. Collette welcomed them, telling Brian these were off-duty policemen hired to guard the front door until noon. The door would have to be open a good deal of the time while the TV people prepared everything, and Nazir had wanted to ensure the public didn't wander in when no one was paying attention.

The morning was busy. While Collette, Jason and Brian cleared the center of the showroom and set up over a hundred folding chairs, the Discovery Channel men installed a huge screen in the back of the store, facing the front windows. They brought in projection equipment, which they connected to the cables which now ran through the front door. Then they hooked everything up and tested the video and audio feeds from Egypt.

A split screen was set up. The bulk of the screen showed the television feed which was the live Discovery Channel broadcast. A smaller screen on the lower right showed the feed from a camera aimed at the podium in the tent where the auction was happening. Similarly, the tent in Egypt had a small television monitor which showed a view of the dais which had been erected at the New York store.

At ten the caterers arrived, bringing in canapés and other refreshments, and setting up a champagne bar. Just before noon, they unloaded and set up a beautiful ice sculpture in the likeness of the pharaoh Inkharaton, as depicted on his sarcophagus. Brian thought it was incredibly beautiful and a great addition to the celebration about to commence.

Brian was moving about in the showroom, doing last minute adjustments on chair rows, when he heard, "Good morning, Brian," through speakers set up by the electronics men. He looked up and saw Darius on the small screen, standing in front of the podium in Egypt. One of the workmen told Brian to walk to the dais in the back of the showroom. When he did, the television camera in New York picked up his image and he sent his greetings to Darius, who then could see him on the Egyptian monitor.

Darius said, "It's good to see you, Brian. We're just making last minute preparations here. I think things are all ready to go. As you know, we begin with a tour of the tomb at 1 p.m. your time, then precisely at 1:30 we'll emerge to conduct the auction. It'll be the last thirty minutes of the hour Discovery has allotted for the broadcast." They chatted briefly and Darius signed off.

Brian checked his watch. It was less than half an hour until the public would be allowed to enter. Collette and Jason had set up a table at the front of the store to check invitations and register guests, including the two bidders they were expecting. Brian went to the office to change into his suit and tie, emerging a few minutes later.

A number of people had formed a line outside the gallery, awaiting the noon opening. Precisely at twelve, the door was unlocked. As they were checked in, Collette invited the attendees to have a glass of champagne and hors d'oeuvres. Within twenty minutes the gallery was full of people. Brian had asked Jason to make sure he knew who the two bidders were. By twelve thirty they had not yet been introduced to him, so he knew they were not yet on site. The room was filling with well-known faces, however. Several titans of business had dropped by to see the auction, as well as a few actors who had flown in from California to attend this monumental event. Bijan had hired some plainclothes security guards, and a couple of people arrived with bodyguards of their own.

He stood on the dais checking the microphone while the sound man worked at a monitor. A man who appeared to be in his mid-sixties, a head full of wavy gray hair, had completed the check-in process. Brian saw Collette point in his direction, and the man strode through the gallery toward him, confidence in every step. His suit was impeccable and Brian noted that he wore an Hermes tie, Gucci shoes and a Rolex watch which peeked out from under his highly starched French cuff white shirt.

Brian had already decided this must be the bidder from Canada. He stepped down from the podium, extending his hand, and said, "Welcome. I'm Brian Sadler."

"Good day, Mr. Sadler," the man replied. "It's very nice to meet you. I'm John Spedino."

# Chapter Twenty Five

The look on Brian's face must have betrayed his astonishment. He was at a loss for words. Spedino smiled and said, "I'm looking forward to seeing the auction. I'm a great fan of ancient art and relics, and this is shaping up to be the sale of the year."

Gathering his thoughts, Brian responded, "I . . . I suppose I should thank you."

"For what?" Spedino said. "Have we met?"

Stumbling a bit, Brian said, "I have a feeling you're behind my move to Bijan."

John Spedino looked at him quizzically. "I have no idea what you're talking about, Mr. Sadler. Although I have been a customer of Bijan in the past, it's only been through an agent, so your firm has no record of me as a purchaser in my own name. Perhaps you are thinking of someone else." He smiled at Brian, excused himself and moved to the champagne bar.

Brian stood, trying to put together all the disjointed thoughts which ran through his head. His confusion was interrupted when the production man said, "Twenty minutes to air time, Mr. Sadler."

Within the next ten minutes both his bidders arrived. Paul

Lecroix, the representative from the National Museum of Canada, was brought to him by Collette, who introduced them. Brian thanked Lecroix for attending and received assurances that he would let Brian know if he needed anything.

The second bidder arrived soon after the first. Collette caught Brian's eye from the front of the room and gave a slight nod in the direction of a man picking up his credentials from the table. Brian came forward and was introduced to an attorney from one of New York's leading firms, who was the bidder for Marilyn Lukonen. Collette had checked the power of attorney which would allow him to bid. The dollar amount which was his top bid authorization was covered by a small piece of paper, and would be uncovered only when the final bids were in.

The Discovery Channel production man held ten fingers in the air. Brian went to the podium and spoke into the microphone. "Please take your seats. The tour of the tomb of Inkharaton will begin momentarily." Reading from a card given him by the TV crewman, he told the seated crowd that the tour and auction were being broadcast live to a worldwide audience on the Discovery Channel. He asked all attendees to please remain in their seats except during four commercial breaks which would be signaled by the TV crew. As he finished reading, he looked up and saw one late attendee signing in at the desk. As she turned to find a chair, she caught Brian's eye, smiled and waved at him. Nicole had come after all.

# Chapter Twenty Six

A couple of minutes before 1 p.m. the Discovery Channel's broadcast was displayed on the huge screen as the gallery lights were dimmed. They went to commercial break, then returned. There was a slight murmur of voices in the gallery as a shot of the tomb in Egypt was shown. A deep commanding voice read the words displayed on the screen – "Inkharaton: The Forgotten Pharoah."

An announcer welcomed viewers to the first live broadcast of a new tomb in the Valley of the Kings, to be followed by the auction of the pharoah's unique second casket. Introductions were made and the program was handed over to the Director of Antiquities, whose role it was to be the master of ceremonies for the tour. While the broadcast unfolded, Brian stepped off the dais and went to the back of the room. Nicole was seated on the end of the last row. He bent to speak to her. She looked at him, put her finger to her lips and whispered, "Shh! I want to watch this!"

The tour completed, Discovery took a commercial break. As they had discussed, the producer gave Brian a finger in the air at around 1:30 p.m., indicating one minute until the auction would begin. Both bidders had been given paddles and instructed to make their bids when and if they wished. Brian would announce the bid vocally on his end, and Darius would call out bids on the Egypt side.

# Chapter Twenty Seven

At 3:30 p.m. Brian took a breather and looked back on the hectic afternoon. During a wrap-up phone call, Darius confirmed that the auction had been a huge success. After opening the bidding at $10 million, things had quickly progressed. At the final hammer of the gavel, only four of the six potential bidders actually had joined the auction, and the golden sarcophagus of Inkharaton sold to the British Museum for $19.5 million. The Museum's Director of Egyptian Art, who had been the bidder, was briefly interviewed at the end of the Discovery Channel program.

The sale gave Bijan Rarities a commission of slightly under a million dollars. Darius told Brian he estimated the gallery's total expenses at about three hundred thousand, which netted the gallery a lot of money and publicity that was impossible to value. Already in the past month calls had come from places around the globe, offering rarities to Bijan for outright purchase or auction, that the gallery might not have seen before. The Inkharaton sale put Bijan on the map as one of the major galleries in this field.

Brian invited the Canadian bidder to dinner, but he declined, saying he was catching an earlier flight back to Montreal. The other bidder, the attorney for Marilyn Lukonen, had bid himself, then left immediately following the closing bid. When Brian had looked around the room, John Spedino also appeared to have left, and he saw Nicole at the front of the gallery talking to Collette.

Many of Bijan's most important clients had attended this prestigious auction, and reporters on the sidewalk snapped photos as they left. Several were household names in the finance and entertainment world. Donald Trump and Jack Nicholson were talking as they left, and were captured in a photograph which made page one of the New York Post the next morning.

Several clients made their ways to the dais and spoke briefly to Brian. Many of them knew about his imminent arrival with the firm, having spoken to Darius. Each expressed how pleased Nazir seemed to be that he would have a partner for the first time. Brian received hearty congratulations and promises of lunch and drinks down the road.

Jason caught his eye, motioned him to the side and said, "Mr. Nazir is standing by his cell phone in Egypt. He'd like you to give him a ring as soon as you can, please." Brian looked again at Nicole, who was still across the gallery from him, and unsuccessfully tried to get her attention. He went to the office and called Darius for their wrapup meeting. He knew Nazir would be exhausted, and by the time he got back to his hotel in Luxor it would be long after midnight.

After a short review of how everything went, Darius again told Brian how pleased he was that they had partnered together. At the end of the conversation, he said, "I'm staying an extra day in Cairo before I head home, Brian. There's a rumor that something's been found that's the biggest rarity to hit the market in years. I have no idea what it is. Everything's pretty hush-hush right now, but I want to look further into it. More news as I get it."

Brian raced back into the gallery, anxious to find Nicole. There were only a few people left, talking in small groups. She was not on the floor. Collette told him she'd been asked to pass along a message that Nicole would catch up with him later. He thought he'd try her cell phone, then remembered that although she knew his number, he didn't know hers, nor had she ever called him from her phone, so he didn't have her number stored. How, he wondered, did she intend to catch up with him?

# Chapter Twenty Eight

Thinking maybe she intended to stop back by the gallery, Brian stayed, spending over an hour writing a summary memorandum for Darius, which were Brian's observations on the auction from the New York side. At six p.m., Collette and Jason stuck their heads in the door, asking if he was ready to close for the night. There were no customers left. Since Brian had neither key nor code to the gallery's sophisticated burglar alarm system, he was forced to leave when they did.

He stood on the sidewalk for a couple of minutes, thinking Nicole might stop by. Then he placed a call to Carter and Wells, reaching Ryan Coleman. He asked for Nicole's cell number and Ryan replied that his instructions were, if you don't already have it, I'm not allowed to give it to you. He thought about asking Ryan to call her himself, and pass along a message, but Brian decided if she had left without knowing how to find him, he wasn't going to appear to be chasing after her.

Walking through the Inter-Continental's lobby to the elevator banks in the back, he caught himself glancing right and left, seeing if perhaps she was waiting for him there. The bar was completely open to the lobby, so he would have easily noticed her blond hair if she'd been there. He went into his room, setting down his briefcase in the hallway. He heard, "Well, it's about time you got here." He looked at the bed. Nicole was lying on it, wearing nothing but a pair of tiny pink panties.

# PART THREE

## Chapter One

THE HILLS NEAR QUMRAN
JANUARY 2004

Two teenage boys hiked in the midday sun. Sons of shepherds, they were no strangers to the hills around the ancient ruins of Qumran. They lived at the edge of the Dead Sea, only a few miles from where they stood today, and had spent their lives roaming the hills and valleys nearby.

Since 1947, when the first scrolls were found, the residents of this area had become de facto treasure hunters. Not many days went by without at least a few people combing the hills near Qumran, hoping to uncover the next cache of earthenware and parchment. These boys were no different. They had packed lunches and planned to spend the day enjoying the outdoors and searching for caves. Everyone in the area laughed about it, but secretly many of them believed there had to be more hiding places than the ones found so far.

After hours of roaming, they stood on a hilltop overlooking the Dead Sea in the distance. "It looks as if there is an old trail below us, maybe," one said to the other. They worked to find handholds as they inched down the rocky hillside. Finally they landed on an area about fifteen feet below the mesa on which they had stood.

"Doesn't look much like a trail to me," the other boy said. They looked around, walking twenty feet to the east until they came to a small hole at the side of the makeshift trail. One of the boys found a stick, knelt and began to dig out the hole, careful lest a snake emerge. With very little effort, the boys dislodged rocks to make the hole bigger. Instead of digging them out, they were heartened that the rocks fell down inside the hole, indicating there could be a cave beneath.

Once they had removed sufficient rubble, they could see that a cave went down, then straightened out. They could see an opening in the rear of the cave indicating a second room behind it.

They quickly saw that the room wasn't big enough for both of them. Renewing their pact that whatever one found belonged to both of them, they drew straws and one was soon sliding down into the hole they had made. He was able to crawl on all fours when he hit the floor, and moved the few feet to the second space. "It looks like just an empty room," he called back to his friend on the outside. He pulled a small flashlight from his pocket and shone it through the hole in front of him. He didn't want to stuff himself through the small opening only to come face to face with some desert creature.

Determining the room was empty, he squeezed through the doorway dividing the two areas of the cave. It was claustrophobic. The walls were within a foot on each side, and the ceiling was not far above his bent back. "I don't see anything," he said, turning slightly so his friend could hear.

"Look around closely," came the reply.

The boy raised up off his hands, holding the light in one while he ran the other along the back wall.

The wall felt smooth as his hand moved along the sandstone. He came to a ridge almost in the middle of the wall, stopped and dug his finger into the indentation. It ran up and down, almost eighteen inches. Along the top, the ridge continued left and right. These are rocks, not the wall, he thought excitedly. He took a Swiss Army knife from his pocket and inserted it into the ridge. The knife went in easily, all the way to the hilt. His adrenalin began to pump as he feverishly used his knife as a lever to see if he could move the rocks.

"What's going on?" his friend yelled into the cave.

"I . . . I've found something," the boy replied. "I'm trying to dislodge a rock. Give me a minute."

As he pried with his knife, one of the rocks suddenly began to move without warning, popping out toward him. It wasn't particularly large, but in the tight space it startled him as it began to fall, and he let out a yell.

"Are you OK?" his friend asked, concerned.

"Hang on!" The boy's voice resounded with excitement. He could see the corner of an earthen jar protruding into the space where the rock had been. It was sitting on a ledge, and had been hidden by two rocks carefully placed side by side and smoothed over.

At this point he had no trouble moving the other rock out of the way. The earthen jar now stood in front of him. He was transfixed as he stared at it.

"What's going on in there!" his friend yelled.

"I've found a scroll jar, I think," the boy yelled back. "I'm going to try to get it out without breaking it!"

Raising up to the maximum height, his back against the low ceiling, he reached forward with both hands, bringing the jar down to the floor. He thought he had sufficient room to turn around, and he tried to do so. It didn't work. Instead, he decided to back out just like he had come in. So he moved slowly backwards, feet first, crawling along and pulling the jar with him as he moved.

Once into the larger front room of the cave, he turned and for the first time, his companion got a glimpse of the jar, sealed tightly with an earthen plug. The boy outside took the jar from his friend, who scampered out quickly.

"Let's look inside," one boy said, his voice quivering with excitement.

"No!" the other one replied. "We have to make sure we are believed when we show this to someone who might buy it. Let's take it to the market and let someone there open it!"

That plan in place, the boys walked to their homes, carefully carrying the jar between them.

# Chapter Two

One day less than a week later, the boys and their fathers had driven to the marketplace in Jericho. Although the town was small, many tourists came through on their way from Jerusalem to the resorts of the Dead Sea. Consequently, there was a thriving market, run mostly by Arabs who sold bananas and citrus fruits, spices and rugs, along with a hodgepodge of miscellanea as would be found in any large bazaar in the Middle East. People sat in garden restaurants which lined the town's main street. No one gave a second glance to the four, one of whom was carrying a large earthen jug.

The fathers had agreed that the jar should remain sealed. Although they still did not know what was in it, they could hear a muffled sound inside when they moved the jar. There was a rock or something else solid inside. That was disheartening, because to their knowledge, no other authentic scroll jar had contained anything but the Biblical scrolls of the Essenes. Regardless, someone had gone to a great deal of trouble to hide the earthenware pot, so they had high hopes that something good would emerge.

The fathers and sons had decided not to tell anyone specifics about where the jar had been found. They would refer generally to the Qumran hills, but that was it. The first dealer to whom they had gone told them they stood to gain far more by opening the seal than by selling it as it was now. "No one knows its true value," he said. He offered to open it, but they declined.

They got much the same response from another man, and at the third, while they sipped coffee and talked generally of where the boys found the jar, they agreed to allow the man to carefully remove the plug that sealed the top of the vessel.

The dealer, a very fat man with a scraggly black beard, took a sharp knife and began to dig carefully at the seal, careful not to damage the pot itself. It took nearly twenty minutes before he had dug out the chunks, doing his best to keep debris from falling inside and possibly damaging whatever was in the jar. Once open, the boy who had found the jug was given the honor of using his flashlight to look inside. He did so. "There's a scroll in here!" he said.

No one could see what had been making the muffled noise as the jar was moved. With great care the dealer tipped the jar on its side, sliding the scroll out onto a table. Shivers of anticipation went down his back as he thought of what he might have in front of him. I must be calm, he told himself. *If today it is my destiny to become wealthy, I must be able to bargain well with these simple people.*

The scroll was rolled, but not tightly. They tipped the jar and out poured a round black object that resembled charcoal, and a much smaller piece of parchment. The dealer looked at the object. *This is a coin.*

"What is that?" one of the fathers asked. "I don't know," the dealer replied casually. "It looks like a small piece of coal." He handed it to one of the boys and the visitors passed it among themselves.

While they looked at it, the dealer held the small scrap of parchment in his fat fingers, closely examining the writing on it. It was obviously very, very old, and was not a language he immediately recognized. *It looks a bit like Hebrew,* the Arab thought, *but somehow different.* He had an idea what language it was, but without a translation, there could be no real estimation of the value of the items before him. It was now his job to part these strangers from their find for as little money as possible.

"What do you want for these scraps of paper and this chunk of coal?" the fat dealer said offhandedly. "I have no use for any of them, but perhaps I could find some tourist on which to pawn off the jar. It's obviously very old."

One of the fathers responded first. "We want to know if these are more of the Dead Sea Scrolls," he told the dealer. "And this round black thing . . . I think that might be a coin, although I didn't hear of coins being found in any of the other scroll jars."

The dealer tried to appear disinterested. He said, "To save you the time and trouble of finding people to interpret the writing, I will offer you five hundred shekels for all of this. I hope I can recoup my money, and at least the items might be interesting to some collector of old things."

Five hundred shekels, around a hundred U.S. dollars, was a good deal of money to the men. But they were shrewd, like the dealer. And nothing was finished until the negotiating was done.

"Thank you for your time," one said. "But we will take the items to the university in Jerusalem and see if someone can translate them. If they happen to be more of the Biblical texts, they may have more worth than your generous offer."

One of the men began to gather the items, returning them to the jar.

"I have an idea," the dealer said. "I will take these things to a friend of mine who is here in Jericho, but who specializes in ancient artifacts. He can value them without your having to make the trip to Jerusalem. For this service, I would like a reasonable percentage of the ultimate sale price, perhaps forty percent?" He sat back and folded his hands in front of him.

"That is a very good idea, sir," the other father replied. "I am certain you are completely honest and trustworthy beyond measure. However, we have only just met, and as co-owners of the items, the four of us would have to accompany you. For your service, we would be pleased to offer ten percent of the ultimate price."

The dealer did not want them tagging along. After considerable haggling, they agreed that he would take only the small scrap of parchment, leaving the four with the jar, large scroll and small black lump. If it were proven that something of value potentially existed, the dealer would receive fifteen percent of the ultimate sale price. If not, he would receive nothing. He called to the shopkeeper across the way to watch his stall. Lifting his enormous girth with some difficulty, he finally stood, took the small piece of parchment and walked away.

# Chapter Three

Taking a circuitous route, the dealer ended up in a stall not two hundred feet from his own. He spoke quietly in Arabic to a man there who was smoking a cigarette, and handed him the small piece of parchment. The fat dealer knew that this man could speak Aramaic. He was virtually certain, if this scroll were from the period as the others, that was the language written on the scrap.

The man sat, staring at the parchment, then handed it back. "It is nothing," he said, looking down.

"Look in my eyes!" the dealer said sharply. "I am not your customer. I am your friend. What do you see on this scrap?"

"Friends come and go," the seated man said quietly. "Sit down. The writing is Aramaic. If it is genuine, and it certainly appears so, there are two interesting sentences written on this scrap. But first, we must talk about compensation for me. I want you and me to be good friends."

Once the fat dealer managed to get himself seated, the haggling began. The dealer found himself at a distinct disadvantage. He was negotiating for something about which he knew nothing. After a cigarette each and considerable discussion, the dealer asked the interpreter to give him more information about what he was looking at. Taking a long puff on his cigarette, the interpreter said, "Where is the coin that you found with this parchment?"

He refused to say more, and the dealer, working hard to control his excitement, would not admit there was a coin. At last the two agreed that they would equally split the dealer's commission on the sale of the items. He told the interpreter his cut was ten percent, keeping the extra five for himself. *After all,* he thought, *I am the one who brought this opportunity to the interpreter. Allah would wish me to have the lion's share of the proceeds.*

Once agreed on the terms, the interpreter said, "I will tell you generally what this scrap says. If I need to give you the exact words, it will take a little research. The two sentences say this. As the man began to talk a breeze arose, quickly cooling the bazaar. He said, "'I, Benjamin, saw with my eyes the baby Messiah in the stable behind The Four Horsemen in Bethlehem. I handed him this coin, which he took in his own hands, and Yeshua, which is the baby's name, returned it to me.'"

The men suddenly noticed that the breeze was blowing much harder now. The previously sunny sky had darkened, and the hot day had turned cloudy and cool. The wind blew the parchment the interpreter held in his hand, and he struggled to hang on to it. "What is happening?" the fat dealer said. "The sky has been clear all day. Where did the clouds come from?"

Within a moment, the clouds had passed and the day was bright and warm again, the air as still as it had been before. The men made no sense of the event, although it had sent chills down their spines. At last the dealer said, "You say this scrap talks of the baby Yeshua and the coin?"

"It does," the interpreter said. "You do have the coin, do you not?"

Without responding, the dealer stood, retrieved his scrap of parchment and said, "I will come back to you when I know more."

*Indeed you will,* thought the interpreter. *I will make certain of it.* He reached into a pocket of his galabeyeh and took out his cell phone.

# Chapter Four

The dealer thought of how he would talk to the four visitors as he waddled through the narrow lane separating stalls, finally ending back at his own. When he arrived, he saw them standing in the passageway, showing the rolled scroll to another dealer. Startled that he might be losing his customers, he grabbed one of the men's arms and whispered, "Come with me!"

He ushered the four into the back room of his tented stall. "The man could not read the parchment. It appears to be an unknown language, or perhaps only a lot of markings," he told them. "He does say it is old, perhaps as ancient as the Dead Sea Scrolls which were found. It therefore has value, although nothing like if it were easily translated, say from Aramaic." One of the fathers stared closely at him, and the dealer averted his eyes.

"Thank you for your trouble," one of the fathers said, rising. "Let us go, children. This man has been kind to give us his time."

"One moment," the dealer responded. "As I said, the scroll obviously does have some value. I can give you five thousand shekels for it right now, and I will take the chance that perhaps I can recover that huge sum from such a scroll."

"We will continue to search for an answer to the scroll," the father said. They rose and walked out of his tent, one of them bearing the jar with the scroll, scrap and coin back inside. They walked down the narrow passageway. The interpreter stood nearby, watching them closely as they left the bazaar. He spoke quietly into his phone.

# Chapter Five

"That fat swine was lying. I could tell it by looking in his face," one of the fathers said to the group. "He knows more about the scrap of parchment than he was willing to tell, and he was trying to cheat us!"

"But father," his son said. "What do we do now?"

"I think we must go to Jerusalem, my boy, and see what the scholars at the university can tell us. At least they will be honest."

Having spent a good deal of the day in Jericho, and not wanting the expense of a night away from home, the four got into their old truck and began the short journey back to the Dead Sea. The men talked about taking off work in a couple of days and driving up to Jerusalem, a journey of less than thirty miles from their homes.

Not far outside Jericho, they were passed on the highway by a black pickup moving at a high rate of speed. One of the fathers cursed at the man and shook his fist at his dangerous driving. Topping a hill a few miles down the road, they saw the vehicle parked at the side of the road, its hood raised, and a man looking at the engine. "I'm going to tell this man a few things," the driver said angrily. He pulled in behind the pickup, got out and walked to the front.

As he walked around, the pickup driver greeted him with a small pistol. "Go back to your truck now," he said.

Both men walked to the truck. "Do as I say and no one will be harmed," the gunman said to the four. "Give me the jar."

One of the boys saw the man's gun and immediately held up the vessel.

"Open your door slowly, and hand it to me."

The boy did as he was told. Taking it, the man gestured for the driver to get in the truck. "Go down the road now, and do not stop until you reach your homes. If you contact anyone, I will come to your houses and kill you all."

The fathers and sons drove quickly away from the gunman and his pickup, knowing that they had lost any chance to ever profit from the incredible find.

# Chapter Six

THREE DAYS LATER

Alim Shakir was the name of the man who had interpreted the Aramaic writing for the fat dealer. He sat in the restaurant of the Hilton Hotel in Jericho. Its location on the main highway put it a few blocks away from the bazaar. Today, he did not want to be spotted by other dealers in the marketplace.

Shakir waited for one of the hotel's guests to join him for coffee. He was dressed in a western suit, having foregone his galabayeh for today's meeting. As he waited, he nervously rechecked the shopping bag he had set in the chair next to him. It had cost him a small fortune to hire his nephew to follow the strangers out of town and steal the jar.

After Shakir had seen the writing on the scrap, he knew that the stupid dealer would never understand the true value of what he had. And until the nephew brought the jar back to him, Shakir was not aware that the large parchment existed. He was expecting only the shard he had seen, plus an old coin.

As soon as his nephew dropped off the stolen urn, Alim took the items from the earthenware jar and sold it immediately for one thousand shekels to a dealer nearby in the bazaar. Ancient pots were not that rare, but they did command a decent price. He therefore recovered all of the money his nephew had earned for snatching the jug. Now the jar was just one of several sitting on display in the marketplace, and no one would ever identify it as this particular scroll jar.

A man walked into the coffee shop. He was obviously not Arabic, although his pockmarked face set him apart. There were no other customers in the restaurant at this mid-morning hour. Alim stood and asked in English, "Mr. Jackson?"

The man approached his table and sat down. Prepared for the usual banter prior to discussion of business, the Arab asked, "Would you like sweets and coffee?"

"Show me the things you have," the Westerner who called himself Jackson responded curtly.

Alim looked in his face. The man looked menacing. "Of course," he responded. "It is so typical of you Americans to want to do business first. You are American, correct?"

The pockmarked man said, "I asked to see what you have. I have come a great distance. Show me these things now."

Alim retrieved the shopping bag and pulled out the small scrap of parchment and the blackened coin. "Do you read Aramaic, Mr. Jackson?" he asked.

"What does it say?"

Alim gave him the translation of the two sentences.

Pointing to the parchments still rolled and in the shopping bag, Jackson said, "And what does that scroll say?"

"I have not opened it, sahib," responded Alim. "It is undoubtedly fragile, and should be handled very carefully. Since it was found with the scrap and coin, I am certain it is also of the time of the Christian Messiah, around two thousand years ago."

"What is your price for these items?" the man asked. From his accent, Alim wasn't sure whether the man was American or not. From his dealings with Westerners in general, he was prepared for their "get down to business" attitude, but this man had been with him only a few minutes. This was disconcertingly fast, and the man was unbelievably rude.

"I want five hundred thousand U.S. dollars for the three items," Alim responded, sitting back in his chair and folding his arms.

Jackson looked him squarely in the eyes. "I'm sure you do," he responded at last. "I am going to give you ten thousand dollars today, in cash. Then I am going to take these items to be authenticated. If they are what you say, you will receive one hundred thousand dollars more."

Alim began, "No, that is much too low . . ."

The pockmarked man interrupted him. "Mr. Shakir, listen carefully to me. I am not a man who negotiates. And you are not a man who wants to trifle with me. I am offering you more money than you have ever seen in your miserable life, and you think you are going to sit here and barter with me?" The man stood, pulling a thick envelope out of his inner suit coat pocket. "Here is your down payment," he said to Shakir.

Alim decided to be aggressive as well. "You cannot have the items," he said, picking the shred of parchment and the coin up off the table, and putting them back in the shopping bag. "And I will call the authorities if you attempt to steal them from me. You will never leave Jericho if you do."

Alim Shakir threw a few shekels on the table to pay for the coffee. He walked confidently out of the hotel without looking back, and started toward the town square a couple of blocks away. He was certain the man would catch up with him and give him far more money than he had offered.

As Shakir walked along, the driver's door of a car parked parallel to the sidewalk suddenly opened. A Semitic man emerged from the car, closing a cell phone, and said, "Mr. Shakir, please do not be too hasty. Mr. Jackson just called. He has what he thinks is an acceptable trade for you to consider."

Reaching to the door, the driver lowered the darkly tinted back window slightly and said, "Take a look inside."

Shakir stooped slightly and looked through the window opening. In the back seat, his wife lay stripped naked, bound and gagged. He could see the terror in her eyes. "We will release her once Mr. Jackson has left Israel," the man told Alim.

"All right," he stammered. "I'll take the deal. Give me the ten thousand."

"Oh no," the driver laughed. "The deal now is that you get your wife back. That's all, you greedy bastard." He took the shopping bag, looked inside to confirm its three contents, and left Alim Shakir standing on the sidewalk.

Even though he knew it was futile, Shakir memorized the license number of a car that had been stolen only moments before, and which would be found in the desert a few days later, with his wife's naked, ravaged body in the back seat. He never related his story to the authorities. He knew his only hope to live, was to keep quiet.

And he too knew he would never see this amazing find again.

# Chapter Seven

CAIRO, EGYPT
TWO YEARS LATER,
MAY 4, 2004

The pockmarked man who yesterday at the museum had posed as a police inspector now sat in his apartment in the fashionable Giza District of Cairo. He thought it fitting that he could see the Great Pyramid outside his bedroom window. He had over the past few years become somewhat of an authority in ancient things.

Over the past five years he had acquired nearly a dozen priceless objects. Some he had purchased. Most had been stolen. Until now, he thought there would never be an item he couldn't sell, but this time might be the exception. His forte was the network of people in bazaars across the Middle East who knew of him. When Alim Shakir had interpreted the small piece of parchment, Shakir had known where to turn. He had called a contact in Jerusalem, who in turn called Cairo.

The man in Jerusalem had received one thousand dollars for doing nothing more than to make a long distance call to Cairo. Everyone was happy, the pockmarked man decided. Well, maybe not the pig Alim Shakir, who could have briefly had ten thousand dollars before he probably lost his own life. Instead, he still walked the earth but his wife was dead.

Although he was an American, the man had lived in Cairo for so many years that he spoke Egyptian like a native. As he sat on his couch, the three items lying on a table in front of him, he thought of what to do next. He had used one of many fake credentials he had accumulated, and had convinced the Museum director to get the scroll translated while he waited. "It's a key to solving an important case," he had told the director. And even though he knew what the two sentences on the small shred of parchment said, he was truly unprepared for the shock he felt when he read the translator's notes.

In his lifetime he had held in his hands some truly unique artifacts, highlighting the glories of ancient Rome, Greece and even Egypt, his adopted country. But never in history had anyone imagined the existence of a scroll written by a person who had seen the baby Jesus, the Christian Messiah Yeshua, with his own eyes.

He took his time to determine the best course of action. The man had been working lately for a client in America, doing mundane tasks as he directed. None of it was related to his passion, which was to broker artifacts. Instead, he had found himself being nothing more than a glorified secretary doing what the boss ordered. He was paid well to make phone calls and tie up loose ends, but with the artifacts he had in his possession, he could break the tie with this client forever. And that, the man thought, was a good thing. A continued association with this particular client could come to no good.

The man had plenty of money in several bank accounts across Europe. He would be in no hurry to dispose of these three things, which would provide him the opportunity to retire in splendor and enjoy life to the fullest. He put the items back into the same shopping bag and went to the Giza branch of the National Bank of

Scotland, where he maintained a large safety deposit box. There he secured the items, safe until he could determine his client's interest in them.

---

Two days later, the man placed a call from Cairo to New York City. He described in detail the three artifacts he possessed, and faxed a copy of the notepad from Achmed, the translator at the museum. As he had expected, the client in America was very interested in the items.

What he did not expect was that he would be paid nothing more than a finder's fee for his efforts, and the items would then belong to the client. But the man in Cairo had had no choice, and quickly agreed that he would turn over the items to his New York client for less than a hundred thousand dollars. He knew how persuasive this client could be. And he was not interested in finding out the extent to which he would exercise his persuasive tactics to get these items. The pockmarked man decided the best policy was deference.

# Chapter Eight

NEW YORK CITY
APRIL, 2006

It was after midnight. Brian and Nicole sat in the middle of the king sized bed, eating hamburgers and French fries they'd ordered from room service. Both wore hotel bathrobes.

"I was starving," she said, "and I thought you were never going to get around to buying me dinner."

He laughed. "Who was the one that kept pulling me back every time I tried to move even an inch?"

"Hey!" she responded. "It didn't seem to be too much of an inconvenience for you."

Up to this point, nothing had been said about her being in the hotel room when he had arrived over four hours earlier. He had undressed quickly - his clothes were lying all over the chair - and had joined her in bed. It took only a few minutes of intense kissing before her pink panties joined the pile of discarded clothing. They took their time for the rest.

For over an hour they explored each other, touching, gently rubbing and lightly moving over sensitive skin and moist areas ready for more. She took him in both her hands, rubbing up and down for long minutes as he groaned. He felt her hard nipples and tight, firm buttocks.

There was nothing they missed as the hours passed and one orgasm came after another. Finally around 11 p.m. they came together, she on top. Her back arched, then she fell off him onto the bed. Both of them were sweating and exhausted.

"Wow," she said. "I need a cigarette."

"I didn't know you smoked," he responded in a whisper.

"I don't, but now seems like a hell of a good time to start." They laughed and laid on the bed as the moonlight through the hotel window outlined their two naked bodies.

Finally she had arisen, gone into the bathroom and turned on the shower. When she emerged, she wore nothing except for a towel around her wet hair. "You forgot your clothes," he joked.

"I have a towel," she said. "That's enough."

He looked at her. She was beautiful, and obviously a natural blond. She stood at the end of the bed and said, "Let's order something to eat." They did, and in the thirty minutes he had to kill, Brian showered too.

Brian looked at her and smiled.

"What?" she asked.

"How did you get in my room?"

"It was easier than I thought it would be," she replied. "I told Collette I was your attorney. She recognized my name and law firm because you put me on the guest list. I asked her where you were staying, so I could get a room there too. I ended up here, and gave one of the bellmen $100 to let Mrs. Brian Sadler into your room as a surprise. The rest is history."

"Where's your luggage?" he asked.

"I have a hang-up that has everything I need. I left it at the gallery during the auction, and now it's in your closet!"

"One more question," he said. "What made you think I would

be alone, and that I'd be interested?"

"That part was strictly woman's intuition," she responded, smiling. "I think I can tell when there's a chemistry, and there damn sure is between us. And were you alone? I checked the room when I got in, saw nothing but man-things, got undressed and waited for you. If you'd shown up with some bimbo, I guess my intuition would have been wrong about you. But you didn't, and I wasn't, and I'd like to congratulate us on the great sex we just had!"

They drank a six-pack of beer that had come with their order from the restaurant, turned on a classic movie and watched very little of it. They laughed and talked for a couple of hours, then turned off the lights and ended up right back where they had started.

# Chapter Nine

On Saturday morning Brian retrieved the New York Times from the floor outside his door, ordered coffee and bagels and laid around in bed. He had put on his bathrobe to let the room service waiter come in, while Nicole dived under the covers, but now they were naked again, lying next to each other drinking coffee and reading.

"I have to say, in Dallas I received distinct vibes from you indicating you didn't like me very much," he said to her.

"I still think you're a total idiot for what you did in your deposition, Brian. But I have a professional side and a personal side. My personal side thinks you're hot, and I wanted to sleep with you."

"Well, it looks like you got what you wanted."

She looked at him and laughed. "I think maybe you also got what you wanted."

"No doubt about that," he said, leaning over and kissing her deeply. One thing led to another, and shortly the action started up once again.

They awoke with sunlight streaming into the room. Nicole sat up and looked at the clock on the nightstand. It was after 2 p.m. "Shit," she said. "I have a flight in two hours."

"I'd say you're screwed," Brian responded.

"Yeah, that's a fact. But regardless, I'm going to miss my flight. When are you going home?"

He got up and grabbed an itinerary from his briefcase as she searched the room for her cell phone. She called American Airlines and switched to the Sunday flight Brian had booked. She upgraded to first class and said, "I'll sit by you. We'll make whatever little hottie's in the seat next to you switch seats with me."

Brian said, "Actually, you'll be the little hottie in the seat next to me."

"Oh," she said. "How rude of me. I forgot to ask if it's OK if I spend one more night with you."

"I thought you'd never ask," Brian Sadler replied.

She smiled and laid back on the bed, running her fingers down his chest until she reached where she wanted to be.

# Chapter Ten

They were watching CNN Headline News when Brian's cell phone rang. It was Darius. "I hope you're outside enjoying the beautiful day I hear you're having in New York," he said.

"Actually," Brian replied, "I've stayed in until now, catching up on some things." Nicole's muffled giggle came from the pillow where she'd buried her head. "But I am going out shortly." He hit her playfully on the back as she laughed.

"I told you I was chasing a rumor about something big that may be coming on the market," Darius began. "I wasn't able to confirm anything. It's like this much of the time. Shadows, whispers, rumors may be all you hear for days or years. Then something hits the street that makes your heart race. All I can find out is that there may be some ancient Jewish relics that have never been offered before."

They talked a bit about how that could happen - a reclusive collector who dies, and whose collection sees the light of day for the first time. Or a relic stolen by the Nazis and presumed lost for seventy years, suddenly found in a Bavarian mine. "Don't get excited about this yet," he cautioned Brian. "If it happens, it happens. That kind of thinking keeps your feet planted firmly on the ground, where they belong." He told Brian he hoped, if the relics did exist, that the publicity generated by Bijan over the sarcophagus sale would give the gallery a chance to be on the short list of potential buyers.

Darius told Brian once again how pleased he was with everything. "Collette gave you the complete stamp of approval," he said. "That means a lot. She's a discerning woman and I trust her instincts about people. She's helped me land a big deal more than once, and also to steer away from some that could have caused big headaches."

They talked about upcoming plans as Nicole went into the bathroom. Lying naked on the bed, Brian could hear the hair dryer through the closed door. The offering was tentatively scheduled to go public in two weeks. Brian would quit the firm then, move to New York and hopefully be settled in a month or less.

Brian hung up and knocked on the bathroom door. "Come in," Nicole yelled over the buzz of the hair dryer. She stood in front of the mirror, naked.

He walked over and stood directly behind her, pushing against her back.

"My God, Brian," she said, turning off the dryer and setting it down. "I'm not going to be able to walk by tomorrow."

"That's my goal," he said, laughing, as he led her back to the bedroom.

They finally went outside around 4 p.m. and walked the streets. The day truly was gorgeous. It was warm and there was a light breeze as they strolled and window-shopped. They ended up on Madison Avenue in the 60s, and popped in to one of the small Italian sidewalk cafes that dotted the landscape in that area. They sat on the sidewalk, had a few glasses of Pinot Grigio and some pasta.

Brian mentioned that in this morning's paper he had seen an open house for a recently opened apartment building in Gramercy Park. "I have to find something soon, so let's go down there tomorrow morning before we head back to Dallas. That is," he looked at her, smiling, "if you can keep your clothes on long enough."

"Me??" she retorted. "It takes two to tango, buddy. I'm up for it if you are. And while I'm on the subject, may I say you've been up for it quite well so far!"

# Chapter Eleven

DALLAS
FOUR WEEKS LATER

Bijan Rarities Limited went public the third Friday in May without a hitch. Brian submitted his resignation from Warren Taylor and Currant effective the same day. The guys on the trading floor threw a combination celebration and going away party at Cru, a nearby wine bar. As the party got into full swing, Brian looked for Nicole.

They'd seen each other often since the trip to New York. She'd thought the Gramercy Park apartment looked great, and he put a ten thousand dollar check down to pay for deposit and rent. He was planning to move next week.

His impending move to New York made their relationship a little awkward, he thought. They really couldn't make serious plans for the future since they'd talked about how long distance relationships rarely worked. So they had gone out for a few dinners, spent a few nights at one apartment or the other, and met for drinks every other day or so.

This afternoon he had left her a voicemail at work, asking her to come to Cru for the party. They'd been drinking at the bar for over an hour already and she hadn't arrived. He was a little surprised how much he hoped she'd come. They hadn't talked much about how they both felt deep inside, but he knew he was getting seriously interested in her. He was glad he had both the money and the upcoming travel schedule that might allow him to get together with her every few weeks, at least. He didn't want to spend much more time than that away from her.

His reverie ended suddenly. "Snap out of it, buddy!" his cubemate Jim Palmer said. "I get someone new next to me. I should be the one daydreaming about the beautiful college graduate who's going to sit next to my cube, fall in love and whisk me away to her daddy's villa in France!" Brian laughed and clinked glasses with a number of well-wishers.

At eleven the party began to wind down. Brian grabbed a cab. He'd come back and get his car tomorrow. As much as he had had to drink, driving wasn't a good idea. As he rode back to his place, he pulled out his cell phone. He had a voicemail. In the noise on the sidewalk outside Cru, he didn't hear it come in.

"Brian," Nicole started. "I'm not coming to your going away party. We have less than a week before you leave. I've never lost control of my emotions before, but it's happening to me now. I don't want to share the time we have left with anybody else. Let's have dinner tomorrow night someplace quiet. Call me Saturday and let's figure it out. Hope your party was fun. Brian . . . " there was a long hesitation. " . . . oh nothing. I'll talk to you tomorrow."

# Chapter Twelve

NEW YORK CITY
LATE OCTOBER 2006

Leaving his Gramercy Park apartment at 8 a.m., Brian walked to the 23rd Street subway station and took the northbound train to Grand Central. He wore a topcoat. The trees had lost all their leaves by now, and a crisp fall wind heralded the beginning of the winter season.

Emerging from the cavernous station on Vanderbilt Avenue, he walked north and west, moving with pedestrian and vehicular traffic to avoid long waits, until he reached Fifth Avenue and Bijan's front door. He punched in a security code to disarm the alarm system and used his key to enter the building, locking the door behind him.

In the back of the building was a vault with a time-delay lock. As always, that was his first stop. Along with many other things, the rare objects which would be displayed in the gallery sat in this vault, and would be removed and put in their places prior to the gallery's 10 a.m. opening. A twenty minute wait was required before the security system released and the combination could be entered to open the huge door. Brian pushed six small buttons in sequence to start the countdown, then walked to his office.

In the five months since he had come on board, many exciting things had happened. Brian had been to China and western Europe once each and to London twice a month. Darius had introduced him to many of the firm's contacts for the purchase of rarities. Their newfound fame after the Inkharaton sale had resulted in dozens of new opportunities for Bijan. Darius was thrilled to turn over the international travel and likewise, Brian was very pleased to be going. Travel was new to him, and every single day of his work in this exciting field exhilarated him beyond measure.

Darius had showed Brian everything. He gave him reams of documents to read. There were customer profiles, showing who bought what, worldwide lists of contacts and sources from whom the firm had bought objects or received important information. Darius told Brian the firm had bank accounts in New York, London, Geneva and Cairo.

Slowly, Darius had introduced Brian to the firm's secrets. "Sometimes it's necessary to make a discreet payment to a high-ranking public official to gain information we need," Darius had said. "So we also have untraceable funds in cash stored in our London bank's safety deposit box."

Bribes, Brian had learned, were part of the way Darius chose to extract information. Darius gave him everything. Brian even had the means to withdraw the gallery's cash from the London bank if he wished.

Darius had explained the horde of cash in the U.K. only after exploratory discussions to see how open Brian was to doing things on the gray side of right-and-wrong. Darius believed in paying income taxes, but he also believed there were many ways to circumvent such payments, and that most companies engaged in such practices.

Brian learned how untraceable cash got into Bijan's hands. Darius had explained that he often purchased groups of items from estates or individuals. The more prominent of those were listed on Bijan's records. The rest were not. The full purchase price was allocated to the few items that were on the books. That meant that the others were shown nowhere, and had no purchase price allocated to them.

When the time came to sell, Darius made sure those sales were outside the United States to insulate Bijan from possible tax consequences, and that those sales were in cash. That cash, stored in London, was Bijan's own private slush fund. At the moment, there was a half million dollars there. It was money that had to be used carefully, to avoid creating even a hint of suspicion of unreported income in the United States.

Darius and Brian's personal friendship quickly grew. Though there was a thirty year age difference, they bonded immediately and frequently dined together after a day at the gallery. Darius became Brian's mentor in business but also in his personal life.

Nicole, the primary focus of Brian's life away from work, had come to New York at least once a month since he moved from Dallas. Her hectic schedule, combined with his travel around the world, made it difficult to get together very often. Darius had met Nicole several times. The three of them met for drinks most of the times she was here.

Sensing how much she meant to him, Darius had insisted that the firm pay for first class tickets for the trips she made to New York. "It's important for your well-being," he told Brian. "Think nothing of it. Besides, you're a shareholder. Forty percent of that ticket price comes from your share of Bijan."

Brian absorbed everything Darius could teach him. The older man told him how good he was becoming at every aspect of the gallery's operations. "I'm confident if I were to retire this moment,"

Darius said recently, "that you could carry on Bijan's work with not a single interruption."

One evening, the talk turned to Nicole. "It's none of my business, I know, so feel free to tell this meddling old man to shut up. What discussions have you two had regarding the future?" Darius asked.

Brian told him things had been a little strained, as he had expected with two people who saw each other rarely, and lived two thousand miles apart. "She told me we should date other people," he said, "and we're pretty open about discussing that. Only trouble is, I have to make up the ones I'm dating, and I'm certain she's really doing it."

Darius asked him if he wanted to consider opening a gallery in Dallas.

Brian was amazed and flattered that he would suggest such a move. Telling him so, Brian dismissed the idea as quickly as it had come up. "I love New York," Brian said, "and I want to work here with you. Dallas could never be the same for me."

"If you are truly in love," Darius said, "and I think you are, then you should let nothing stop your quest to win her heart."

Brian finally told Darius that he also thought he was in love, but until they had time to be together for a long, uninterrupted stretch, there was no way either of them could know for sure. "And I'm not even certain how she feels," he said at last.

Darius said, "I believe in fate. If your love is meant to be, something will happen to allow it."

# Chapter Thirteen

The day the call from John Spedino came was in December. The gallery was adorned with beautiful golden Christmas decorations, and Fifth Avenue was crowded with shoppers and tourists. A few blocks to the south, the windows of Saks portrayed animated scenes of Christmas past, while across the street the Rockefeller Center Christmas tree was ablaze in lights as ice skaters glided along the frozen rink below it.

Darius had left the store early to pick up some presents in anticipation of his trip to California in a couple of weeks. He was spending the holiday with his children, both of whom had adopted the Christian religion after marriage, and their families. Brian was in the office working on paperwork when Collette buzzed and said, "John Spedino is on line two for you, Brian."

Brian had neither seen nor talked to Spedino since the auction in May. He answered the call. Spedino told him he had a job for Brian. "I want to acquire some artifacts," he said, "and I want Bijan Galleries to act as my agent on the deal." He refused to say more on the phone.

Brian suggested that he and Darius meet Spedino to discuss the project and Spedino agreed, but with Brian only.

"This is not a project for Darius Nazir," he said. "I want you to say nothing to him about this until I give you approval to do so. Is that clear?"

Brian said yes without thinking. They agreed to meet in the King Cole Bar at the St. Regis Hotel the next day.

After the call ended, Brian felt ashamed for having so easily agreed to keep a secret from Darius, who could not have been more open with him. He had been flattered that a powerful man like Spedino wanted to entrust a confidence to him, but vowed to inform Darius about everything as soon as they had met and he had more information.

Brian arrived first. Spedino came in twenty minutes late, sitting down without apology. He shook Brian's hand and said, "I don't have a lot of time. I'm going to give you some information, and I want you to get back to me as soon as you have worked out the details." A waiter stopped by their table. They both ordered coffees, and Spedino started talking.

"Have you heard that a scroll was found a couple of years ago, which is rumored to be a complete account of the visit by shepherds to the inn on the night Jesus was born? And that two other relics accompany it? One is a scrap of parchment identifying a coin which a shepherd boy presented to Jesus in the manger, which He held in His hand. The other object is the coin itself."

The stunned look on Brian's face must have been obvious. "I'm not surprised this is news to you," Spedino said. "I think your boss has heard a few rumors, but I'll bet he doesn't know as much as I just told you."

"How do you know about this?" Brian responded.

"I don't want to sound arrogant, Brian, but I'm not answering questions about this. I'm going to tell you what you need to know."

He told Brian that he had confirmed that the relics did in fact exist. Spedino wanted to acquire the objects and present them to the Vatican, to allow them to rest in the holiest of places in Christendom. "Call it an atonement for my sins," Spedino said. "I'm a good Catholic, and I've done things in my life like everyone else. This is a way to make myself feel better about things."

"What I want is for Bijan Rarities to acquire the items first, then sell them to me," he continued. "And if your first question is, 'Why', then just know that I have my reasons, and your gallery will benefit from the transaction. Thinking of nothing but the publicity, it'll be even greater on this one than on the Egyptian sale. And there's a fat profit for Bijan."

Spedino continued. He told Brian there were several loose ends to tie up, including determining how much money it would ultimately cost to buy the relics. Brian asked if he had a ballpark number.

"I figure around twenty five million," Spedino replied.

Brian looked at him blankly. "How could Bijan ever swing a deal like that?" he said. "The gallery doesn't have that much money."

"Oh, but you will," Spedino said. "I'm going to put you in contact with a friend of mine who has Israeli government-issued bonds for rent. They're used to prop up balance sheets so companies can make deals like this."

He told Brian that the plan was that Bijan would never actually put out any cash. The entire transaction would happen very quickly – in a matter of days. A bank would issue a letter of credit for say $25 million, based on Bijan's balance sheet which is improved by $25 million in Israeli bonds. The letter of credit allows Bijan to buy the relics and and pay for them immediately. Bijan then has time to flip the relics before having to come up with the cash to pay for them.

"When you sell to me at a guaranteed profit, Bijan pays for the relics, cancels the letter of credit, returns the Israeli bonds the firm borrowed, and pockets a profit of two million dollars. It's all cut and dried," Spedino said. "Nothing can go wrong. And I'll even pay the rental fee for the bonds."

"I'll need to talk to Darius," Brian said.

"No," Spedino replied. "In fact, you won't need to talk to Darius. This is strictly between you and me. It'll be over and done with before Darius hears about it, and you'll be the hero of the day at Bijan Rarities."

Brian protested. "Darius is not only the majority shareholder, we're a public company," he said. "How can I get by with rented assets on my balance sheet, and what bank will loan money against them without asking how we got them?"

"Bijan has to make quarterly reports to the SEC," Spedino replied, "so all that matters to a public company is what's on your books on the last day of the quarter. Anything that happens between day two and day eighty-nine makes no difference at all. The public never sees it.

"This transaction will take place *during* a quarter, not over the end of a quarter. These bonds will be on and off the books before you have to file your quarterly report with the SEC. As to the bank, you're going to borrow the money from First InterCity Bank. They'll be happy to serve a new client of your caliber. And one of the loan officers there owes me a favor. You just need to relax, boy," Spedino concluded. "I've covered everything."

He told Brian that any discussion about this transaction would be referred to by a code name - "The Project." Spedino cautioned Brian once again to say nothing to Darius Nazir. He promised to have someone make contact shortly to discuss the transfer of the bonds. Thanking Brian for his time, he rose, handed Brian a card with his phone number on it, and walked out of the bar.

Brian sat in his chair, thoughts racing through his head. *I don't think I ever agreed to this,* he said to himself. *But it's a done deal anyway.* He didn't feel right keeping this from Darius, although the way Spedino laid it out, it really did seem foolproof. And if it worked, Darius would see that Brian truly did have the capacity to make decisions on his own, and do what was best for the firm. But somewhere in the back of his mind nagging fears arose. Looking down, he saw his hands were shaking. John Spedino seemed like a cultured, sophisticated businessman. Brian knew what he really was, however, and that a person like Spedino should never be trusted. *With that kind of guy,* Brian mused, *things are never as they seem.*

A cocktail waitress came over and asked if he was finished. He ordered a martini, just to have a moment to settle down and think. Ever the optimist, Brian Sadler began to formulate a plan. With some forethought, he could make sure nothing went wrong on this deal. And he could tell Darius just enough that he wasn't betraying him.

# Chapter Fourteen

A week later, Brian sat in the Grill Room of the Four Seasons Restaurant on Park Avenue and 52rd Street, having lunch with Chaim Weisenberg. The man had called Brian on his cell phone and suggested they meet at the restaurant regarding the short-term transfer of Israeli bonds to Bijan.

The men met for the first time as Weisenberg was ushered to Brian's table by the maitre d'. He wore a yarmulke and a black suit, and appeared to be in his forties. Pleasantries out of the way, Brian asked who had given Weisenberg his name.

"Actually," the man responded, "I get a lot of second-hand introductions. I'm not certain, but I think perhaps I learned of your need through a contact at First InterCity Bank."

"And not from John Spedino?" Brian asked. Weisenberg raised his eyebrows, and looked at Brian with a surprised expression. "John Spedino, the Mafia guy? Do you know him?"

Brian replied that Spedino was an occasional customer of the gallery, but he didn't really know him.

Weisenberg changed the subject. He launched into a description of how the bond loan worked. He said the bonds were bearer bonds, which meant they belonged to whomever had possession of them. The owner, a European company, did the short-term loan transactions to make a significantly higher return on the bonds than interest alone would have garnered.

"How it works is this," Weisenberg said after they ordered lunch. "You'll pay a commitment fee of half a percent of the face value up front, and the bonds will be transferred to you on paper. Physically they will remain in the vault of a major British bank, but any CPA or auditing firm who wished to verify their existence may do so by contacting the bank."

He explained that the bonds would pass muster as an asset for any company, because in reality they were exactly what they were supposed to be – bearer bonds issued by the Government of Israel, in the amount of twenty-five million dollars. The only hitch was, they were temporary assets – only on a company's books for the short period during which the company needed a hike in assets for a particular project.

When the project was over, Weisenberg told Brian, the transfer agreement was cancelled, another fee of half a percent was paid, and the parties went their own ways. "In your case, Mr. Sadler, you will have borrowed $25 million in assets for a sufficient time to do a major transaction, paid $250,000 for the loan, and presumably made much more than that on the deal you consummated."

Spedino had agreed to pay all fees, Brian remembered, so literally no costs were coming from Bijan's funds. "I'll need to get an attorney to review the documents," Brian said. "When can I get them?"

"I have a sample set here for you," Weisenberg said, handing a thick manila envelope across the table. "Save yourself some money. There's a letter inside on the letterhead of Maurins and Catchpole, one of Britain's largest law firms. The letter both attests to the validity of the transaction and certifies that the bonds are in existence as stated. That's all the verification you should need."

They finished their lunch. Brian asked Weisenberg a few questions about what sort of business he was in. The man offered no concrete response to Brian's inquiry. He merely responded that he was a facilitator for the party who owned the bonds, and he was paid a fee by them for deals he closed.

"Will these bonds pass a certified audit by an accounting firm if they're on my books?" Brian asked.

"I expect they will," Weisenberg responded. "Just remember one thing – you're borrowing these bonds for a very short period of time. That will be clear to anyone reviewing your books, since you didn't actually have $25 million on hand to pay for them. The transaction is perfectly legitimate. It just needs to be on and off your books as expeditiously as possible."

Walking back to the gallery after lunch, Brian thought about his conversation with this man. He'd never actually said where he got Brian's name, and when they parted ways, he advised Brian he would be in touch in a week or so, leaving Brian no way to initiate contact himself.

# Chapter Fifteen

Back at the gallery, Brian placed a call to Nicole's direct line. "Ms. Farber's office," Ryan answered.

"Hey, Ryan. Is Nicole there?"

Ryan replied that she was in a deposition this afternoon, and was not expected to return to the office today. Brian ended the call, dialed her cell phone and left a voicemail asking her to call him. He asked Collette to photocopy the documents he'd received from Chaim Weisenberg, added a short cover letter to the copies, put them in a Fedex envelope and sent them overnight to Nicole.

He didn't hear from her that night, although he checked his cell phone every hour or so to make sure he hadn't missed the call. He decided her deposition had run over, then wondered if the client had taken her to dinner, or maybe they were working late at her office. He stopped his mind from wandering places he didn't want it to go, and ordered Chinese food at 10 p.m. from a place around the corner that delivered. He finally went to bed, still wondering why Nicole was so busy she couldn't return his call.

The next morning he checked his cell phone first thing. There was no message, nor was there a voicemail when he called in to

Bijan's office and checked his phone there. He went to work, finally deciding around noon to call again.

He reached Ryan, who said, "She hasn't been in this morning, Mr. Sadler. She's pretty tied up with this deposition, and I think she and the client were huddled up somewhere last night working on strategies. It's a pretty big case."

Brian wanted to ask who it was, but knew he'd get nothing from this guy. "OK," he said, as cheerfully as he could. "It's nothing, really. Just ask her to call when she takes a look at the stuff I sent her."

Ryan confirmed that the package had in fact arrived, and that he would give it to Nicole as soon as he saw her.

Darius had flown in from a trip to Chicago the evening before. As soon as he reached the office, he and Brian met for an hour so Brian could be brought up to speed on a pending deal to sell an Etruscan vase to the Field Museum. Darius was excited and spared no detail in telling Brian about the opportunity the gallery had to be a broker in this deal. "When we sell to these major museums, it's more good press for us," Darius said.

When Darius asked him what had been going on in his absence, Brian mentioned the call from Spedino, and his revelation that there were three relics that could be acquired. He didn't mention the Israeli bonds, or that Bijan might actually become the owner of the items, because he didn't want to muddy the waters at this point with facts he didn't totally understand himself just yet.

Darius reacted differently than Brian had expected. His eyes darkened, and he looked troubled. "Do you know who John Spedino is?" he said to Brian in a loud voice. "Do you know how dangerous it is to even *talk* to a man like John Spedino?"

Brian stammered for a moment, then said, "I'm not saying we're going to be partners with the guy. I'm saying he's got a legitimate deal for us to be part of, that'll give us more press than the Inkharaton deal ever did."

Darius became angry. "I don't want you talking to John Spedino again," he said, his voice cracking in a manner Brian had never heard before. "Promise me you will stay away from him. He's dangerous, Brian. You need to start fresh with Bijan. Don't play with fire." He stood and without another word, walked out of Brian's office.

Brian was almost in shock. He knew Darius had done deals that, to put it mildly, wouldn't pass a close inspection. Darius had told him about some things he'd done that involved artifacts from questionable backgrounds, things he thought might have been stolen, but he did the deal anyway because the deal passed the smell test on the surface.

He had told Brian to rely on his gut. This time, Brian wanted this deal to work badly, and his gut was telling him to go for it. He had to prove to Darius that he knew how to do a deal on his own. And he would.

# Chapter Sixteen

Darius Nazir was furious. He left Brian's office, then stormed out of the gallery to the street. Walking a couple of blocks to the Peninsula Hotel, he went into the lobby and sat at a table there. It was noon. The lobby was busy but not crowded. Removing his cell phone, he placed a call. John Spedino answered.

"What in hell do you think you're doing, involving my new man in one of your projects?" Darius hissed quietly into the phone. "It's bad enough I'm involved with you. Now you're pulling Brian Sadler into your deals too!"

"Wait a moment, Darius," Spedino responded calmly. "If it weren't for me and my 'deals', as you call them, you wouldn't have met Brian Sadler in the first place, so you wouldn't have his million and a half personal investment. Nor would you have $4 million of public money which Warren Taylor and Currant raised for you. Thanks to me, this archaeology buff got the investment proposal from Bijan Rarities in the first place. Thanks to me, W&T did the offering without hesitating. Keep all that in mind, my high and mighty friend, and remember that you have 'deals' of your own. Think about whether you want Sadler involved in *those.*"

"Listen to me, Johnny," Nazir said. "Back off this transaction now. Stay away from Brian Sadler. He's the best thing that's happened to me and this firm in years. Keep your greasy hands off him."

There was silence on the phone for perhaps thirty seconds. John Spedino said calmly, "Darius, if you ever call me Johnny again, I'll send someone around to talk to you. You know what I mean. You've seen my people talk to others. What nerve you have, telling me what to do. And calling me greasy. My, my, Darius. You really don't want to get on my bad side."

Spedino's voice turned hard. "You would be nothing without me, you little prick. You needed help with money, and I helped you. Not once, but over and over. Now your firm, and this new *boy*, as you call him, are going to help me."

"You leave me no choice," Darius said at last. "I'm not going to let you continue to make me your hostage. Maybe you can take me down, Johnny. But you won't take the firm and Brian Sadler down. Just wait and see." He hung up.

---

By 5 p.m., the man who would cause Darius Nazir to die had spent a half hour looking at the alleys behind Nazir's apartment building. In the early afternoon, the man had received a call and begun to prepare for the job he was assigned. He was told that Nazir ate his dinner away from home every evening around 7:30 p.m. Armed with a photo, the man stood at the intersection of Park Avenue and 86th Street, half a block away from Darius' building, and watched until Nazir left.

Shortly thereafter, the intruder used a lock pick and easily gained access to the building through a delivery door in the alleyway. He locked it behind him, then took a service elevator to Nazir's floor, again easily gaining access to his flat. There were no security alarms on the door. An apartment building such as this had a doorman - that was comfort enough for most residents, including Darius Nazir.

The man had a number of possible ways to do the job with which he was tasked. Hoping the easiest way would work, he went to the bathroom and looked at medicine bottles sitting by the sink. One had large capsules filled with liquid. The instructions said, "Take three before bedtime."

Pleased with his luck, the man counted the capsules in the bottle. There were five. He took one of the capsules and, holding it in his gloved hand, injected it with a small amount of liquid from a syringe he had pulled from his coat pocket.

There was no guarantee Darius Nazir would take his medication tonight or that one of the three he took today would be the right one. Whether today or tomorrow, he would eventually take the pills. Death would occur within a couple of hours, leaving no suspicion of foul play.

# Chapter Seventeen

Brian spent the afternoon in his office with the door closed. In Weisenberg's envelope were a description of how a sample transaction worked, photocopies of the bearer bonds themselves, an example of a transfer document and the letter of attestation from the London law firm.

He read the documents which Chaim Weisenberg had given him, made notes and laid out the entire proposal in flowchart format, finding that easier to understand. When he finally took a break, he saw that it was nearly 6 p.m. He wanted to find Darius and tell him good night – they needed to smooth things over before they left the gallery.

He walked out into the showroom. Collette and Jason were closing things up. She had just closed the vault and set its alarm. "Is Darius here?" Brian asked.

"No, Mr. Sadler," she said. "He left the gallery around noon, right after he talked with you. We haven't seen him since. I presume he had errands to run, since he just got in from Chicago. Should I try to reach him on his cell?"

Brian declined, saying he'd catch Darius in the morning.

Brian put on his overcoat and muffler and left the building - it was lightly snowing. On the sidewalk, he absentmindedly checked his cell phone again to see if he could have missed Nicole's call. While he held it in his hand, it rang. He saw her name and number displayed. "Hey," he said. "I thought you'd forgotten about me." He began walking toward the subway station on Lexington Avenue.

"I've been busy, Brian," she said sharply. "I read these documents you sent me. What the hell is all this about?"

"What do you mean?"

"My God, Brian," she said. "Borrowing somebody's bearer bonds? Who in hell would do that? If this deal blew up, whoever did this would be stuck holding a big bag of problems."

Brian had intended to lay out the acquisition program for her to consider, including Spedino's proposition. He saw that course of action was futile at this point, and instead said, "I was talking to a guy the other day and he told me about this method of using assets short-term. I thought the firm might borrow some assets, make a major acquisition, pre-sell the deal to a client before we buy it, and pass it on to the buyer, all in a matter of days. Sounded like a win-win deal to me."

"Sounds like a wishy-washy deal to me," Nicole replied. "I've never seen anything like this before. If you have a pre-sold deal, just take the deal itself to the bank and they'll loan you the money against it."

He explained that if the deal were huge, the bank likely wouldn't allow Bijan to borrow the money, because of the chance something might go wrong. But a huge deal, Brian explained, carried with it the chance for Bijan to make a huge profit.

"A little free advice for you, Mr. Sadler," she said. "If it looks too good to be true, it probably is. You can choose to take my advice or leave it – it's up to you – but to say this kind of deal is out of the ordinary would be a massive understatement. Do you see where I'm coming from?"

Brian said he did, and was merely looking at every deal that came along. "There's nothing in the works that we'd need that kind of transaction for anyway," he said casually, closing the conversation.

He asked her where she'd been. "I thought you might return my call last night," he said.

She explained that she was in a deposition with a client who owned one of Texas' largest private oil companies, and had been sued by the Equal Employment Opportunity Commission for hiring illegal aliens. "He stands to lose a couple of million dollars if the EEOC prevails," she said. "We've been working night and day to get his testimony nailed down. But it's nice you miss me," she said at last.

Unsatisfied with her response, Brian asked if she and the client had gone to dinner last night. He was surprised at the jealousy that ran through him as she explained her working so closely with another man.

"No, Brian," she replied. "We skipped dinner completely. We went over to his place and screwed until after midnight. I was so exhausted I couldn't talk, so I didn't call you. Satisfied?"

Brian stopped suddenly. A man behind him nearly ran into his back, giving him a gesture as he walked around Brian on the busy sidewalk.

After a moment of silence, Nicole said tersely, "Brian, I'm a lawyer. I have clients and I have to work late sometimes. I'm also a red-blooded American female. I have drinks with guys now and then. I have dinner with guys now and then. We both agreed that we would do that since we're so far apart. I'm not screwing my clients, so lighten up a little on the schoolboy jealousy. I'd rather be with you, but I'm not. So long as we both want to keep up this here-today-gone-tomorrow relationship, we have to live with being apart."

"I don't like it," he said at last, crossing Park Avenue as a cold wind picked up and the streetlights came on. "Come up here this weekend. I miss the hell out of you."

"Brian," she said, "I miss the hell out of you too. Christmas is next week. You're coming back to Texas – right?" Both his family and hers were in Texas, so she knew he would be there.

"Yeah," he said, "but with your schedule I feel like I need an appointment to spend a day with you."

She laughed and said she'd reduce her rates for him. "I'll call you in a day or two, but I have to go now," she said, telling him she had to attend a cocktail party at the office of the firm's largest client, a major South American oil cartel. "I'll be home late, but don't worry about me. I'll be good if you will. Let's spend some quality time together next week when you're here."

She paused for a moment, and he finally said, "Good night, Nicole."

"I miss you a bunch" was her response, after which she ended the call.

# Chapter Eighteen

Brian arrived at Bijan Galleries a little earlier than usual the next morning. It was the week before Christmas, and he and Darius had a major sale in the works. A long-time customer who ran one of New York's major mutual funds had been in to look at a gold necklace which was reputed to have been worn by Anne Boleyn. Although not ancient by Bijan's standards, it was a truly historic piece which the firm had on consignment from a client in London. The provenance for the piece was a portrait painted in 1535, the year before Anne lost her head, literally, when Henry VIII decided it was time for a new wife. In that portrait, she was wearing what appeared to be this necklace.

Much work had been done by London firms to establish the age of the piece, and it had been determined in fact that it was sixteenth century. That was enough for most collectors. Bijan had a price of $1.5 million on the piece, and the mutual fund executive was scheduled in this morning for his third and hopefully last visit to see the extraordinary necklace.

By 10 a.m. Darius had not arrived, and the customer was due in thirty minutes. Coming in late without calling was unprecedented for

Darius. Brian tried his cell phone but it went straight to voicemail, indicating it was probably turned off. At 10:30 the customer arrived and Brian spent an hour with him in a private viewing room off to the side of the showroom. The fund manager used a jeweler's loupe to examine the piece and read closely the paperwork that authenticated it.

At last, the deal was consummated at $1.3 million. This would be a stunning Christmas gift for his wife, the man said. *A good Christmas gift for Bijan as well,* Brian thought. The profit to the firm on this item would be over four hundred thousand dollars. The man took Bijan's wire transfer information and made arrangements to pick up the necklace the following day, giving him time to obtain insurance to cover the piece when he accepted it. Until then, it would remain in Bijan's vault.

By mid-afternoon, Collette, Jason and Brian were very concerned about Darius. There had been no word whatsoever, which was totally unlike him. At Brian's direction, Jason was sent to Darius' apartment house while Collette began calling hospitals in Manhattan. When the two reported back, Collette said she had no luck with the hospital calls.

Jason said the doorman at Darius' residence had not seen him all day. The doorman had sent the super upstairs to ring Nazir's doorbell, but said they were not allowed to enter the apartment. No one had answered the door.

Brian went to Darius' office, looked in the massive Rolodex on his desk, and called Darius' son Christopher Nazir, an internist in San Francisco.

Once Brian told the receptionist it was an emergency, Christopher came on the line quickly. Brian explained that Darius had not been in the gallery today and they couldn't reach him. "Have you heard from him?" he asked.

The doctor said he had not, but that he would call his brother and phone Brian right back.

Within ten minutes Brian knew that Darius had made no contact. "I'm going to call the police," he told Christopher, who agreed that was a good idea. They exchanged cell phone numbers.

Around five p.m. a plainclothes detective from the Eighteenth Precinct rang the front buzzer. Collette admitted him. Brian saw a modern version of Columbo. The detective was dressed in a gray suit and a heavy black wool topcoat. It was snowing outside. He dusted flakes off as Jason took his coat from him. Brian introduced himself and the man said, "I'm Detective Simon Patterson. Is there some place we can talk?"

They settled in Brian's office and he gave the detective all the information he could about Darius Nazir. He furnished his home address, home and cell numbers, the contact information for his children, and spent half an hour talking about Darius' normal routine. He told the officer about today's sale, and how important it had been to Darius. Brian said Darius would not have missed that appointment. He said they had checked both apartment and hospitals, to no avail.

The detective asked Brian about himself, how long he had been with Bijan and how he had come to be there. He asked about the ownership of the gallery, and how it was doing financially. He told Brian he might need financial statements. Brian said, "Why are you asking all these questions that have nothing to do with Darius Nazir?"

The detective replied that there were lots of possible reasons for a person to disappear, and it was his job to think about all of them. Sometimes, he said, people disappeared when things were going badly. Other times, people disappeared when things were going well, and someone wanted them gone.

Brian assured him things were going very well financially at the gallery, and offered to provide financial statements if the detective wanted them.

After an hour the detective rose, shook Brian's hand and said, "You've been very helpful, Mr. Sadler. I may need to talk to you again soon. Do you plan to be in the City over the holidays?" Brian said he would stay in New York until the middle of next week, when he was flying to Texas for Christmas. He and the detective exchanged contact numbers. Patterson left, promising to be in touch when he knew something.

# Chapter Nineteen

As Brian exited the subway station for Gramercy Park, his cell phone rang. He recognized the San Francisco number as Christopher Nazir's.

"My brother Tom and I are coming on the redeye tonight," the doctor said. "We'll be at JFK tomorrow at 6:30 a.m."

Brian agreed to meet them at the gallery when they called.

At 2:45 a.m. Brian awoke from a fitful sleep, filled with disturbing dreams he couldn't quite recall. His cell phone was ringing. He answered and heard, "This is Detective Patterson, Mr. Sadler. I'm afraid I have some bad news for you. We've found Mr. Nazir's body." Brian fell back in bed, tears welling in his eyes.

The detective told him they had been required to wait twenty-four hours from the last known contact, before they could use force to enter Mr. Nazir's home. Since no one had heard from him all day yesterday, they went to Nazir's East 86th Street apartment after midnight and had the super open the door, after getting no response from repeated knocking.

Nazir appeared to have died in his sleep, the Detective said. Initial post-mortem examination by the medical examiner indicated he had been dead for at least 24 hours, and there were no visible signs of trauma on the body.

Brian told him that Nazir's two sons were en route to New York. Peterson said he would get the final medical examiner's report in a few days, but at this point the death was being considered to have been by natural causes. Still at the apartment, Peterson said he would leave a message for the Nazir sons to call, to wrap up a couple of things. He advised he would leave a uniformed officer at the scene until Nazir's sons arrived and determined where the body should be taken. Thanking him, Brian hung up, then dialed Christopher Nazir's cell number and left a voicemail for him to call as soon as they landed in New York.

Although Brian tried, there would be no more sleeping that night. Around 4, he finally gave up. He turned on his TV and sat transfixed in front of it, hearing nothing and thinking only about what would happen to Bijan Galleries now that Darius was gone. Brian couldn't possibly afford to buy Nazir's stake, so it was likely at this point Brian would be finding something else to do.

Thoughts of the excitement he felt every morning in the gallery mixed with the last days he had at W&T. He was so happy now, traveling around the world to make acquisitions for such a respected gallery – his gallery – that he couldn't imagine going back to a mundane life. But he was certain that was his next step. He could see no alternative.

# Chapter Twenty

Christopher Nazir called Brian as soon as the plane landed at JFK. Brian related what the policeman had said and offered his heartfelt condolence at the loss of their father. Dr. Nazir thanked him, then said they would go directly to their father's apartment instead of coming to the gallery this morning. Once they had made arrangements, they would call Brian to talk about short-term plans.

When Collette and Jason arrived at the gallery, Brian broke the news to them. They all shed tears at the loss of a good employer, and in Brian's case, a newly formed good friend. They tried to work, but found themselves discussing Darius with a few long-time customers who dropped in. It was difficult to concentrate on the office work he had to do, Brian discovered, so finally he stopped trying. Instead, he spent the rest of the morning on the showroom floor, talking with customers. A deep sense of sadness permeated every corner of his body. He would miss Darius Nazir very much.

Around 2:30 p.m. Christopher Nazir rang Brian and made arrangements for the brothers to meet him at the gallery in an hour. When they arrived, Collette and Jason hugged the two men, whom they had met before. Brian was surprised at the resemblance to their father, and again told them how much he would miss his friend and mentor.

Not sure whether to discuss business at this early stage, Brian ushered them in his office and waited for the men to begin. Christopher told him that he had spoken with Detective Patterson, who asked if there would be an autopsy. Since they were given a choice, and given the circumstances of his death, they decided against having it done. His body was taken to a funeral home, Christopher said. His father not being a religious man, Tom Nazir said the service would be on Monday at the funeral parlor. He also mentioned Darius was being cremated, which had been his wish.

Tom Nazir told Brian how fondly his father had spoken of him, and how much sincere friendship Darius had found since Brian's arrival a few months ago. "My father is a fairly private man," he said, "but we could hear the delight in his voice every time we talked. He was truly happy, which he had not been in a long time, perhaps even since our mother died."

The Nazir brothers explained to Brian that in the past month their father had made provisions for succession. He had done this only after he was convinced Brian was the right partner for him and the gallery. "Bijan owns a $5 million life insurance policy on my father," Christopher said. "It's payable to his estate, for the purpose of repurchasing his stock."

Brian sat dazed before the brothers. He understood how it would work - once the corporation paid $5 million to Darius Nazir's estate, the share certificate owned by Nazir would be cancelled, leaving Brian with 100% of the gallery's stock. A very simple plan, Brian thought, put into place by a very generous man. Darius had created a way for Brian to own the gallery without having to pay anything. And he hadn't even mentioned it to Brian. Tears flowed once again as Brian expressed his gratitude to his mentor. "It's exactly what my father wanted for you," Tom said. "He would be so proud to have you carry on the Bijan tradition."

They talked for another half hour, then the Nazir brothers left to visit relatives on Long Island for the weekend.

# Chapter Twenty One

Bijan Rarities closed Monday for Darius Nazir's funeral. Many of Bijan's clients were on hand, since an obituary had run in Sunday's New York Times. Since the Inkharaton sale, Darius had become much more high profile, especially in the small community of rare artifacts collectors. Brian had his cell phone turned off during the service. When he turned it on afterward, he had a text message. Clicking on it, he read "Payback completed."

"Mr. Sadler!" Collette took hold of his arm as she stood next to him on the sidewalk outside the funeral home. "You look as though you've just seen a ghost. Are you all right?"

"Yes . . . yes, I'm OK," Brian stammered, closing his cell phone. "I . . . I just ..."

At that moment John Spedino approached him, extending his hand. "My condolences at the passing of Mr. Nazir," he said. Thoughts swirled through Brian's head. First the text message. Then Spedino thirty seconds later. Brian couldn't respond to Spedino. He was speechless.

John Spedino smiled, turned and walked to a sedan waiting for him at the curb. The driver opened the door for him and they moved into traffic.

That afternoon, Brian took his cell phone to a computer tech center and asked a technician how he could tell the number from which the message was sent.

The tech looked things over and said, "It appears to have been sent from a blocked number in the 306 area code." Looking it up quickly in an online cross-reference, the tech said, "That's Saskatchewan, Canada."

Walking back to the gallery, Brian thought about the calls he'd received from the man with the gravelly voice, which appeared to come from all over. He knew that anyone can route a call using Skype or something similar, so the recipient would no idea where it really came from. The caller could be next door, and you'd think the call came from California.

# Chapter Twenty Two

The death of Darius Nazir began a new chapter in the life of Brian Sadler. In under seven months he had gone from investment banker to business owner. For a boy from Longview, Texas, he had come a long, long way, he thought to himself. Sitting alone in the darkened showroom after the funeral, gray afternoon slowly turning to drizzly winter evening, he looked around him at the gallery Darius Nazir had created, that now was his. Thoughts swirled through his head.

It was Monday, December 18. Christmas day was a week away, and he found himself randomly moving from highs to lows in his mind. Things *had* happened almost too easily: one day he worked for Darius, the next, thanks to a fortuitous set of events, he owned the gallery. One day he was a guy learning the ropes, next day he was the boss, calling the shots.

He thought about the words on his cell phone. Was someone trying to make him think they'd killed Darius to pave his way to becoming Bijan's owner? The police said Nazir died of natural causes. If there had been any hint of foul play, wouldn't the detective have been all over it? And now the body was gone, cremated. Regardless, he thought, who would want to kill Darius Nazir? It just didn't make any sense.

Ever the optimist, Brian Sadler consciously set aside the negative thoughts and began thinking about Christmas.

His phone rang. It was Nicole, saying she hoped he'd had an OK day, under the circumstances. Earlier, he had told her about the insurance policy and his sudden ownership of Bijan. He decided not to mention this afternoon's text message about payback. Some things were better left unsaid.

On this call they finalized earlier discussions they'd had on when to meet during the holidays. Bijan was closing Friday through Tuesday, as was Nicole's firm. They agreed to spend Thursday night together after he arrived in Dallas. By late Friday he wanted to be home in Longview, about a hundred miles east. She wanted to see her dad in Fort Worth, then she would fly to Houston on Saturday to spend the holiday with her mother and sister. They agreed to meet back up in Dallas on Christmas night, then he would fly to New York on Tuesday.

"Get some rest, honey," Nicole said as the call neared its end. "You've been under a lot of pressure, and now you've got a new set of things to think about as the sole owner of the gallery. I'm proud of you, and I can't wait to see you next week."

When the call was over, Brian took a quiet walk through the gallery, locked everything up and walked to Peking Duck House on 53rd Street for dinner. It was the place Darius had taken him the day they met, and it had become his favorite Chinese restaurant. He considered it a fitting tribute to go there on the day of Darius' funeral.

# Chapter Twenty Three

Thursday came and Brian headed to Texas for Christmas. He picked up a rental car at the airport and drove to her apartment. She had only been home a few minutes when he arrived, but she had his XO Martini waiting. Since they had been apart awhile, there was a brief period of hesitation on both their parts. Nicole had consciously decided not to mention the proposition Brian had considered, where he would rent bearer bonds. *Bringing that subject up won't help our short time together,* she had decided.

They discussed where to go for dinner, decided neither was that hungry, and shortly ended up where they both wanted to be, naked and entwined in her king sized bed.

Friday morning was crisp and cold. Nicole went for a run most mornings. Today Brian accompanied her, commenting on how few cars there were on the streets. A lot of people had obviously already started a long Christmas weekend. They ended up at Starbucks for coffee, then walked a block back to her place. "I'd like you to open your gift," she told him when they were back in bed with the morning paper and a fresh cup of coffee. She went to the closet and came out with an envelope. "It's not much, but I think it's something you'll like."

Brian tore the envelope open. Out fell two tickets to what had been advertised everywhere as the Honest-to-God, last ever, Pink Floyd Final Concert. Entertainment websites said the concert, scheduled for London in the spring, was the hardest event in history to snag a ticket for.

"Incredible! How on earth did you get these?" he asked, dumbfounded.

"I know what a fan you are, since his posters are on your bedroom wall, and I've obviously been in your bedroom," she laughed. "The firm represents a company that's responsible for booking the concert, and I was able to get two tickets. Do you like my gift?"

"It's fantastic! I can hardly wait. But I wonder who I can get to go with me?"

She hit him on the arm and jumped on top of him. *"I'm* going with you, unless you have some little twenty-something up there in New York you're hiding away."

"Well, I guess I have to take you," he responded. "After all, you gave me the tickets. Seriously, thanks so much. This will be a wonderful trip."

He got up and walked to his computer case. He pulled out an envelope. "Now open your present," he said, tossing it to Nicole.

"Another envelope? You're copying me!" she said, sitting up in bed and tearing it open expectantly.

Inside was a booklet Brian had made on the computer. The front cover said, "Join me at the 4-S Resort."

Nicole stared at it for a minute. "The 4-S Resort? I've never heard of it."

"Keep going," Brian said.

The first page had a big S, and a clip art picture showing snow falling. "So the first S is snow," she said. The next page featured another big S and a picture of people skiing. "Oh, boy!" she said. She turned the page. There was another S and a clip art photo of the Alps. At the bottom it said, "Welcome to Switzerland." She was getting really excited, and turned the page. The last big S had no picture. At the bottom were small words that said, "Let's go to Switzerland and Ski in the Snow. When we get back to our room, I bet you can figure out what the fourth S is."

She looked at him, laughing. "Yeah, I would say our sex is so good, it should have a capital S."

"You got it, babe," he said.

She turned to him, pulling off her sweatshirt and unhooking her sports bra. "That's a great present, Brian. And you're so incredibly clever, doing it yourself on the computer. I just love the idea of a ski vacation! I've never been to Switzerland, but I'm ready to go with you whenever we can work it out."

She tugged down her sweatpants and panties, kicking them off onto the floor. "Get your clothes off, buddy. Let's practice on the last S, then we can talk about when we're going skiing!"

# PART FOUR

## Chapter One

EZE VILLAGE,
FRENCH RIVIERA

Eze Village is a beautiful medieval town situated high on a cliff overlooking the Mediterranean Sea. The busy Moyenne Corniche, one of three main roads between Nice and the principality of Monaco, runs below it. Tourists sometimes stop to see the ruins of the twelfth century fortified castle and have lunch on tiny winding streets in the adjacent village.

The man sat sipping a coffee and reading *Le Monde,* as was his custom each morning. He lived nearby and strolled each day to the restaurant. As he read, he failed to notice the two men dressed in suits who were standing half a block down the narrow street, watching him. Comparing his face to a picture one of them held, they confirmed his identity and crossed the street.

There were only a few patrons sitting in the outdoor restaurant at this early hour. The man looked up from his newspaper as the two approached his table. "Francois Rochefort," one said in French, "we are from the Surete and you are under arrest."

# Chapter Two

Other than a long weekend in London for the Pink Floyd Final Concert, Brian and Nicole managed to see each other only four times in five months. Twice Brian returned from a trip to Europe and hopped on the American flight to Dallas instead of going directly back to New York. He was able to spend the weekend with Nicole both times. She had a business trip to New York once, and went a second time on the spur of the moment.

The date for their ski trip had been set and postponed twice. They finally decided to put it off until the fall because of the difficulty coordinating their schedules. Nicole and Brian talked about where things were going with them. They decided their relationship, if it could be called that, was far less than ideal, but they were career professionals.

"If we're meant to be together one way or another," Nicole said one evening in New York, "then it'll all work out. Absence makes the heart grow fonder, they say."

Brian snorted, agreeing that this beat nothing, but not by far. Neither of them could see a way to change things, so things stayed as they were.

# Chapter Three

In mid-February Chaim Weisenberg left Brian a message, asking him to return the call, and referring to "The Project." Interesting, Brian thought. That was John Spedino's code name for the bond deal – Weisenberg obviously was hooked up with him somehow.

The bonds were set to be transferred whenever he wanted, Brian learned from his call, once he executed the paperwork. Weisenberg told Brian it would take about ten days from start to finish.

Brian had heard nothing from Spedino about the relics themselves. The rumors of the existence of a Jesus scroll surfaced from time to time. And in the past couple of weeks, a contact had called from Cairo, asking for Darius. Brian looked him up in the Rolodex as he told the man that Darius had died, and that he was now the owner of the gallery.

"But I do not know you," the Egyptian said. "We must meet when you are next in Egypt. Until then, I will say that I have some information about a scroll naming Jesus himself which may become available. I can tell you no more until we have met."

Collette had told Brian recently that he needed to make a trip to Egypt. "You've met so many of our contacts and sources already, but only in western Europe and China," she said. "I can set all your appointments and in a week, you can establish all the contacts Darius had in Egypt."

Learning from Collette's call that the new owner of Bijan Rarities was coming to Cairo, Salid Mushtaf spent hours considering how best to approach the sale of the rarities. He was nothing more than an intermediary, but he had solid information about who owned the three relics. He placed a call to the man. As always, the man's voice shook Salid for a fleeting moment. It was rough, steely and menacing.

Salid told the man he could help him sell the relics. The man did not acknowledge having them, but instead said, "What business is this of yours?"

Salid responded that he was in contact with one of the top galleries in the world, a firm which likely could and would purchase the items.

The man laughed. "You? Do you think a man like yourself can have contacts that I do not possess?" The laughter stopped. "Perhaps a worm like yourself may have value to me after all," the man finally said in a quiet voice. "Make your contact. If you have anything interesting to report to me, do so at once." He hung up, leaving Salid to wonder if his having made the call was a good idea or not.

# Chapter Four

Three weeks later, Brian sat in the lobby of the Nile Hilton. Beautifully decorated in white marble, the expansive area was a quiet haven from the bustling activity just outside the front doors. He wore a tan linen suit with a yellow tie. He had described what he would wear to the contact with whom he had spoken in New York, and he saw a man approaching him, wearing a white galabayeh and a light blue scarf on his head. "Mr. Sadler?" he asked.

Brian stood, introducing himself and asking the man if he wished to move into the bar for a drink.

"Not for me, sir," he said. "I am a practicing Muslim and I must abstain in order to be ready for evening prayers shortly."

They sat in the lobby. The contact, who said his name was Salid Mushtaf, asked Brian about Darius. He told Brian how much he had personally respected Nazir, one of his countrymen, and a man of high integrity when it came to making deals. "I have located artifacts for him. I have given him clues about the whereabouts of others. I have passed along rumors. Always, he generously rewarded me for the value of the thing I did to help him. He made us Egyptians, his fellow countrymen, proud to be associated with him."

Brian had heard similar comments from others with whom he had spoken after Darius' death. He knew Nazir had played the relics game close to the edge – and maybe over it sometimes. But he certainly treated his contacts well, paying attention to those who could help. It meant they might call you first when the unique artifact turned up.

After coffee and small talk about America, Brian eased into the topic. "Tell me about the Bethlehem Scroll," he said.

Mushtaf looked all around him, then lowered his voice to a whisper, even though there were only a dozen other people in the massive lobby, none of whom was nearby. He told Brian that there was a man who was reputed to have three relics associated with the birth of Jesus. "One is said to be a scroll like the others found near the Dead Sea. It is the Bethlehem Scroll – the one which relates the shepherd boy's tale. The second is a small piece of parchment which describes the third thing, a coin said to have been held by Jesus himself."

The astonishment on Brian's face was not lost on his guest. "These things will be very costly, Sahib," the Arab said, using the traditional term of respect. "I am a humble man. I know how to acquire the relics, and for my knowledge you will pay me one hundred thousand American dollars." As he spoke, Salid glanced around the lobby again, obviously frightened of something.

Brian followed his eyes, wondering what he was looking for. "That is a great deal of money," Brian responded, negotiating. "I have other brokers with whom I am meeting. I doubt the information you have for me will be worth nearly that much."

Brian asked how the owner of the relics had come into possession of them.

"I am not at liberty to say," was the response. Salid's evasive answer worried Brian. Did this man have any information at all?

Was he merely fishing for a commission? Brian knew Darius had dealt with Salid at least twice in the past, although the deals had involved funerary relics from pharonic tombs of the twenty-second dynasty. These had been nothing on the scale of the scroll relics. But then, if the scrolls and coin were real, there had never been a sale in history which would rival this transaction.

Brian told Salid that authentication of the relics was the key to determining his interest in making the purchase. Salid responded that authenticity was not an issue, and Brian asked him if he had seen the artifacts personally.

The Egyptian dodged the question. He merely said, "All things in good time, Mr. Sadler. I will contact you when the time is right." He glanced right and left again.

His nervousness finally caused Brian to ask what was wrong. "I must go now," was all Salid would say in response.

He watched Salid leave the hotel. He doubted this shabbily dressed individual was truly involved in the transaction to move the relics. Brian had spent enough time negotiating in Cairo's Khan el Khalili bazaar to recognize Salid for what he was – a man who had a piece or two of information, perhaps enough to generate a small commission for himself, and which would likely result in Salid's introducing Brian to the owner of the relics.

Brian headed across the lobby to the elevator banks, heading to his room to check emails on his laptop. Near the front desk, a man called his name. Turning, Brian saw Phillip Edmonds, Sothebys' primary acquisitions man for ancient Middle Eastern items. Edmonds was headquartered in London. Brian had met him twice in the past few months, most recently when they both attended a sale at Sothebys in New York.

"Checking in?" Brian asked as they shook hands.

"In fact, I am," Edmonds responded. "Fancy meeting you here.

What's up in your world?"

"Just working on some deals," Brian said casually.

The desk clerk handed Edmonds his passkey. "Want to join me in a cup of tea?" he asked Brian.

Getting a nod, Edmonds walked to the concierge desk and dropped his luggage with instructions to put the cases in his room. As the men walked toward the restaurant, the front door of the Hilton flew open and the doorman shouted a command in his native tongue. "My God," Phillip Edmonds said. "He just ordered the front desk clerk to call an ambulance."

They walked to the door. A crowd had gathered a block away from the hotel, where the short street serving it adjoined the bustling Nile Corniche. Brian and Phillip moved closer. A policeman walked around the corner and took control, pushing the crowd back. "What happened here?" he asked the onlookers.

Phillip translated for Brian as the response came. "It seems a man was struck by a hit and run driver," he said. "This is extremely common in Cairo, I'm afraid. No one watches the pedestrians, and no one controls the maniacs who drive."

As the policeman gestured with a nightstick, the throng moved back. Brian looked at the figure lying on the ground. His galabayeh was bloody, and Brian immediately recognized the light blue head adornment. It was Salid Mushtaf and he was not moving.

"I . . . I just had a meeting with that man," Brian blurted out. "Should I tell the policeman who he is?"

"My advice? Keep out of it," Phillip said. "If you say anything, you'll spend the rest of today at the police station. Who is he, anyway?"

Brian hesitated, then said, "A man who said he had some information for me."

"About the Bethlehem Scroll?" Phillip replied, staring at Brian.

Brian jerked his head around and looked at Edmonds.

"Hey, old man," Phillip said, taking Brian's arm lightly and moving him back toward the hotel. "You have a lot to learn about this business. It's a small world out there, especially in Egyptian circles. Who was this guy? Was it Ahmed? Mohammed? Salid?"

All these names were people with whom Brian had appointments. "Yeah, Salid," he responded quietly.

As they reached the hotel, the increasing rise and fall of a blaring siren indicated the ambulance was very near. The two westerners stood in front of the Hilton and watched as the vehicle arrived and the crew took a look at Salid. They lifted him onto a gurney and covered his body with a sheet, closing the vehicle's back door and moving back into traffic, no siren now required.

Brian was speechless. His face was ashen. Phillip Edmonds said, "Come on. Let's have that cup of tea. You need to get hold of yourself." They sat and talked. "I'm sure you and Salid were talking about what he knew, or said he knew, about the Bethlehem Scroll. I had a meeting with Salid tomorrow myself, so don't feel too privileged, my boy," Phillip smiled.

"But . . ." Brian said, "do you think there's any significance to Salid's accident and our meeting just moments before?"

"Don't be too hard on yourself, old man," Edmonds responded. "It was a coincidence, I'm sure. I'd wager ten or twenty people a day die in Cairo after being struck by vehicular traffic. You were unfortunate enough to have witnessed one first-hand."

The conversation shifted to business. Phillip told Brian that there was a network of people in northern Egypt who made a livelihood of watching and listening. Sometimes they had good intel, sometimes not. Darius, he said, was a master at dealing in Egypt, because he was a native and was trusted. "I have to say," Phillip said, "I was as shocked about Darius' untimely passing as anyone, but he was the most formidable opponent I had in the business, and life will be easier without his one-upping me all the time." He looked at Brian. "In seriousness, Darius was a good man, Brian. He played close to the edge most of the time, but he was not a cheat. His word was his bond."

They talked about how small the world of Middle Eastern antiquities really was. "I win some deals, I lose some to you or others," Phillip told him. "But we're all gentlemen, graciously accepting our victories, and not crying over our defeats."

They finished their drinks and promised to meet up again during the week if time permitted. Back in his room, Brian instructed Collette by email to change the venue of the remaining meetings. He had no intention of parading his guests into the lobby for Phillip Edmonds to see, and he was sure Edmonds wouldn't do so either. He also informed her of the death of Salid Mushtaf.

Collette moved Brian's meetings to the Sheraton Cairo hotel in Galae Square. Over the next three days, Brian met ten other men like Salid. Some of them were dealers in their own rights. Others were obviously middle-men, intermediaries who could facilitate a deal between a willing buyer and seller. Although the Bethlehem Scroll was of paramount interest to Brian, he chose not to initiate discussion of it with any of these men, knowing how things would go. They would feign knowledge, gathering as much information from Brian as they could, then go into the marketplace and try to ascertain how to get hold of these relics themselves. It could do nothing but muddy the waters, Brian thought.

Brian met Phillip Edmonds for a quick drink on Thursday evening. They talked about business in general, consciously avoiding discussing their whereabouts and meetings during this week in Egypt. Phillip left for a dinner. Brian had a steak and a bottle of Cabernet Sauvignon in the hotel's dining room, then went upstairs to pack for his departure the next morning.

Brian was taking the Delta flight to Paris and changing planes for New York, arriving Friday evening. His wake-up call came sooner than he expected. As he groped around for the phone he glanced at the bedside clock. It showed 3:30 a.m., three hours earlier than the time he had requested.

When he answered, he heard the gravelly voice which had awakened him at this same time back in New York. "Mr. Sadler," the man said, "I have the items you seek. Come to the Muslim Quarter, to the entrance of the Citadel, at noon today." The caller disconnected abruptly as usual. Brian bolted out of bed, wide awake. His heart was racing. He had to stop and think about what he was getting into. He associated nothing good with the calls from the gravelly voice. How did this person know what items Brian sought? For that matter, what items was he even talking about? Brian presumed the Bethlehem Scroll was the topic for discussion, assuming he chose to change his flight and go to the meeting place. But Brian also knew this was a meeting he could not afford to miss.

# Chapter Five

The concierge efficiently handled swapping all of Brian's flights from Friday to Saturday. By mid-morning, Brian was wandering the narrow, winding streets of the Muslim Quarter. Some were cobbled; others were unpaved. Many people he passed held out their hands, asking for a coin. Others touched him lightly. Being an American, this close proximity to people made him extremely uncomfortable. *I need my space*, he unconsciously thought.

He avoided eye contact, moving quickly along. He wanted to get to the Citadel early enough to figure exactly where he should go. He wondered how he would recognize his contact. He thought the voice was American, so he figured perhaps it would not be so difficult.

He held a map in his hand as he moved through Old Town, as the area was known. He had asked the taxi to drop him ten blocks from his destination so he could tour the area, but he wondered now if it had been a bad decision. He consciously avoided the eastern fringe of the Muslim Quarter. The hotel concierge had advised him the city's worst slums were there and told him it was no place for a westerner. As he moved closer to the Citadel, he found himself deeper and deeper into crowded streets with ragged men, women and children, all pushing and shoving. With only a block to go, he weaved his way through a throng of people, many of whom groped at his sleeves or touched his hands. At last he emerged onto the spacious square where the Citadel stood.

He looked at the building, begun by Salah-ad-Din, better known to westerners as Saladin, in 1170 as a fortress against the invading Crusaders. Its towers rose nearly a hundred feet into the air. Brian walked toward the entrance, which was marked by a ticket booth and signs in English and Arabic. He reached into his pocket for money to purchase a ticket and realized his pocket had been picked, probably in the melee of people just before he got to the square. He was glad he had planned for such an event and had therefore lost only a few Egyptian pounds.

Brian bent down and reached into the top of his sock, pulling out several twenty pound notes. He used one of them to buy a ticket, then entered the massive fortress. There were hundreds of tourists milling about, most of whom were westerners. He heard English being spoken all around him and he wondered how he would ever link up with this man. He found a shady spot near a drink vendor and sat on a low wall to wait.

Precisely at noon, a short Egyptian in a galabayeh walked to Brian and said, "Mr. Sadler?"

Brian acknowledged, and he said, "Follow me, please."

They walked out of the Citadel and crossed the square to a small restaurant filled with tourists. The man took Brian to an empty outdoor table and said, "Sit here, please." As Brian did, the man abruptly left.

Brian saw a man crossing the square. He was portly, wearing a faded suit that had once been a lighter shade of tan than now.

He wore a hat which covered his face. He walked directly to the table, sat down and removed his fedora. Brian looked at him. The deep pockmarks on his face were startling. Brian struggled to avoid looking surprised.

The man appeared not to notice. "You seek the Bethlehem Scroll," he said, the gravelly, raspy voice unmistakable to Brian.

"You! I want to know who's directing you to make your phone calls to me," he blurted.

Without warning, the fat man slammed his hand down on the table. "You will not talk!" the man said. "You will listen!"

The man pulled a sheaf of folded papers from inside his jacket. "This is a photocopy of the scroll. You may take this back to New York. Also I have given you copies of a rough translation. You may authenticate any way you wish."

Brian took the papers and opened them. The copy of the scroll was hard to read. Obviously the original had been faded from age. It was filled with writing in a language which appeared from Brian's experience to be Aramaic or ancient Hebrew. The two were very similar, but he felt this was probably Aramic.

The translation was a copy of a notepad on which someone appeared to have taken a stab at translating the document.

"Where are these documents now?" Brian asked.

The man looked at him. "Did you understand me when I told you not to talk? Say nothing to me. Nothing."

"There are three items. The scroll, of which you have a copy and translation; a coin; and a scrap of parchment which identifies the coin as having been held by the newborn Yeshua. The price for these three items is twenty five million U.S. dollars. It is not negotiable. You are the only person to whom I am making this offer at this time. If you do not purchase the items within thirty days, my offer is withdrawn. I will contact you on Friday, two weeks from today. You will tell me then if you are buying the items. If so, you will meet me in Cairo exactly two weeks thereafter. I will provide instructions for the transfer when I speak to you in two weeks."

The man stood. "Please do not be foolish, Mr. Sadler. Do not attempt to ascertain who I am, or how I came to acquire the artifacts. You are in a truly unique position. Take advantage of it. If you fail to do so, you will never see me or this opportunity again."

The man walked away, turning immediately into one of the crowded side streets off the square. A waiter brought the check. Brian used another of his bills to pay for it, then hailed one of the taxis sitting in a queue near the Citadel. During the ride to the hotel, he thought through the instructions the man had given him, and the things he had to do to make this all work.

# Chapter Six

Brian's excitement was almost uncontrollable as he read the translation while flying to New York. Back in his office, Brian made yet another copy of the scroll document, then used scissors to cut all but a few lines from it. He asked Collette to run the document over to New York University, where Bijan retained the services of a man who was fluent in several ancient languages.

By the next morning, Brian had confirmation that the translation he had received was accurate, at least insofar as it pertained to the small portion of the scroll text Brian had been willing to show to someone else. Brian could hardly keep the information to himself. He wanted to share it with Collette and Jason, to tell them the incredible good fortune which was coming to Bijan, but he felt compelled to keep things quiet for now. He knew Collette would wonder how the firm could afford to swing a deal like this, so it was best not to say anything yet.

He called Chaim Weisenberg and asked him to set in motion the Israeli bond rental, in the amount of twenty five million dollars. Since it was late July, Weisenberg suggested they date the transaction, and he would deliver the documentation for the transaction, on

August 1. Brian calculated that the bonds had to be on and off his books by mid September at the very latest, to allow him to present a clean balance sheet for his quarterly report to the Securities and Exchange Commission.

Brian called the number John Spedino had left for him. It was answered on the second ring.

"Yes?"

Brian said, "I'm calling about The Project." He told Spedino of his meeting in Cairo and the photocopies he now possessed. "You need to see these, to convince yourself of their authenticity, before we move forward," Brian said.

Spedino's response surprised Brian. "They're real," John Spedino said. "How much is he asking for them?"

Brian told him, then asked, "How do you know they're real? You haven't even seen them."

Ignoring his question, Spedino said, "As we agreed, I will give you two million dollars' profit, making my total purchase price $27 million. How have you arranged to retrieve the documents?"

Brian outlined the instructions he had received from the pockmarked man.

"Call me the minute you have the artifacts," Spedino instructed. "I'll wire your money to Bijan's account in London, and you can bring the items back to New York to me."

Brian asked for the name of the contact at First InterCity Bank. Spedino gave him a name and number.

"Don't call the banker until you have the bond documents and are ready to do the transaction," he told Brian.

"You mentioned the favorable publicity which Bijan will get from this transaction," Brian reminded Spedino. "Will I make the initial announcement when we have purchased the artifacts?"

Spedino told him the announcement would come, but only

after Brian had handed the items over to the Vatican. "I'm staying out of the picture," he said. "Your publicity will come when you hand the scroll and the coin to the Archbishop of New York. He'll be expecting you."

When the call ended, Brian was astonished at the trust Spedino had put in him and in the man from Egypt. He hadn't hesitated a moment before declaring the items authentic, even though he had seen nothing which would assure himself of that. As he thought about it, he began to figure out what was going on.

# Chapter Seven

The day he received the original Israeli bond documents, Brian took them to the banker he had contacted at First InterCity Bank. The man gave the documents nothing more than a cursory glance. He opened a file, then had Brian sign loan documents for $25 million, including his personal guarantee – "it's only a procedural thing," the banker said when Brian questioned the personal indemnity, which had not been discussed previously. The whole thing was as simple as getting a car loan, Brian thought to himself. His hand shook as he signed for more money than he had dreamed possible only months ago.

Brian gave the banker the wire transfer instructions for Bijan's London account. He had decided the entire transaction would be done from there instead of in New York. Perhaps it made no difference, Brian reasoned, but in a pinch, at least a U.S. banking transaction couldn't be hung around his neck by regulators. Stifling such negative thoughts, the optimistic Brian Sadler moved ahead.

At the gallery, Brian confirmed receipt of the funds from First InterCity, then he instructed Collette to wire $250,000 to a bank account in the Isle of Man. Chaim Weisenberg had provided instructions on where to send the first installment on the rental fee for the bonds.

Brian awoke at 3:30 a.m. the Friday morning which was two weeks after his meeting in Egypt with the pockmarked man. He stared at his cell phone, surprised when no call came.

Around ten that morning, Collette advised Brian he had an overseas call. Brian took it, and the raspy voice said, "Do we have a deal, Mr. Sadler?"

"You already know we do," Brian responded. There was silence for a moment.

"Whatever you think you have figured out, Mr. Sadler," the man said slowly, "remember this. Curiosity kills not only cats. And people who become too smart are liabilities, not assets." The man told Brian he would meet him at the same restaurant outside the Citadel in Cairo in two weeks, and gave Brian instructions how the money was to be transferred.

# Chapter Eight

Several days later Brian received a call from an attaché at the Embassy of Israel in New York. The man told Brian that he had received word that Bijan was acquiring some artifacts that may have been stolen from Israeli soil, and the Ambassador was interested in speaking with Brian before any potential sale of the relics occurred. Brian asked for specifics on the items in question. The attaché responded that he had been told there were relics that had been found near the Dead Sea and which were attributed to Jesus. "It is our understanding, Mr. Sadler, that these items may have been exported illegally from Israel," he said.

Brian told the man that he was unable to comment about any such artifacts, or to confirm whether any transactions were imminent. He was sure, however, that his response was not the end to this inquiry. A quick call to the attorney who represented Bijan provided Brian the path he needed to take. Brian placed a call to John Spedino and within forty-eight hours, he was told that when the artifacts were delivered, original export documents, duly processed by Israeli customs, would accompany them.

# Chapter Nine

Settled back in his seat on the British Airways flight to Cairo, Brian ran through the scenario he had figured out. The first clue Brian had that something was fishy was a set of notes he had found in Darius Nazir's desk.

John Spedino was far more than an occasional, indirect customer of the gallery. He had invested significant money in the venture and, prior to the public offering, Darius had bought him out. Brian figured that even though Spedino was no longer an investor and partner, anyone who got into bed with a Mafia figure had to plan on staying there forever. At least from what Brian had read, there was never a way out. It was a deal with the devil, made for life. And Darius Nazir apparently had made it. Brian surmised that Nazir had paid the ultimate price.

It was obvious that the pockmarked man with the raspy voice worked for John Spedino. All of his calls and text messages were either veiled threats or payback announcements – things Brian had decided long ago were the orchestration of the mobster. But if the man from Cairo worked for Johnny Speed, why hadn't he just handed the artifacts over to Spedino himself? Why the need for this complicated set of financial transactions, where Spedino basically ended up paying $27 million for something he could have had for nothing?

The answer had come to Brian late one night. It was all a big, complicated money laundering scheme, with a way for Spedino to use clean money for a massive tax writeoff. Brian figured John Spedino had pocketed around $25 million from the Bellicose Holdings public offering. When Francois Rochefort, the puppet head of the company, had disappeared with the company's funds, everyone – even the FBI – believed the cash went to Spedino. But no one could ever prove it.

And now Spedino was paying $25 million plus a two million dollar kicker to Bijan, for the privilege of buying artifacts he already owned. That purchase both established that the scrolls and the coin had been purchased legitimately, and it created an established value in the marketplace for the relics. Both of those would be required in order for Spedino to make a tax deductible donation to the Vatican.

Twenty-seven million dollars of Spedino's legitimate income was paid out in a tax deductible transaction. He could therefore earn a great deal more legitimate income without paying income tax on it, thanks to this one donation.

And when things were all finished, Spedino still had $25 million, all of the money he had paid less his commission to Bijan, because whatever Brian wired to the pockmarked man went right back to Spedino, ultimately.

Brian felt certain that delivery of the artifacts would be accomplished without a hitch. If the pockmarked man was actually Spedino's associate, there was no reason for things to go wrong.

# Chapter Ten

The gravelly voiced man had set the meeting time for noon, presumably so that a wire transfer could take place that same day. Brian sat at the same table in the square surrounding the Citadel. The massive building blocked the sun, throwing that side of the square into shadows. He watched for the arrival of the portly man. Instead, a ragged beggar approached his table. Brian reached into his pocket for a coin, but the man whispered to him, "Follow me."

The beggar took Brian through winding streets, stopping suddenly at a wooden door. He pushed the door open and motioned for Brian to step inside, then wandered off down the street. Brian was in a courtyard. The fat, pockmarked man sat in a chair under a date tree about fifty feet from him. A briefcase rested on the ground at his side.

There was an empty chair next to the man. Brian sat down, and the man reached in his valise, pulling out an oilcloth and a small cloth bag. He dumped the black lump into Brian's hand and said, "This is the coin. In the cloth are the scrolls." Brian opened the cloth and looked with wonder on the larger scroll. Shivers went down his spine as he thought of the hands that had penned the words over two thousand years before.

The man handed Brian a set of formal documents, printed in Hebrew and English, which he said were the export papers the Embassy would require. Brian looked them over. They were identical to many others he had seen since he had begun his work with Darius Nazir.

As agreed, Brian took out his cell phone and called Collette in New York. It was very early there, but she was standing by as he had instructed. He gave her the go-ahead to initiate a wire transfer from Bijan's bank in London, per instructions he had left for her.

He then called John Spedino and told him to wire his money to London. Within minutes, Brian received an email confirmation on his cell phone that showed Spedino's $27 million had been received into Bijan's account from National Bank of Switzerland's Geneva head office.

While they waited, the fat man took out a cigarette and smoked it. Brian looked around the courtyard. There appeared to be no one nearby, and he could hear no sounds from any of the second-story windows that opened into the area in which they sat. The entire building appeared to be deserted.

About twenty minutes later, the pockmarked man's cell phone rang. He answered, speaking quickly in Egyptian, and hung up. "Done," he said to Brian, standing up and walking out of the courtyard into the street. He closed the door behind him.

Brian stood, picked up the briefcase and followed him. By the time he reached the narrow roadway, he saw no sign of the man.

# Chapter Eleven

*Once I'm finished with this transaction, I'm sticking with the straight and narrow,* Brian thought to himself as he lay in the first class SleeperSeat. The British Airways 777 was winging its way from London to New York, the last leg in his trip from Cairo with the artifacts. Brian kept the briefcase lightly tethered to his wrist, even though the first class section was quiet and people were napping or watching movies at their seats.

He had made a decision to break ties with John Spedino. The transaction they were completing with Brian's delivery of the artifacts was an incredible windfall to Johnny Speed, by Brian's calculations. He could now declare an incredible amount of legitimate income without having to pay income tax on it, and have almost all the money left when it was over.

Even though dealing with Spedino was distasteful in one respect, Brian felt a sense of pride in knowing that he was helping ensure that the world's most precious documents, the account of Jesus Christ's birth, would end up in the Vatican where they would be preserved and kept safe for generations to come. At least that was the plan.

The afternoon sun shone through the windows of the restricted area as Brian had walked from the plane to the customs booths in the Arrivals Hall. After removing the tether from his briefcase as instructed, he sat it on the floor next to him as he waited in line. The Semitic family who had been in first class moved along in a line next to him. The man smiled and nodded absently as Brian's eyes met his for a moment. Then their line curved away from his. Brian had picked up his case and moved along in line, thinking of nothing but the future.

Now Brian sat in a small room with only a table and two chairs, in a holding area for United States Customs at JFK Airport. "Why are you detaining me?" Brian asked. "The Arab family who stood next to me in line has switched cases with me. Why aren't you trying to help me? I'm a U.S. citizen, and the items in that case are priceless!"

The agent explained carefully that although Brian now apparently had nothing to declare, his earlier statements, the tether on his wrist, and his agitation at seeing the empty briefcase caused them to determine that they would temporarily detain him until they reviewed videotapes and got to the bottom of the matter. He took detailed notes as Brian described the three artifacts which had been in the briefcase.

Brian asked if he could call his attorney. The agent said that was OK, but that Brian probably would be there less than a half hour longer if everything turned out satisfactorily. Brian decided to wait. From her location in Dallas, Nicole couldn't have moved things any faster than that even if she started immediately.

Leaving Brian alone, the agent left for about thirty minutes. "Mr. Sadler," he said upon his return, handing Brian his passport, "I want to take you to the office of the Airport Police. Your story checks out in every respect. The videotape clearly shows what appears to be a Middle Eastern family next to you in line. The man does in fact switch briefcases with you, then within a couple of minutes, he switches lanes. The people who apparently formed his family are now in their line, and he is by himself in his. He moves quickly through Customs, since he has no baggage to declare. He is actually an Israeli. We have his information but were not able to locate him, as he left the airport by a private car which our videotape shows had diplomatic license plates.

"His so-called family is a different story. We also have videotapes of them as well. They exited Customs, but then went straight to check-in for Air India's flight to London and presented return tickets. We have them in custody now."

The agent opened the door and accompanied Brian to the JFK Airport Police desk, where for another thirty minutes an officer completed a report. The customs agent remained there, giving the policeman all the information he had earlier provided to Brian, including the license number of the embassy vehicle which had whisked away the thief.

As Brian left the police desk, the customs agent gave him a phone number and promised to be in touch if they heard anything more. He apologized for detaining Brian and wished him luck in finding the artifacts.

Once the agent left, Brian stood outside the terminal and called John Spedino's number on his phone. In five minutes, he gave Spedino the facts of where things stood at the moment, hoping he could find the Israeli thief easier than the police could. But the response was unexpected.

# Chapter Twelve

"You don't have the artifacts?" John Spedino said slowly. "You're telling me the goddamned artifacts were stolen?"

Brian could feel the hatred in his words.

"Let me tell you something, mister," Spedino said. "You are going to wire my money back on Monday morning. Do you understand me?"

Brian hesitated.

"DO YOU UNDERSTAND ME?" Spedino shouted.

"Mr. Spedino," Brian said, his voice quivering, "you know all about the transaction that I just finished to get this whole thing done. You know those Israeli bonds won't stand up to scrutiny if I have them on my books September 30th. You helped me set this whole thing up. I can't wire your money back. I need you to help me find the guy who stole them."

There was a lengthy silence. "Brian," John Spedino said evenly, "your mother and father live in Longview, Texas. Your father runs the newspaper there. They're nice people. They're both healthy. I presume you'd do everything in your power to keep them that way. Listen to me. It's Friday. On Monday, you are going to either deliver the artifacts to me or wire my money back, you little bastard."

"Mr. Spedino," Brian said, his voice shaking. "I need your help. You have to find the relics. You have the resources to do it. I don't." Spedino said nothing else. He merely hung up. Brian stood at curbside, staring at his cell phone. He was terrified, and had nowhere to turn.

As Brian rode the cab to Manhattan, his mind raced. He had to figure a way out of this mess he was in. His optimism couldn't fail him now, although he couldn't think of much to be optimistic about.

# Chapter Thirteen

Brian lay in bed. The 3:30 a.m. call had unnerved him almost to the breaking point. The raspy voice said, "Remember how Darius Nazir just died in his sleep? He dared to tell somebody to stay away from you, Mr. Sadler. Something as simple as that, and now he's dead. For you it's much more serious. If you don't perform on Monday, you better never sleep again with both eyes closed."

"Hey," Brian responded. "Remember me? I bought the scrolls from you." There was no sound. Finally the call disconnected. It had come from the 319 area code. Brian didn't even bother to look it up. He knew the caller was in Egypt.

On Monday Brian called the customs agent, who told him the woman and children had been deported to Israel. "We spent quite a bit of time with them," the agent said, "and it was obvious they were recruited to do nothing more than accompany the thief on the flight and pose as his family. The woman's family was given ten thousand dollars, and she got a free ride to New York City and back, with her two kids."

He further said that the Israeli Embassy had gotten involved in the mechanics of her deportation, as was customary, so he had also asked them about the diplomatic vehicle that had taken the man away from JFK. "They advised that that license plate was not registered to the Embassy. We figure the driver could have altered a stolen plate. At any rate, we have nothing on this individual. His passport was fraudulent, although a very good forgery."

Going online, Brian checked to see that Spedino's funds were still in the London bank account. The money was there, but Brian couldn't return it to Spedino. If he did, he would be required to cash in the Israeli bonds to repay his bank loan with First InterCity. He felt certain that transaction would never occur. Whether real or not, the bonds were meant for one thing only – to be used as assets to prop up a balance sheet. They weren't going to be cashed in to help Brian or anyone else, he was sure.

If he defaulted on the loan with First InterCity, his personal guarantee would kick in, and he would lose Bijan Rarities. If the SEC or any other agency looked closely at the bond transaction and it failed to pass muster, Brian was afraid that he might face jail time for fraud. He knew when he did the deal the bonds weren't great, but this was a quick in-and-out deal, and nobody would get hurt. At least that had been the plan.

At 1 p.m. Collette forwarded a call to Brian. "The caller says its urgent, and he won't tell me who he is," she said.

Brian took the call and heard John Spedino's voice. "I don't have my money," he said tersely, "and I don't have my scrolls and coin. So what's the plan, buddy boy?"

"Do you have any idea where the artifacts are?" Brian asked.

"I'm not your errand boy. I'm your client. I wired you the money to deliver me some relics, and you failed to deliver. But I'm going to do you a favor. Why? I don't really know why. I'm going to give you twenty-four more hours to deliver, because I think I know where the relics are. If I find them before they leave the United States, you're off the hook."

# Chapter Fourteen

A junior clerk at the Israeli Embassy encoded a transmission going to Tel Aviv. It confirmed that Lev Cohen, an Israeli citizen on a mission for the Mossad, had in his possession a set of artifacts he had stolen from a man at JFK Airport. Although the clerk knew nothing of the items themselves, she was surprised that her government was involved in such a crime, and that it merited encryption. Encrypted messages usually involved high security transmissions with strategic, usually military, significance.

The coded message made such an impression on her that, lying in bed that night, she told her boyfriend Eli about it. She was surprised that he appeared interested in something besides sex for once. He sat up in bed and asked her to tell him everything about it. She told him all that she could recall - the name of the man and the location of the safe house where he was awaiting return to Israel, were two of the things she remembered.

It was impossible to keep information from John Spedino once the word got out that he was interested. The rewards he gave to those who furnished what he wanted were legendary. To collect a ten thousand dollar bounty, Eli Avraham, a member of a local gang of Jewish thugs who were involved in petty crimes, called a man who wanted to know where the artifacts were. This man had put the word on the street only a few days before. Thanks to his girlfriend's information, Eli received a cash payment of more money than he had ever before had in his possession. He promptly dumped the girl, spent the cash on drugs and booze, and was broke again in three weeks.

Spedino moved quickly. He had no idea how much time remained before the thief would be on a plane to Israel, and the artifacts lost to Christianity forever. He made a phone call and put things in motion. Within hours, the three relics were safe, and the thief was eliminated.

John Spedino's house was in a gated community far out on Long Island. It had an expansive view of the Sound. Spedino and his wife enjoyed sitting on their patio, a fire blazing in their outdoor fireplace, watching sailboats move serenely past.

Spedino heard the distinctive ring of the phone from the gatehouse. One of the staff answered the call, then walked from the house to where the couple sat. "My apologies for the interruption, Mr. Spedino," he said. "There are two Federal agents who are on their way to the house now. The guard at the gatehouse called to advise he had admitted them."

His wife asked what this was about. Like many other wives in her position, she asked few questions about her husband's business. She was a modern woman in many respects, but had become content in one area that was a throwback to the old days. She had a great life and John Spedino cared for his family well. She heard the news, and saw the tabloid headlines. But she chose to ignore what the public said, or what in her heart she knew was true. She knew a different John Spedino, her provider and husband. A good man. And that was good enough for her.

"As usual, it's a harassment visit," he said, leaning down and kissing her. "I probably will have to go into the City, but expect me back soon." John Spedino rose from the chair and went into the house. He went into the bedroom and changed into a coat and tie, as he heard the doorbell ring. He knew from past experience it was likely he would be taking a ride into Manhattan. He had done it before, and he'd do it again. But he also was certain he would very quickly be making the return trip to his house. He had never spent time in jail. Thanks to very good lawyers and very careful activities, John Spedino was sure this would be no exception. He was made of Teflon, after all.

# Chapter Fifteen

Having nowhere to turn for help, Brian could do nothing but wait, panic gradually overwhelming him. He desperately tried to think of something he could do, but got nowhere. He lay in bed in a cold sweat.

Around ten p.m., his cell phone rang. He didn't recognize the Dallas number. Answering the call, he heard his former cube-mate Jim Palmer say, "Well, Brian, you better consider yourself lucky you bailed when you did." Palmer told Brian that after close of business that afternoon, a cadre of U.S. Marshals, along with agents from the FBI and the SEC, had arrived at Warren Taylor and Currant.

"We're shut down," Jim said. "Nobody knows exactly what happened, although the rumor mill has it that Francois Rochefort has turned up. I don't know if that has anything directly to do with us or not." He said that the Feds had removed records and computers from the firm. "We can't survive another round of negative publicity," he continued. "I got a call about an hour ago from one of the VPs. He says don't bother coming to work tomorrow. The firm's closing and filing bankruptcy."

Afterwards, Brian surfed the business channels but couldn't

find any news about W&T. Likewise, the internet sites that usually carried this type of story had nothing to report. He finally went to bed but lay awake almost all night, wondering how this was all going to play out.

Around six a.m. Brian began checking the internet while he listened to CNN News. The business sites had nothing, but the homepages of all the news agencies displayed versions of the same major headline. "TEFLON TWO ARRESTED," read the article's banner. John Spedino, reputed head of New York's crime families, had been arrested the night before on charges of extortion, fraud and murder. Brian felt a glimmer of hope.

The story related that the Federal case against Spedino was based largely on the testimony of Francois Rochefort, a convicted criminal and former associate of Spedino's, who had been sought for his role in the downfall of a public company called Bellicose Holdings. Rochefort had been arrested earlier in the week by officers of the French police agency, Surete Nationale. He had been living in hiding in Eze Village, a medieval town in the south of France nestled on a cliff overlooking the Mediterranean Sea. It was a perfect place for a French-speaking Canadian to hide. He would fit in well.

Brian read that Spedino was being held in a Lower Manhattan jail without bail, Federal agents having convinced a judge that the mobster was a flight risk. In a related story, the Dallas brokerage firm of Warren Taylor and Currant was raided by authorities yesterday. Two years ago, W&T's top executives had provided damaging testimony and records, which showed the firm's ties to organized crime, through Spedino.

The U.S. Attorney's office believed the testimony of the W&T executives alone was not sufficient to corner Spedino for good, so the FBI had bided its time, waiting for the right opportunity. They kept the men in protective custody, knowing they would otherwise be ordered killed by John Spedino.

Now that Spedino was in custody, the Feds had raided W&T to get computer and hard copy documents which both Rochefort and the two executives had steered them toward. These records would confirm the involvement of W&T with Spedino. The SEC, the news story reported, was withdrawing W&T's license to sell securities pending a hearing. Brian knew that meant the end of the firm.

Rochefort had waived extradition. Once the cooperating agencies had him safely inside the United States, they had offered a plea bargain which would allow him to serve a few years in prison. In exchange, Rochefort agreed to testify against his boss and mentor, Johnny Speed, the man everyone wanted to put behind bars. And Rochefort had the goods, including where the bodies were buried. He had already begun talking to the FBI, and this time the U.S. Attorney was certain Spedino was down for good.

Buoyed by the news, Brian went into the gallery with a plan in mind. At his instructions, Collette wired twenty-five million dollars to First InterCity Bank, who released the Israeli bonds Brian had offered as collateral. That transaction was now finished.

She then wired $250,000 to Chaim Weisenberg. After an hour, Brian called and Weisenberg confirmed receipt of the money, emailing Brian a complete release. That transaction now was also complete.

Except for John Spedino's artifacts, things were all as they were intended to be. And so long as Spedino was in jail, he had other things to think about, Brian figured, than getting his money back.

# Chapter Sixteen

That afternoon, Brian received an unexpected call from the office of Archbishop Francis McGann, head of the New York Archdiocese of the Roman Catholic Church. The caller put Brian on hold while he got the Archbishop on the line.

"Mr. Sadler," he began. "I am calling to thank you for your efforts in helping get the priceless Bethlehem Scroll and its accompanying artifacts into the hands of the Church. I'm confirming that the relics are in my possession, and I will be taking them to Rome tonight to deliver them to the Pope himself."

"How did you get them?" Brian stammered, totally taken by surprise.

The Archbishop explained that a man had delivered the relics in a briefcase to the Diocese office around 4 p.m. yesterday.

"Was it John Spedino?" Brian asked.

Archbishop McGann's voice sounded surprised. He told Brian that he had never dealt with John Spedino in his life. "The Vatican advised me months earlier that I should expect the artifacts someday. The donor would be a wealthy Catholic and the gift was given anonymously. I have no idea who the delivery man was. I only knew to contact you because the Vatican had said the transfer of the relics to the church would be handled by an intermediary - Bijan Rarities."

Shortly thereafter, the customs agent who had detained Brian at JFK called him at the gallery. "I just wanted to give you some news," he said. "The man who stole your briefcase was on a high priority watch list, and he turned up last night. His body floated to the Queens side of the East River about six p.m. Some boys were fishing there and it scared the hell out of them."

Piecing it together, Brian figured Spedino's boys must have found the man, killed him, retrieved the artifacts, and had them delivered to the Archbishop. Then John Spedino had been arrested, and all that happened within about an eight hour period. Regardless of exactly how it all transpired, things had certainly fallen into place for Brian Sadler, the eternal optimist who had almost played the game for keeps.

Brian looked back on the last few days with relief. Determined not to repeat his past, he vowed to concentrate more on the things that mattered to him – building a relationship with Nicole and building a business of which he could be proud – and less on the glamour and fame that required living too close to the edge. Brian Sadler, the eternal optimist, decided he had almost paid too high a price to get what he wanted. He wouldn't do it again.

# Epilogue

## ONE YEAR LATER

Brian Sadler and Nicole Farber sat in the Grill Room of the Savoy Hotel having lunch. It was autumn in England, a beautiful time to see trees changing color, gusty winds announcing change in the air. From their table, they could see boats moving lazily down the Thames River below them.

Brian found himself in London more and more, and he had decided to open a branch of Bijan Rarities there. Collette was being promoted to gallery manager. She and Jason would run the New York operation while Brian headquartered in London. He was negotiating for space in Old Bond Street and was excited about the prospects of spending more time in his favorite city.

Nicole had taken a week off to join him. They were hopeful of having at least a few free days to visit the countryside. Brian had developed a friendship with Oscar Carrington, owner of a gallery in Knightsbridge. Carrington invited the two to his country home in Oxford, a twelfth century structure reputedly built by a son of William the Conqueror.

The publicity John Spedino had promised Bijan for handling the hottest artifacts in history never materialized. It was for the best, Brian figured. The gallery was doing very well and continued to be recognized as one of the world's top resources for ancient pieces. And the Vatican was obviously not interested in making the artifacts public.

As Brian and Nicole sipped glasses of Sancerre, a man entered the dining room with a cardboard mailing tube under his arm. He searched for a moment, eyes landing on Nicole, and he made his way to their table. Without waiting for an invitation he sat, extended his hand and said, "Mr. Sadler, I'm here at the direction of David Cardone."

Brian and Nicole knew who Cardone was. After the fall of Johnny Speed, the papers had reported that Cardone had taken over as New York City's new godfather. "We're having lunch," Brian said.

"I can see that," the man replied, unabashed. "I bring a message from John Spedino. He asked me to look you up. He has something he knows you will be interested in."

"Spedino?" Brian responded sharply. "Isn't he in prison?"

"Of course," the courier responded evenly. "But that doesn't mean he can't communicate."

Irritated, Nicole looked at Brian. "Can't this be dealt with at another time?"

"With all due respect," Brian said to the man, "please let us finish our lunch. I'll be happy to talk to you at my hotel if you'll make an appointment through Bijan in New York."

Ignoring him, the man took a yellowed sheet from the tube, unrolling it on the table in front of Brian. "Mr. Spedino would like to sell this document to you."

Brian glanced at it. "What is this?" he said at last.

"It's a copy of the Declaration of Independence," the courier answered.

"Of course it is," Brian said. "It's the kind of copy anyone can buy in the gift shop of the Capitol."

As though he had not heard, the man said, "Mr. Spedino is certain you will be willing to buy this copy of such a revered document. He is asking one million dollars for it."

Brian laughed aloud, noticing that the courier did not smile. "It's worth a couple of dollars," Brian said, tossing the yellowed parchment back to the man.

"With all respect, Mr. Sadler, you made a two million dollar profit when you did the deal on the relics. And now they're locked away somewhere, doing you and Mr. Spedino no good. Mr. Spedino finds himself needing to sell some assets to, shall we say, pay his expenses. He therefore insists that you buy this document."

Brian looked at the man intently. "You want me to give a million of Johnny Speed's money back?" He was incredulous.

"His name is John Spedino, Mr. Sadler. And no, you aren't giving anything to anybody. Mr. Spedino is going to sell you this document for a million dollars, wire transferred to a Swiss account within a week. And, Mr. Sadler, you're going to buy it."

## THE VATICAN

Joseph Ratzinger sat in his favorite chair in the library, reading for the hundredth time the translation of the Bethlehem Scroll. Known to the world as Pope Benedict XVI, Ratzinger thought of himself as nothing more than a humble servant of God, and not the leader of the Roman Catholic Church, every time he read the electrifying words. As soon as the artifacts were safely in the Vatican, the Pope had put scribes on the task of performing a detailed translation of both the scroll and the parchment scrap that accompanied the coin.

Those men spent painstaking hours checking and double-checking every word of Aramaic, ensuring the meaning was exactly as it had been intended. The result was the English translation of an incredible story, told through the eyes of a child, who spent a night of wonders like no other in history.

Other men used the latest techniques to clean the coin. After the residue was removed, it was shown to be a common shekel, dated to the Herodian era around the time of Jesus' birth. This shekel, however, was anything but common. It had rested in the Messiah's hand. The Pope was certain of it.

The three relics were placed in an air-tight container and locked in a vault which contained other priceless things collected over the centuries by the Vatican. The existence of the vault was known to only a few trusted individuals. Each Pope learned about it only upon his succession to the papacy.

Benedict wished that the artifacts which confirmed Jesus' birth could be viewed by humanity, but he knew that keeping the unique relics safe and secure was the only possibility. There were many who would steal and destroy them, to extinguish the message contained in these relics. So he chose to keep them locked away, never to be seen again unless another Pope, years in the future, had reason to view them.

Benedict had placed the relics in the vault himself. No one had accompanied him, and only a handful knew what the items were. Inside the vault, a yellowed ledger sat on a table by the door. The pontiff made three entries on the list, describing the artifacts and dating their addition to the safe.

Looking at the entry just above them, he saw that the last time the vault had been opened was in April, 1946, when a number of treasures stolen from churches by the Nazis were shipped to the Vatican. Benedict knew, therefore, that no eyes would likely see these relics again for decades. They would rest on a shelf, hidden from everyone.

Sitting by the fire, he looked at the translation. Every time he read the story, it filled the pontiff with wonder. He never tired of hearing the first-hand account of Benjamin, a Jewish boy who saw the Messiah with his own eyes. The Pope slept well that night, comforted as always by the knowledge that locked away in the most secret vault on earth, the original account of the Messiah's birth was safe and secure inside the Vatican, forever.

A few moments after the vault door was closed and sealed, the artifacts simply disappeared from the shelf on which the pontiff had placed them. And the three entries carefully penned by Pope Benedict XVI on the list, disappeared as well.

Far away, a wealthy Lebanese and his wife wondered who had stolen an ancient urn they had purchased in the Jericho marketplace, which now was missing from their front porch.

THE QUMRAN HILLS NEAR THE DEAD SEA

It was hot and dusty along the little trail that ran down the side of an outcropping in the hills near the ancient site of Qumran. The entrance to the small cave had been virtually obliterated over the years. It would take some effort to locate the entrance.

In a wall of the small cave's second room stood two stones. They blended well with the wall, so completely in fact that no one could tell they hid a clay urn, sitting on a small ledge. Except for a short time, the jar and its contents had sat in the cave for over two thousand years, and now they were resting here once again.

*It was not time.*

CPSIA information can be obtained at www.ICGtesting.com
Printed in the USA
BVOW01s0840180315

392232BV00004B/83/P

9 781432 738921